"Like Isabel Allende… Kassabova has a gift for measured, eloquent, no-frills storytelling."
– Scotland on Sunday

"Excellent… well-written, psychologically intriguing with an exotic setting and a mystery plot."
– The Guardian

"Like her poetry and memoir, Kassabova's fiction is taut and evocative. […] Inspired by the landscape of Ecuador as well as the end of a personal relationship, Kassabova's latest novel is a commentary on human strength. Elegant prose and unusual plot lines will intrigue the reader to the finish."
– The Herald

"A wonderfully intriguing story about relationship dynamics, our innermost fears, and a *Lost*-type plot that keeps building momentum with every page."
– The Scottish Review of Books

"Intelligent, psychologically compelling… a truly mesmerizing read."
– The Scotsman

"Reminiscent of Maugham's Borneo stories and Bowles' *The Sheltering Sky*… ultimately, however, concerned with individual relations."
– TLS

ALMA BOOKS LTD
London House
243–253 Lower Mortlake Road
Richmond
Surrey TW9 2LL
United Kingdom
www.almabooks.com

Villa Pacifica first published in New Zealand by Penguin Books NZ in 2010
A new, revised edition first published in the UK by Alma Books Limited in 2011
This mass-market edition first published by Alma Books Limited in 2012

Printed in Great Britain by CPI Group (UK) Ltd, Croydon, CR0 4YY

ISBN (PAPERBACK): 978-1-84688-186-2
ISBN (EBOOK): 978-1-84688-218-0

VILLA PACIFICA

KAPKA KASSABOVA

VILLA PAC

PUERTO SECO

MALECON

CAFE FIN DEL MUNDO

PACIFIC OCEAN

NATIONAL PARK

CLIFFS

LOOKOUT POINT

WATER CAVES

1200m

AGUA SAGRADA CLOUDFOREST

CLIFFS

FICA

LEGEND:

- PUERTO SECO = Fishing village.
- VILLA PACIFICA = eco-resort /animal shelte
- AGUA SAGRADA CLOUDFOREST = artisan community in the cloudforest hills.
- MANTEÑO NATIONAL PARK = dry tropical forest.

AIN
ATE

VILLA
PACIFICA

MAIN
HOUSE

ANIMAL
SHELTER

MAIN ROAD

MANTEÑO
NATIONAL PARK
ENTRANCE

IATIONAL
PARK

MARSH/
MANGROVES

Like any Romantic, I had always been vaguely certain
that sometime during my life I should come into a
magic place which in disclosing its secrets would give
me wisdom and ecstasy – perhaps even death

Paul Bowles

Two roads diverged in a yellow wood
And sorry I could not travel both
And be one traveller, long I stood
And looked down one as far as I could
To where it bent in the undergrowth

Robert Frost

For my parents, Nik and Diana,
with love and gratitude

Part One

1

UTE WAS NOT JUST well travelled, she was professionally well travelled. So she of all people shouldn't have been surprised that sometimes the road to hell begins with an ordinary bus ride, in an ordinary South American country, at the end of the ordinary year 2009. And on that bus, we sit next to the one we ordinarily love.

Ute and the one she loved had taken the last bus of the day from what the guide book, penned by Ute herself five years ago, called "the regional centre". That was guide-speak for hideous industrial dump with a car yard at one end and a bus station at the other. Having the transport to get away is its only saving grace, Jerry pronounced. The station was full of squat hustlers with dirty nails who waved bus tickets and yelled in high-pitched voices, "Guaa Guaa Guaaaaaa!" and "Jipi jipi jipiiii!"

"What's this hippie place they're selling?" Jerry enquired.

"Jipilini. Small transport hub a few hours down the main road. Been there once, and that was plenty."

"Guaa Guaa Guaaaaaa!" the taloned hustlers kept squealing, but nobody paid attention.

"They're paid commission by the passenger, aren't they?" Jerry snorted.

"Well spotted," Ute said.

"I'm an old South American hand, me. Any questions about South America, I'm your man." Jerry was good at self-parody. This was only his second time on the continent.

They had just spent two dust-choked days in the "regional centre", long enough for Ute to trawl around hotels and eateries and update the practical section of the guide, while Jerry stayed behind in cafés, nursing fruit juices and a jet lag headache. They didn't sleep much at night. The noise was diabolical, and it seemed to ooze from every pore of the city: traffic, car alarms, motorbikes, music, people shouting, dogs barking, and car alarms again. Every night, Ute cursed herself for leaving behind in an Andean village three thousand metres above sea level her box of silicon earplugs, the only type that really seals out noise.

There was a new, "revolutionary" government with great plans, which had just been re-elected that year. Along the road, giant billboards announced in excited letters "THE CITIZENS' REVOLUTION IS FORGING AHEAD!" and "THE FATHERLAND NOW BELONGS TO ALL!"

In the rickety bus, the citizens were asleep as usual, mouths agape, while the loudspeakers above them blared out Cumbia and advertisements at eardrum-shattering decibels.

"Are they deaf or brain-dead?" Jerry looked around at the inert passengers.

"All of the above," Ute said. "Round here you either go brain-dead from lack of sleep or from the music."

"You mean the same fate awaits us if we hang out here long enough?" he snorted. "Which we won't, thank God."

Jerry took things personally. He thought the world was out of joint if it didn't coincide with him. He was already not enjoying himself. He was normally great company, but outside his comfort zone he became ratty – another reason why they didn't travel together much, except for pleasantly uneventful holidays to France, Italy and Greece. Four hours on a potholed road, in a stinky clapped-out bus with seats that spilt stuffing was definitely outside his comfort zone.

Ute was worn down after seven weeks on the go and what felt like seven hundred days of broken sleep, but it was a habitual fatigue. Sore buttocks and broken sleep were part of the job description.

Jerry had joined her for this leg of the journey along the coast, to soak up some sunshine in the middle of December. It was his winter holiday.

They rarely travelled together, because his academic holidays never complied with her schedule. Besides, she always travelled alone for work.

She had covered the Andes, which ran along the centre of the country like a spine, and the better part of the coast. They were now headed for the last stretch of it, in the south. It was the least visited.

Puerto Seco wasn't in the guidebook. But it was on a newly printed local map she'd picked up somewhere further up the coast. It seemed to be the closest point to a local attraction – a recently established national park which consisted of dry tropical forest and cloud forest, an unusual combination. Ute was curious. Every travel-guide writer, even when updating their own guide, wants to discover something new. Who knows, she thought, maybe Puerto Seco was worth a look. Jerry agreed to stop overnight, or maybe for a couple of nights. He just wanted a nice beach, somewhere to warm his bones for the second half of the English winter. Ute had a feeling they weren't going to find his dream beach along here, simply because all the good beaches were further up north. But they were already on their way, no point in bringing the mood down.

An hour into their bus journey, when it was still daylight, a salesman got on. The bus slowed down, and on he hopped with his suitcase. He was a young man, well groomed, with slicked-back hair and a buttoned-up pink shirt under his jacket. His baked-earth face glowed with sweat. He addressed the lethargic crowd.

"*Señoras y señores*," he shouted over the music, holding in one hand a tiny bottle and gripping a seat with the other as the bus dived in and out of potholes as big as moon craters. "Can any of you here honestly say that you are completely healthy? That you have never experienced aches and pains, mental and physical? No, of course not. Can any of you tell me how many green vegetables you eat every day, how much broccoli, tomato, carrots?… Ah, you'll say, but we eat banana and plantain. *Señoras y señores*, do you know the nutritional value of a plantain?"

He went on like this for a while. People's heads bobbed up and down, and he staggered about the front of the bus like a man on the deck of a ship in a sea storm.

"That's one hell of a sales pitch," Jerry said. He didn't understand Spanish, but it was obvious that the man was blabbering. The salesman didn't make eye contact with any one person; his glazed eyes hovered over their heads. He finally came to the point.

"Have you heard the magic word 'ginseng'?" He held up the tiny bottle for everyone to see. "Ginseng means health and long life. The Koreans and the Chinese take this regularly, and do you know that China's oldest man, who is a hundred and twenty years old, has a lover of twenty-five? *Sí, señores*, you too could enjoy that if you started taking ginseng regularly."

Someone chuckled.

"What I have here is pure extract of ginseng," the vendor went on. "You can buy it or not buy it, it's your choice. You can buy health and a long life for three *dolaritos* apiece, five *dolaritos* for the pair, or you can continue to suffer fatigue, anxiety, arthritis, indigestion, uterine cramps, cancer, erectile dysfunction and early death."

He cheerfully distributed tiny bottles to the audience. Jerry took one too. A couple of women were already reaching for their bags.

"Thank you," Ute said to him when he passed to collect the unwanted bottles, "we already have some." Lying is a form of politeness. Ute had learnt this long ago.

"Thank you, *señora*," he lied back, for he knew this too, "you're very kind."

His business completed, he sat in a free seat across from them, to wait for the next stop. They were enveloped in a damp cloud of cheap eau de cologne. After a while, he leant towards them and spoke to Ute, glancing at her inflamed face.

"*Señora*, ginseng is also excellent for skin ailments."

Ute grimaced a smile. "*Bueno*," she said. "I'll remember that."

The faces of women were open to judgement everywhere in the world. Something about a woman's face made it a free-for-all. Anybody with half a brain had the right to comment on female beauty or the lack of it. Not that Ute was ugly. It was just hard to see her face properly when the evil flower of eczema blossomed over her cheeks, nose and eyelids.

"What's your destination?" the man shouted over the music – which, unbelievably, had just got louder.

"Puerto Seco," Ute shouted back. The salesman fixed her with his cherry-black eyes.

"Are you visiting someone there?"

"No, just stopping for a day or two. Do you know it?"

"Yes, I'm from a village further down the road. Not for tourists. Puerto Seco is not for tourists either. But the national park is nice."

"Is there anywhere to stay in Puerto Seco?" Ute asked.

He shook his head. "I don't know, there used to be..."

A fresh explosion of Cumbia from the loudspeaker above their heads wiped out some of his words. "I don't know... still... animals... Pacifica..."

"What?" Ute shouted.

"Villa Pacifica," he shouted back. Then he got up, waved goodbye and moved to the front of the bus. The bus slowed down without stopping, and he jumped off nimbly. Ute and Jerry looked out the grubby window. He was already walking along the road with his case. He didn't look up at the bus as it passed him.

"What was that about?" Jerry asked. "Were you asking him about Puerto Seco?"

"Yeah, places to stay. Apparently there's none. It's not a touristy place."

"There's a surprise," Jerry snorted.

"But there's one place called Villa Pacifica, or something like that. I'm not sure if it's for people or animals though. He wasn't actually sure if it's still there. I didn't hear everything he said."

"First he's keen to talk to you, then suddenly he's keen as hell to get moving."

"It was his stop. Anyway," Ute said brightly, always bright when faced with Jerry's fussiness, "it's good to have at least one recommendation about a place to stay. It could be interesting – this Dry Port."

"Good name anyway. And we might get a couple of nights' decent sleep out there. This noise and dust are driving me nuts. Have you got any water left?"

They took a last sip each from the warm plastic bottle, and he put a sweaty hand on her thigh. They had another bottle of water in her pack, somewhere in the viscera of the bus. She leant into him and sniffed his familiar sweaty, chicken-soup smell.

And she thought, quite out of the blue, that she would leave the last sip of water for him if they were both dying of thirst. But would he, she wondered hazily, would he do it for her? Then she berated herself for thinking such neurotic thoughts.

2

IT WAS SUDDENLY PITCH-BLACK. Unlike everywhere else in the world, here on the equator things didn't cast shadows in the falling dusk. Darkness didn't creep over you crab-like, from the side. No, it hit the land vertically, at a right angle, and without warning it was suddenly night.

The bus driver hadn't heard of a place called Villa Pacifica, and he dumped them in the middle of an empty road. They had passed no signs for the last half-hour. The driver just slammed the brakes and grumbled "Puerto Seco".

They were the only passengers to get off. Not surprising, since most people had already got off a while before. Only a few men remained scattered inside the dark, smelly bus, fast asleep and snoring. Ute knew there was a special kind of poverty in some parts of the world where sleep is the only commodity left to people. And even their sleep is somehow threadbare.

The driver barely waited for them to extract their packs from the trunk on the flank of the bus, and started moving before they'd even shut the trunk door.

"Wait, wait," Jerry shouted and, running after the bus, slammed the door, which nearly dislocated his arm. "Dickhead," he spat out. The bus left them in a cloud of grit and dust.

They took out the large water bottle and drank for a long time. It was dead-dark and dead-quiet, except for the distant barking of a dog. On the other side of the road was the outline of what looked like a forest.

"Well," Jerry said, "I feel like we've crossed the whole continent, but on the map it's nothing. Now what?"

"It's the roads," Ute said. She too felt a bit disheartened by the lack of any discernible village. "They make it longer than it needs to be."

"They're a shocker. Never seen anything like it. This *puerto* better be good," Jerry said, and helped her put on her pack. "Now what? Where the hell are we?"

"Well, we didn't pass anything resembling Puerto Seco or any other *puerto*, so let's walk this way." They started walking in the direction the bus had gone.

"Have you got your torch handy?" Jerry said.

"I think it's at the bottom of my pack."

"Hmm. Might have to stop and dig it out. That dickhead of a driver was a maniac. Do you think he just dumped us in the middle of nowhere to spite us?"

"No. Drivers here can be a bit rude, but they wouldn't do that. Let's not panic yet."

"True, true." Jerry went quiet. "I'm starving," he added after a few minutes of silent walking.

And just then they saw the lights of a village to the right, and the dog was barking somewhere close ahead. Ute realized why Puerto Seco wasn't in the guidebook. Because unless you knew it was here, you wouldn't find it. And last time she hadn't found it. A dirt road branched off the main road, and they took it.

"This Puerto Seco is really just a bend in the road," Ute said. "That's why the driver dropped us there."

Jerry was peering ahead into the darkness. They walked for another fifteen minutes before the first houses started to form out of the darkness. They were all built on stilts. Apart from the invisible barking dog and some salsa music blaring out from an invisible house, there was no sign of life. They walked along the dirt road until they suddenly came to what looked and sounded like a beach. It took Ute by surprise because, normally, she could smell the sea from a mile.

There were dim lights along the waterfront, and it felt good to be able to see, at last. They were standing on something resembling a waterside promenade, what the locals called a *malecón*.

"I'm confused," Jerry said. "Isn't the ocean that way?" He pointed to their right.

"It should be," Ute said. "It must be a very curvy coast around here..."

"This place stinks," Jerry said. "And we're stuck here."

He was looking around. There wasn't much to see apart from the shuttered front of a seaside café and a couple of shops. The façades were different colours and heights. There was a gaping hole where a house had been before, like a missing tooth in a smile. Just then, a motorbike tricycle revved along the dusty road.

"Life!" Jerry exclaimed. "There is life in this dump!"

"*Hola*," Ute waved to the chunky driver. He stopped and looked at them in dismay.

"We're looking for somewhere to stay," Ute shouted over the noise of his engine. "Is there anywhere in the town?"

He shook his head. He was lost for words.

"No hotel, nothing?"

Again, he shook his head. He looked a bit wary.

"What about Villa Pacifica? Is it somewhere nearby?"

"Villa Pacifica," he said and spat thickly. "Yes, I can take you there." He spoke with that lazy, hard-to-understand coastal drawl that sounded more like Portuguese than Spanish.

"That's OK," Ute said, "we can walk. Which way is it?"

"It's too far to walk," he said, and turned off the engine. "It's beyond the end of the *malecón*, that way." He waved behind him. "But there's no lights. You'll get lost in the forest."

"I don't like the look of this guy," Jerry said.

"Do you want to walk then? It's either walk or take a ride with him. I'd rather get a lift. And he's a taxi driver. Doesn't get much safer than this."

"OK," he gave up. "He's smaller than me if it comes to that."

Ute scoffed. The idea of bespectacled, uncoordinated Jerry getting into a fist fight with this phlegm-spitting, thick-limbed ruffian was comical. She dumped her heavy pack on the tricycle's seat.

The man started the engine again. They rode along the *malecón*. The sea was to their right, when it seemed as if it should have been behind them. But soon she didn't even know whether there was any water at all, because there were suddenly no street lights. They rode along a bumpy dirt road plunged in complete darkness, then seemed to get back onto the main road.

They soon swerved off the road again and into a forest. Jerry squeezed Ute's hand. She glanced at him in the dark. She too hated disorientation. Lose your north and south, and who knows what you might lose next.

Suddenly, a bright spot appeared in the shrubs ahead. A massive wood-panelled gate stood before them in a clearing.

"VILLA PACIFICA", said the large wood-carved letters over the gate.

Some people were standing outside. Two men, locals. They were watching the approaching taxi intently, perhaps even grinning. Ute paid the driver, who rode off without a thanks or goodbye.

"*Buenas*," the men greeted them, and let them through the heavy wooden gate. After the rudeness of the bus and tricycle-taxi drivers, this was five-star politeness.

Inside the gates, Ute and Jerry stopped in their tracks, stunned. They were inside a live tropical garden, heaving with exotic plants twice their height.

"Oh, hello!" Jerry said. "I think we've come to the right place."

"This way," one of the men said. He must have seen his share of new arrivals with mouths agape like this. He led them along a white, pebbled path, and they crunched along behind. The warm, moist air was filled with the sweet, intimate smell of rotting vegetation, reminding Ute of the smell of the Brazilian Amazon. Tiny water jets purred among the plants. Insects screeched and fluttered around them.

Unlit pebble paths were leading off in various directions. There were carved signs painted with wild animals. One sign had a tortoise, others had pictures of a lion, birds, monkeys and an armadillo. She glimpsed an empty hammock at the end of a path.

They eventually came to a large terraced bungalow. It stood on stilts, the way most coastal houses here did, to protect them against floods. They went up the wooden stairs onto the terrace. The man who'd shown them the way had vanished. There was nobody around. In the darkness Ute stepped on the tail of a large collie-like dog lying across the veranda like a pile carpet. The dog growled, shook its heavy fur and padded softly away. The inside of the house was dark, and through the enormous glassless windows Ute could glimpse the outlines of a bar, and some wicker chairs and tables. It looked like a communal lounge.

"*Bienvenidos*!" a voice startled them. They turned the corner of the veranda, and saw a middle-aged couple peering at them through a cloud of smoke. The woman was elongated and spindly. Her face of a wilted sun-worshipping beauty was framed with frizzy reddish hair threaded with silver strands. A pile of ledger books and a large seashell full of cigarette butts lay on the table before her.

"English? Deutsch? Français? Italiano? Español?" The man sprung to his feet and grinned with nicotine-stained teeth.

"English and French," Jerry said, visibly relaxing, and then pointed at Ute, "Español and Finnish."

"OK, OK," the man said. "*Sehr gut*. My English is not so good. My girlfriend speaks English and Espanish. And you speak Espanish?"

"I pretend to," Ute said modestly. Her Spanish was fluent.

The man laughed and shed cigarette ash as he waved his hands about. Two tufts of grey hair frizzed up on each side of his bald patch. He had grizzled stubble, and grey hair curled out from the opening of his floral-printed shirt. He flip-flopped inside the house.

"How many nights do you want to stay?" he asked in Spanish.

Ute translated for Jerry. "Ten, twenty?" Jerry chanced. He smiled at Ute. Their host waved his cigarette impatiently.

"Come in, come in, I'll give you a key and take your passports. You can decide later. Stay as long as you like." He switched the lights on inside the lounge.

As Ute passed her, the woman gazed up at her dreamily. There was kindness in her eyes, and also something else, something like a shadow of… wariness. A distant memory. Pity for the flame-faced arrival.

"Well done for finding this place," Jerry said as their host copied details from their passports into a ledger.

"It was the driver, not me," she said.

"You came through the back gate, didn't you?" their host asked.

"I don't know, it was a large gate." Ute said.

"Did you come in a tricycle taxi?"

"That's right."

"From Puerto Seco."

"Yes."

"Those goddamn drivers, they know we don't like people coming through the back gate, especially in the middle of the night like this. They do it to get more money off you, you know. But what can you do?"

"We had no idea. Is there another entrance?"

"Oh yes, just out here, that's the main gate."

"Is it closer to the town?"

"Oh, much closer. It's a kilometre and a half along the beach. Maximum two."

"So which way is the ocean?" Ute asked.

Small ticks worried the man's face and hands.

"Ah, you'll see tomorrow morning," he winked at her. "*Mañana*," he said to Jerry.

"How much is a double?" Ute enquired.

"Depends how long you stay. If you stay two nights, five nights, ten nights, it's thirty dollars a night. If you stay ten days or more, it's twenty dollars a night. If you stay..."

"Ten days!" Ute chuckled incredulously. "We don't have that much time."

"Of course, you can stay as long as you like. Some people stay longer."

"How many guests do you have at the moment?"

"Not many. We're not busy at the moment, it's the off-season. We're going into summer. Normally, it rains quite a lot. We sure hope it'll rain."

"Because of the garden?"

"You got it. This garden needs lots of water, it's a tropical garden. For you of course it's no good, you're here for the beaches and to get away from the rain. Ah, I remember the misery of autumn rains in Spain... But we pray for rain every day here. This region has suffered from increasing droughts. Every year, it gets worse. Climate change. Last year, we had El Niño. It devastated the garden, flooded the front cabins. People lost their houses in the villages, the *malecón* was wrecked, the beach in Puerto Seco was littered with uprooted trees, dead animals, house roofs, all manner of rubbish. Who paid for it to be cleaned up? The local council, you think? No, of course not. It was the rich gringos at Villa Pacifica, as usual."

Tiny bits of spittle sprayed them. His dopey grin had vanished. A frown split his curved forehead. "Yep, we shelled out yet again. Trouble is, it looks like our prayers will be answered only too well this year, and we're about to have another spell…"

"Mikel, *amor*, come," the woman called out softly from the veranda. He seemed to reset himself with an invisible button, and the yellow-toothed smile was back.

"I'll put you in The Tortoise. You'll like it. Breakfast is from eight till eleven. We also have a restaurant, so you can have lunch and dinner here. It's the best restaurant in a radius of 500 kilometres, each way. We have Italian, Spanish, local, and only the freshest produce and ingredients."

"Is the kitchen open now?" Ute asked.

"No, the kitchen is closed now," their host replied, shaking his head sorrowfully. Everything about him was exaggerated. Then his body jerked joyfully. "But we have lemon cake, if you want." He waved at an enticing half-cake along the bar counter. They bought two pieces. Just then, a man materialized in the far, darker end of the lounge and beckoned them over.

"*Buenas noches*, good night," their host said cheerfully, and returned to the table outside.

Ute and Jerry hurried down a dark path behind their guide, stuffing the moist, fragrant cake into their dusty faces. *La tortuga* was a small wooden cabin on stilts with an overhanging thatched roof. It was partially swallowed by huge plants reaching out on every side to the indigo sky. There was a well-used printed-cotton hammock outside. The windows were simply square holes with mosquito nets stretched across. The single light inside was dim. There were a few pieces of wicker furniture, including a small table, and a simple but attractive bathroom with lots of shells and a huge natural sea sponge large enough to towel yourself with. The centrepiece was the large bed, enveloped in a cascading mosquito net suspended from a hook in the ceiling.

They could hear the crickets screeching on their tiny violins outside. A heavy, gritty fragrance, like incense, filled the cabin. There was no luxury here, but such tasteful simplicity that no five-star hotel could have pleased Jerry more. He was partial to creature comforts, though he wouldn't always admit it, because Ute was just so tough by comparison.

"I don't believe this place," Jerry said. "From hell to paradise in twenty minutes."

"Isn't it just?" Ute dumped the dead weight of her pack on the floor. She heard her torch crunch at the bottom, but who cared – they didn't need the torch any more.

"You know," Ute said, "I thought El Niño hit the Pacific coast in 2006 or 2007, I can't remember exactly. Did the guy say 'last year'?"

"Oh, who cares," Jerry said. "What does your guidebook say anyway?" He laughed, and she didn't.

Without unpacking she undressed, washed her hands, swallowed her malaria pill, applied some medicated cream on her raw face and crawled inside the net. Jerry was splashing in the bathroom. She was asleep the second her head hit the pillow.

3

UTE WOKE UP FEELING drugged. Jerry wasn't there. It was semi-dark in the cabin, and Ute couldn't tell what time of day or night it was. She looked at her watch: eleven o'clock. She'd slept for almost twelve hours, a freak event for someone who normally didn't need more than six. And she'd had a bad dream – another freak event. She hardly ever had any dreams. Jerry said it wasn't normal to have so few. He said she must be repressing them.

This time, she had dreamt of her mother. Except her mother was a child in an oversized military coat. She was in a petrified forest where the trees were twisted, unfriendly shapes. Ute was observing her from above, but somehow, in that horrible way only possible in dreams, she also *was* the child. She crunched for ages among the dry branches, lost. There was no path. Ute knew this was a dangerous forest. She wanted to protect the little girl in the military coat from whatever was lurking in this dead forest. She could hear the child's breathing and the child's beating heart like a wounded bird inside her own chest. The dry branches scratched her face and reached for her eyes, her mouth, her nostrils. Somewhere far ahead, she could hear the sea.

Ute sprang out of bed angrily and put her aching head and stiff body under the dribbly shower. How absurd – to come all the way to a godforsaken coastal retreat in South America, and then dream of her mother in 1945.

The water was lukewarm and a sign said in English: "*Care about the water. There are not many left in the world's.*" She smiled and just then she caught a glance of her face in the shell-encrusted bathroom mirror. She instantly wished she hadn't. Her face was ablaze with a fresh flowering of eczema. It must have flared up on the long bus ride here. Sometimes it happened overnight.

She looked like a clown – a big, sad, female clown. The area around her mouth and her eyelids and eyebrows was flaming red. Nothing new of course, but it never failed to make her stomach sink. It had settled down in the mountain air of the Andes. The coast with its damp climate was good for the skin too. But buses and dust and heat were a killer. She applied some Eucerin – she didn't go anywhere without a tub of it – pushed her damp hair into a peaked hat and pulled it low over her face. The practical, unisex look of the travelling Nordic gringa.

The air outside hit her like a Pacific beach wave. It was warm, sweetly putrid and full of insect noises. The giant plants were an intense chlorophyll green, and flowers she'd never seen before peeked from foliage, their faces seductive and predatory. Birds fluttered in a bush nearby. Two locals in Panama hats were hose-watering each plant section by hand. They murmured a muffled hello into the ground in response to her greeting. She crunched along the pebble path. The low-hanging sky was overcast, mushroomy. It looked about to rain.

Ute climbed up the stairs to the veranda of the main house. There was nobody about. Then, suddenly, she saw water through the foliage and – across the water – a glimpse of wooded land. They were right on the seashore! More bizarre yet, across the water came the roar of a large animal, punctuated with the squawks of monkeys – or was it birds?

She walked from the veranda down a gentle slope to the sandy shore. It was a small beach. There was a crumpled towel near the water line. The water was a mossy colour. It looked still, stagnant even, like a lake. Ute took off her sandals and walked to the water's edge. It was warm like soup. To the right, the water continued all the way to the horizon, opening up and losing all land as it went. To the left, there was a sharp bend. The land across was a swimmable distance. It looked like a tropical island. The invisible animal startled her with another roar. She almost felt the land shake.

"She's just a cub," rang a loud voice over her shoulder. Ute yelped and jerked around. She hated it when people crept up on her. A man stood right behind her with a loutish grin. "Imagine what she'll be like when she grows up, right? A man-eater."

He had a loud American accent and a big, square head. He was a bit shorter than her and built like an ox, with a thickset neck, a naked beefy torso covered in curly black hair and thick limbs. His vigorous cheeks were flushed with health. Still, his face had a touch of Latino charisma.

He towelled his hair – his alert, dark eyes still on her. The dense flesh of his olive-skinned body shuddered.

"Didn't mean to give you a fright," he said.

"What's on that island?" she nodded across the water.

"It's not an island, it's the other side of the inlet. It's the deepest inlet along the coast. Used to be a river, but it's been drying up and now it's more like an inlet. Runs for a coupla miles after this bend and stops. What you see up there," he pointed to the horizon, "is the Pacific. Between here and the Galápagos, for five hundred miles, there's sweet fuck-all."

"Really?" Ute said. She was the last person he should be teaching geography to. She'd been to this continent half a dozen times.

"So Puerto Seco is this way, along the shore," Ute said.

"You got it." He tossed the towel onto the sand and started stretching his upper body, not shy to show her the carpet of black hair that covered both front and back. "Where you from, Europe?"

She'd heard Europeans say "South America" and expect to be congratulated for having guessed a person's nationality. It was the same thing.

"Britain," she said.

"Max," he stretched out an arm, "from Miami. What's your name?"

"Ute. Spelt U-T-E," she said, enunciating "ooh-tah" slowly, as she always did. She felt somehow naked even though he was the one in shorts and nothing else.

"Uddar – that's a funny name," he said, crushing her hand into pulp. She squealed involuntarily and withdrew it.

"Sorry." He released her hand. "I always forget." She hoped he was leaving soon.

"So what sort of a name is Uddar?" he said.

"German," Ute said. And to prevent further probes, she asked, "What's over there? Some kind of park or?..."

"*Refugio para animales*," he said in perfect Spanish.

"What, there's an animal shelter there?"

"Right. Right. Villa Pacifica – the peaceful place, get it?" But he was more interested in her right now than the shelter. "Are you the better half of the tall skinny guy with the girl's name? Jenny, is it?"

"Jerry," Ute corrected. He sniggered.

"My wife's over there too, with your Jerry, giving him the guided tour. I hope that's all she's givin' him." He guffawed.

"How long have you been here then?" Ute asked. She was tempted just to wade into the water and swim across – anything to get away from him.

"Ah, let's see. It feels like I've put down roots here. Two days? Yeah, two days and three nights. And I'm bored, man. We've seen all the sights. Like, the dry forest, the beach. Yawn. The animals are kinda cool. For about five minutes, then they get boring. But Eve loves it. I guess I'm doing it for her, doin' it for my lady. Cos I believe in synchronicity, making things happen, you know, right place, right time. Place like this, no way it's not gonna work for us. I offered her a flash vacation somewhere, dunno, in the Bahamas. I said: 'Look honey, you can have a six-star vacation, or I can take you somewhere simple, back to nature and all that. Eco-logical.' And anyway resorts are so boooring, man. But this is kinda boring too."

Ute tried to imagine the sort of woman who would voluntarily couple herself with this man. She couldn't, and this made her curious.

"So how long are you staying?" she said, trying to sound casual.

"Ah, long as it takes. We're working on number four, and aaah, she's not young any more. They say after thirty-five a woman's fertility does a nosedive." He winked at her conspiratorially. "How old are you?"

"Thirty-nine," she said dryly. "And you?"

"Same. Thirty-nine. Getting on. Getting on and there's so much left to do before I turn forty. Nah, don't wanna think about turning forty." Before Ute could ask what he had to do before forty, he shot at her again. "But for you ladies, it's worse. After forty, it's no good. Have you and Jerry, aah..."

"No," she interrupted him, and kicked the water.

"Eve's a baby machine. A super-breeder. It's probably a done deed already. Usually takes only about a week. And how come you missed the train?" He cocked his head, studying her. She felt like a finger was poking inside her.

"I'm sorry. None of your business." Ute strode up the sandy bank, picking up her sandals. This happened very rarely, but she was actually shaking.

"Hey, hey," he said after her, mock-playful. "What did I say! I didn't mean to be rude."

Back on the veranda, Mikel was smoking over a book and an espresso.

"Good morning," he said brightly. "Or, rather, good afternoon."

"Hi," Ute smiled. Last night, after three days in Jerry's company, Mikel had seemed manic, but after Max he was positively sedate.

"Howdy," Max said. He'd come up behind her. Their host crushed out a cigarette in the already full ashtray. Max kept going down the path to his cabin.

"Everything all right?" Mikel enquired, leaning back in his chair. He was like a sprung mechanism. Parts of his body were always moving. Right now, his cracked heel was measuring time in his flip-flop.

"I didn't know there was an animal… shelter across there." Ute sat down in a wicker chair at the next table.

"Oh yeah. We're a sanctuary for endangered species. Animals, humans…" He coughed a warm emphysemic laughter. "Animal trafficking is a massive problem here. The Galápagos in particular. It's big business. Up in the Andes it's even worse, cos nobody gives a shit. Local government will pay thousands of dollars in prize money for cockfights, but they won't sponsor animal refuges like this. Not that we'd ever ask them. But people who are trying to do this elsewhere, they all run on volunteer labour and goodwill, and donations. We give them money too, we sponsor two animal shelters in the Sierra up north. It doesn't take much money. We get a lot of the animal food for free, and we've already got everything else in place. Of course we'd like it to be bigger, but there's only so much space. We can't cut down the forest. It's all protected dry forest around here, for ten kilometres that way." He pointed inland with a nicotine-stained thumb. His fingernails were dirty and broken. "And you know the funny thing? We've got animal traffickers coming here, offering us money for the lion cub, the monkeys, the iguanas, the parrots. The bastards, they just don't get it."

"I guess calling the police would be pointless."

"The police! Did you say the police?" His laughter scratched the inside of his chest. Ute wondered how you get medical help out here. "I prefer to deal with the traffickers. At least with them you know where you stand. You know, once, we had this local family. Rich. They came with their kid for an educational holiday. First thing they say: why isn't there a swimming pool? We explain to them about water, about eco-sustainability..."

The collie ran up from the main gate, followed by the hostess, who was tall and stooped. She gave Ute a crumpled smile.

"Will you have some lunch?" The hostess stood by Mikel's chair.

"*Sí, amor.*" Then he turned to Ute. "Lunch?"

"Yes, thanks. I missed breakfast."

The hostess strode away on her high, lean legs.

"So, anyway, next thing I know," he lit another cigarette, "the kid takes a shine to Alfredito, the marmoset. It's the smallest monkey in the world, really cute. The father offers me good money for the monkey. He starts at a hundred dollars and goes up to five. Then he raises it to a thousand. He can't get it into his thick head that not everything is for sale. I threw them out there and then. The funny thing is, it's precisely to protect animals from people like them that we set up this operation. You know, rich people who buy a lion cub or a giant tortoise for their kids' birthdays, that sort of thing. And when the child is sick of it, the animal gets discarded. Our Jorge was found in a garbage dump twenty kilometres down the coast, almost dead from dehydration, his shell all shrivelled. He's eighty years old, our Jorge!"

"Jorge is our giant turtle." The hostess had returned from the kitchen. Ute heard her American accent for the first time. She was leaning on the doorway of the veranda in a cloud of smoke. "They live up to two hundred years. The oldest specimen is on the Galápagos. So Jorge is not that old, in turtle years. He's younger than Mikel, relatively speaking." She winked at Mikel with both eyes. The deep sun-wrinkles around her eyes were like exquisite tattoos.

"Ah, but I look younger than Jorge, don't I?" Mikel said. He grabbed her hand and kissed its palm sonorously. "Don't I?"

"*Sí, amor.*" She smiled at him.

Their lunch arrived: large plates of spaghetti Bolognese and a bottle of red wine. The young man who served it gave Ute the menu.

"I'll have the same," Ute said. "It looks very good."

"Our chef makes the best spaghetti bolognese on the coast," Mikel announced. "And the best lemon cake, chocolate cake and passion-fruit cake. And the best *arroz marinero*. Have you tried it yet?"

"Yes, we had it up north, but Jerry got an upset stomach."

"Ah, you must try Conchita's. No upset stomachs there." Mikel tucked a large chequered napkin into his open shirt collar.

The three of them ate the spaghetti to the sound of plant sprinklers and birds. The afternoon was sluggish and contented, except for the threat of rain. Ute wondered where Jerry had gone for so long. She was itching to leave the compound and have a look at the dry forest and Puerto Seco itself. And the animals.

"How do you get across to the animals?" she asked.

"By boat," Mikel said. "We have two rowing boats and a big barge for the animals. Didn't you see them?"

"No. Max came up and sort of distracted me."

"Ah yes," he nodded, "Max." They all chewed for a moment. "See the baby iguanas?" Mikel pointed to a high plant right next to our table. She studied its leaves until she saw them: two tiny lizards the colour of the plant, resting in a perfect yin-yang shape on the widest part of a leaf, completely still.

"How did you find this place?" she asked.

The hostess smiled distantly, looking at her as if she herself didn't know and was waiting for Ute to enlighten her. Ute wondered if the woman was on drugs, or just weird.

"A long story." Mikel waved a fork wrapped in spaghetti. "Lucía and I met on the Galápagos. I lived there for a couple of years, managing hotels, doing a bit of tour-guiding. We decided we'd had enough of the Galápagos, all the shit that goes down there, you know. The drugs, the horrible people, the politics."

The name Lucía suited her. Lucía, as in Santa Lucía. There was definitely something otherworldly about her.

"It's an island," Lucía said. "Islands are always... insular."

"That's right," Mikel picked up. "Sooner or later, you realize you're in a sort of prison. We had enough of it. We wanted to settle somewhere along the coast. We wanted to be somewhere green. But the coast is very dry here. It gets green when you start climbing above eight hundred metres, but by then you're not on the coast any more."

Mikel was speaking and slurping his spaghetti simultaneously, spraying the table with specks of sauce, dabbing his stubble with the napkin, his face twitching with ticks the whole time. The most distracting tick was a sudden jerk of his head to one side, always to the right, like chasing a fly from his face. Lucía, on the other hand, was still and opaque like the river outside.

Ute's heart contracted with envy for this untroubled love, for the complete harmony of this couple's life in their gently rotting paradise.

She glanced again at the baby iguanas on the giant leaf. She and Jerry had never had this. Sometimes Ute felt that they lived separate lives, but she quickly told herself that's how she liked it – travelling, compiling the world's opening hours, phone numbers and websites, alone.

"This place was a swamp when we first passed through here," Mikel lit a cigarette and blew the first round of smoke in Ute's direction. He offered her the pack, and Ute reached for a cigarette, the first in many years. He lit it for her. Lucía sat long-necked and still like a sphinx with smoke coming out of its nostrils.

"A swamp along the riverbanks that nobody wanted. It was going to sit here until the end of time. We bought it from the local authorities for a song. We drained the swamp. We had the cabins built on this side of the estuary. Meanwhile, we started rescuing animals from the region. Word of mouth got about and people started bringing us animals. About five years ago, we started building cages. We're the only shelter along the coast..."

Jerry was coming up from the Villa's shore. Alongside him were a rugged stranger in khaki overalls over a bare chest, his face half-hidden by a leather gaucho hat, and a short, cosy-bodied woman with a silvery laugh that ran ahead of her like dropped coins. She had a Latina complexion, and her thighs, squeezed into denim shorts too small for her, were nicely tanned. She wore her bleached hair in a ponytail. Her dark roots were beginning to show. On her tiny ears sparkled precious stones. Jerry was evidently saying something funny. He had found a new comfort zone here, which should have pleased Ute – one less thing to worry about – but somehow it didn't.

"*Hola*," Jerry beamed at the lunchers, creaking up the veranda stairs. The man in overalls disappeared into the back of the building, where the kitchen was, without greeting anyone. "Ute, you've *got* to see the animals. They're amazing." He sat down at the table next to

Ute and the hosts. The woman joined him. Despite the overcast day, she wore enormous sunglasses with a Gucci logo along the rims. "I've never seen an armadillo before, or the smallest monkey in the world, or… or any of them actually. They're all rather exotic."

"The turtles are huge," said the woman. "Shame the kids aren't here, they'd love it."

"Eve, this is Ute," Jerry said.

"Hi," Ute said. Eve got up, stretching out a small, well-manicured hand and stared momentarily at Ute's inflamed face, then blinked away from it, embarrassed. There was something wrong with this introduction, but Ute couldn't say what.

"I'm starving. How's that pasta?" Eve said. Lucía had left most of her lunch untouched on the white plate before lighting a cigarette.

Their hosts were speaking together in hushed tones and sipping their wine. They hadn't offered Ute any, but she was happy with her guava juice. The waiter came and took the new orders.

"A hot chocolate, and ah… the spaghetti *puttanesca*." Eve's loud voice rang.

"When can I see the animals?" Ute asked Mikel.

"You can go across with Carlos now, if you like. Carlos!" he shouted and got up, but only the waiter came out, carrying plates.

"Carlos is gone," the waiter said.

"Ah. Quick as a panther, that Carlos. In that case, this afternoon. The animal carers change over in the late afternoon. You can go across with Pablo and come back with Jesus."

"And Carlos?" Ute asked.

"Carlos lives on the other side. He's always there," Mikel said.

"Jerry?" Ute glanced at her watch: well past one. "When you've had lunch, shall we go to Puerto Seco?"

"Not sure, actually. I don't know if I'll manage a long walk. I've been up since five thirty this morning. And I didn't have a good sleep. I must confess I was rather hoping to sneak into that hammock after lunch… Looks rather alluring."

"Oh, yeah," Eve said.

It felt strange discussing private things, like their afternoon plans and hammocks, in front of these strangers. And she didn't like the way Jerry and Eve were sitting together.

"I feel a bit out of it too," Eve added. "It's the muggy weather or something… I'm feeling real sleepy. By the way, have you seen Maximilian?" She turned to Ute.

"Yeah," Mikel said, "he was here not thirty minutes ago."

"He must be up to something." Eve's eyes narrowed. "Or sleeping."

Ute suddenly had a vision of Eve and "Maximilian" rutting and grunting in the pungent tropical growth like two hippos, their flesh slapping rhythmically in the heavy grind of animal procreation.

"OK." She got up abruptly. "I'm off to Puerto Seco to have a look around. I guess I'll see you later, Jerry." She sounded cheerful, but didn't feel it.

"You will," Jerry lifted his brows mock-emphatically, in that nerdy-cum-charming style of his which sometimes was wide of the mark. Like now. "Be careful out there." He waved his fork at her.

To be fair, he knew she liked exploring alone, and she did have a guide to update. But it stung her how he didn't seem to mind seeing her go.

They had been apart for seven weeks. She would've liked it if he'd kissed her hand instead of waving his fork and pulling a funny face. Come to think of it, he'd never kissed her hand.

"See you later," Eve trilled.

Lucía, Mikel and the collie – or were there two identical collies? – had disappeared. The iguanas hadn't moved from their yin-yang circle.

4

OUTSIDE THE TROPICAL COMPOUND, the air felt dry and dusty, like the savannah. Now the name Puerto Seco made perfect sense.

The beach leading up to the village along the inlet was free of rubbish and cigarette butts. Small palm trees were planted alongside: little imprints of Mikel and Lucía's green thumbs. This strip of the beach had been claimed by Villa Pacifica.

There was no one in sight, despite the fine sand and the tempting water. Ute walked along the waterline, the submissive tide lapping at her feet. The land on the other side of the inlet seemed sparsely inhabited along the shore, and a pale, leafless forest scrambled uphill from the coast. Dark wooded hills rose higher further inland, misted and forbidding. It should have been a beautiful landscape. But there was something exhausted and despairing about the colour or the shape of the land. If it were a wild animal, it would be licking its wounds through torn tufts of fur.

Puerto Seco was about forty-five minutes' walk down the beach and a world away from Villa Pacifica. It was a wheezy dust bowl where homeless dogs rutted in the unpaved streets and rubbish lay about like confetti from some forgotten party. Inside darkened, bare huts on stilts, men lay in hammocks, scratching, their stained singlets peeled off to cool slack bellies on which flies alighted, disturbing their fitful coma.

The women had prematurely wilted faces. They dragged their flip-flops from corner to corner on some drawn-out neighbourhood mission, their legs gripped by snotty kids.

Bare-chested boys with ribs that pushed against their skin kicked a ball on a small football pitch, but even their movements seemed slow, as if they were moving inside a fog. Cumbia blasted out of loudspeakers affixed to the outside walls of a corner shop, to fool the people that something was happening.

Along the *malecón*, Ute crossed a patch of street with empty stalls, which had to be the morning fish market. This was all they had for sale here: fish. The fruit plantations were far away, the artisan workshops too, and so were the Panama hat-makers. All they had here was ocean and twigs.

Ute went into a corner shop to buy a bottle of water. The girl behind the counter was breast-feeding. She greeted the foreigner shyly and without disturbing the plump toddler, who looked at Ute, mouth avidly sucking at the battered young breast. It was like he was saying: "Yes, I too will grow up to be a hammock drone like all the men around here." The girl reached out a hand with bitten-down, painted nails to take the coins. She had delicate features and a disconcerting squint.

Along the deserted *malecón*, the asphalt was eroded on the side of the sea. The steps that led down to the beach were broken. You had to jump. A driver slept in the covered back of his tricycle, baseball hat over his face. Ute couldn't tell if it was the driver from the previous night.

Again, she saw the rubbish-filled hole where a house had been before – unless this was another such house hole. It was obvious that no construction work was planned there. The bare walls of the houses on each side were sporting faded slogans – must be from the last elections, a few months ago, Ute thought. Despite being half washed-out by rain, they were the only cheerful spots that met the eye.

"VOTE FIVE," said one wall, except that a graffiti artist had added his input. The pale letters now read: "VOTE FIVE THOUSAND MINISTERIAL THIEVES. VOTE FIVE YEARS WITHOUT WATER."

"THIS TIME, EVERYTHING!" a man with oiled hair promised from the other wall. Ute had come to know the faces of the various presidential candidates from the remaining slogans around the country, and from newspapers. This one had been the economy minister of a previous government that had bankrupted the country. Someone had edited his catchphrase with spray paint, so it read: "THIS TIME, I'LL STEAL EVERYTHING!"

Ute passed a tiny hole in the wall that bore a chipped, painted sign: "*Salón de belleza*" "Always Happy". It was "always happy" in English, and it was closed. She peaked inside the grimy windows. Chairs, mirrors, sprays. A price sheet half-taped on the glass door told her that for three dollars she could have her body hair bleached or epilated, or get a haircut. Failing that, she could have her nails done for fifty *centavos*. But what she really needed was a shot of caffeine. For some reason, the dog-tiredness of the previous night hadn't left her. Or perhaps she had overslept.

There were a couple of small cafés along the waterfront. One was closed, perhaps permanently, with a corrugated-iron roll-down shutter. The other one looked dark and cavernous inside, but there were two toxic-yellow plastic tables outside. Then she saw the bright sign above: "Café Fin del Mundo". Ute smiled to herself. This sort of thing was a gift to the travel writer.

A petite woman with grey-black hair piled up on top of her head came out from the back of the cavern. She seemed startled by her customer's appearance, or perhaps she was just surprised to have a customer.

Ute sat down at an outside table and asked for a coffee. Her voice sounded oddly muffled, as if her head was filled with cotton wool.

When the woman brought out the pale, dirty-brown broth of unmistakable granulated Nescafé, Ute was stunned at her own forgetfulness. Half a day in the oasis of Villa Pacifica had removed her from the grim realities of the local economy: it was impossible to get real coffee in this coffee-producing country. All the good stuff was for export to the US and, in return, they got the cheap and nasty instant variety. She sipped the rank liquid, smiling at the woman who stood with her arms crossed in the doorway. The woman smiled back. She had a toothy grin that lit up the sad little café. Her ankles and wrists were like dry twigs. Tucked into her crossed arms, against her bird's chest, she had a notepad, and something about it – perhaps the hopeful carbon paper sticking out of it – stabbed Ute with a pang of sorrow.

"Not many people around at the moment," Ute said.

"Yes, it's very quiet. It's this El Niño weather we're having. It puts off tourists." Her voice, like her entire being, seemed too frail for her surroundings. She was like a shadow of what she had been in some previous, plumper life.

"Do you often get storms here?" Ute nodded towards the beach.

"Every now and then. These days it's either drought or floods. We've had El Niño twice in the last fifteen years. A year ago it wrecked the *malecón*. Wrecked our café too. We had very pretty furniture, handmade by my husband. But it was destroyed, everything was destroyed. I wanted to close down the café, but my husband is ill. He can't make furniture any more, and I have to get by somehow. So I painted the front again, got this ugly plastic furniture and reopened." The woman said all this with a brave smile.

"And your husband... Is he better?"

"*Bueno...*" She looked out towards the beach. A ray of sunshine poked through the milky clouds just then. "Not really," she said. "He's up in the hills, across the water." She waved vaguely to the cloud forest in the south. "I think he's OK there, in his own way. The community of Agua Sagrada don't bother him. It's the way he wants it. He doesn't want to die in a hospital. He has his painting, his poetry..."

And she, what did she have? There was no bitterness in her voice. Ute tried to squeeze something cheerful from her sluggish mind. But the woman recovered.

"See these paintings? They're Oswaldo's. He has an unusual style of blending poetry with painting. He's had exhibitions in the capital. He's highly regarded in the art world. But in this country, it's impossible to make a living from art."

Ute got up and peered at the dark walls of the café. They were covered in paintings of varying sizes. They were all for sale, at modest prices.

Bleeding, spidery words she couldn't decipher were woven into the distorted half-animal, half-human figures and landscapes in ochre, yellow, green and blue. The sea was always lurking behind, a pale, murky sea. Ute didn't know much about art, but she knew when she saw a restless soul, and here was one.

"I like them," she said. It was a relief to be honest about something, anything.

"An American couple came by yesterday, they had fried calamari. They're staying at Villa Pacifica. The *señor* is Colombian. He knows a lot about business. He told me to put the prices up. Too cheap, he said. But I don't know who'll buy them. They don't sell much as it is... They're not for the locals anyway. People here are too poor and ignorant. And foreigners, when they come, they come for the beach, for the snorkelling..."

"Did the American couple buy a painting?"

"Oh no, no. I didn't expect them to. To tell you the truth, I keep these paintings up because they make me feel like Oswaldo is here..." She trailed off again. "Such is life, sometimes."

"Yes," Ute said and glanced towards those misty hills across the ditch.

"I'll buy a painting, later," she said, and knew she wouldn't. Even the smallest one wouldn't fit into her backpack. Guilt, that's what it was. She had learnt to manage and suppress guilt when travelling – you had to, you'd crucify yourself trying to save everyone. It was best to give up all thought of helping and distance yourself. But the woman's brave smile and these paintings caught her unawares.

"You're always welcome," the woman said, as if reading her flaky thoughts of a well-meaning gringa. "If the café is closed, just ask around for Consuelo. I live at the other end of the village."

"OK," Ute said. "My name is Ute."

"Ute," the woman repeated. "Nice name."

Perhaps she could buy the smallest one and give it to Jerry to take back with him as hand luggage. Ute got up. The coffee was undrinkable.

"Are you staying at Villa Pacifica?" Consuelo asked.

"Yes."

"There are many paintings by Oswaldo there. I don't know if they're still up, but they're there. He was a very good friend of Mikel and Lucía. We were all good friends once..." She composed herself. "The furniture there is his work too."

All small places have their secrets, Ute thought. She promised she'd look out for the paintings, paid up, left an unreasonably large tip and walked away. Consuelo retreated back into the dark interior.

Some black kids were kicking a half-deflated ball on the beach. The village was slowly coming round from its siesta. Ute sat on a bench not far from the café and sketched in her notepad an outline of the area as she saw it: Puerto Seco, the inlet, the two sides, the sanctuary of Villa Pacifica straddling it. She wasn't too sure about the dry forest – how far it stretched, what was up in those shrouded hills. Ten kilometres that way, Mikel had said. But which way was that? She felt lost without a map, and she didn't like feeling lost.

The kids had spotted her. There were four of them, a girl and two boys of around thirteen, and a tiny girl with something smeared around her mouth who was running behind them across the sand.

"What are you doing?" the older girl stepped forward, the official envoy of the group. She had a chubby face, and her belly protruded over her trousers. She wore a baseball hat, like the two boys.

"I'm drawing." Ute smiled. "It's a picture of the *malecón* and Puerto Seco."

The girl came closer and looked at the pad.

"It doesn't look like Puerto Seco," she declared.

"That's true," Ute agreed, "I'm not a very good artist."

The girl giggled, her hand on her mouth, where a few teeth were missing. The boys smiled shyly, avoiding Ute's eyes.

"Why do you have red all over your face?" the girl asked, rubbing her fingers around her own mouth, to show where she meant. "Are you sick?"

"No, I'm not sick," Ute smiled. "That's just the way I am. You have crinkly hair, and I have red around my mouth. What're your names?"

"Evelyn," the girl said.

"Ricardo," said one of the boys. The other boy mumbled a name Ute couldn't make out.

"And I'm Ute. Can you write your names down for me?" Ute handed over the pad and the pencil to Ricardo. The boys suddenly grew sombre. Ricardo shook his head vigorously. She handed it to Evelyn, who put her hands behind her back and looked the other way.

"Come on."

"We can't," Evelyn said.

"Why not?"

"We can't write our names."

They had dropped out of school for reasons they couldn't explain. Evelyn was ten, and the boys were ten and twelve. The tiny tot was their baby sister. Evelyn lifted her up to show her to Ute, like a toy, and the girl's face soured, ready to cry.

"Where do you live?" Evelyn enquired.

"Over there, in Villa Pacifica," Ute pointed behind her.

"*El Vasco y la Bruja*," she mumbled and looked at Ricardo, and they giggled. The little one laughed too, happily, kicking sand. The other boy remained glum.

"What?" Ute was intrigued. "Who is *la Bruja*?"

"*La Bruja, la Bruja... el Vasco y la Bruja... el Vasco y la Bruja*," Evelyn chanted by way of an explanation. So Mikel and Lucía were the Basque and the Witch. Ute got up. These kids depressed her.

"Are you going to come again?" Ricardo said.

"Of course," Ute said.

"When?" he insisted.

"Tomorrow."

"We'll be over there," Evelyn said, and pointed to the patch of beach where their deflated ball sat.

"OK, see you then," Ute said. But they followed after her, Evelyn carrying the little one. The glum brother tagged behind. Consuelo was leaning in the café entrance, looking their way. From here, Ute couldn't tell if she was smiling or crying. Either way, she cut a disconsolate figure for someone called Consuelo. Eventually, Ute managed to lose the kids and went looking for the tourist agency that sold tickets for the dry forest. It was a newly anointed national park. She had to see if it was worth adding it into her guide update, and she also needed a map of the area.

She tripped over the doorway step of the sleepy little office and almost tumbled inside. There was an elevation fifteen centimetres high at the foot of the door, as if specifically designed to trip up visitors. The swollen-bodied guard dozing on a chair inside the dark room woke up when she entered.

"El Niño," he pointed at the doorstep by way of an excuse. "We have valuable exhibits in here. We can't afford damage like last time."

The only exhibit Ute could detect was him. She bought two A5-sized tickets to the park, plus an extra one to "swim with the fishes of Agua Sagrada", as the guard put it, and for a moment Ute stared at him. Then she realized what he meant and smiled. "Swimming with the fishes" was a local expression for drowning, but of course it also meant snorkelling. She asked him how to get to the other side of the inlet, where the cloud forest was.

"The other side? There's nothing there. The Agua Sagrada beach isn't accessible from there anyway, you have to go onto the main road, and the official entrance to the dry forest is there. Or you can go swim with the fishes from here, and go to the beach as well. By boat. From here."

She was confused. "There's no way across the river further down?"

"You go along the road," he insisted again.

"And what about the community of Agua Sagrada, can I visit them?" It was the sick painter she was suddenly curious about.

"They are too far up the hill. It takes two days to get there on horseback. And anyway, they don't like visitors." He then added, as if it was somehow connected, "They make pottery."

"Careful," he mumbled as Ute headed outside, just in time to prevent her from tripping again over the crazy door stopper. A hundred metres down the street, she realized she'd forgotten to ask about maps, and the exhibits. She was having a forgetful day. She turned back.

The clerk was already dozing on his chair. She looked around for maps or any other information, but there was nothing, except a wad of US dollars behind the glass counter and a wad of tickets.

"What do you want now?" the clerk grumbled. He'd risen from his chair and was attempting to tuck his shirt into his trousers.

"I'm looking for a map."

"What for?"

"Well, to get... oriented."

"If you need information or orientation, you can ask me."

They looked at each other for a dumb moment.

"You are the official agency that sells tickets to the park, is that right?"

"That's right."

"This is a newly established national park." Ute stepped towards him to impress on him the difference in their heights. But clearly he'd seen tall, aggressive gringas before and he wasn't an impressionable type. He just watched her indifferently, waiting for her to finish and leave. His gut hung over his belt.

"You charge twenty dollars per ticket, which I'm happy to pay," Ute continued. "A map and some additional information is not that much to ask for, is it? In a park that's... I don't know how many thousands of square metres, and comprises several microclimates, endangered flora and fauna, beaches and marine life?"

"We do not have the means to provide visitors with maps, *señora*. We have been a national park only for two and a half years, and El Niño hit us hard. As I said, whatever information you need, just ask. That's why I'm here. For example, I can tell you that the park is twenty hectares. It's the biggest park of its kind along the coast, and the only one."

There was a flicker of enjoyment in his eyes now. She had brought a bit of action into his afternoon. "If you'd like to know more about the flora and fauna, just ask the guide when you take the boat trip. And also, you can use these tickets for up to seven days. You can go in and out of the park as many times as you like."

"OK. And can I see the exhibits?" Ute said, resigned.

"Unfortunately, some work is being done on the exhibit room just now. It will be open to visitors in a few weeks. Where are you from?"

"Finland," Ute said.

"Like the vodka," the man said, and smiled lecherously.

"Yes." She felt woozy and aggravated by everything and nothing in particular. It was very unlike her. On the way out, she tripped over the step again.

"Watch out for the step!" a belated drawl followed her out.

5

WHEN SHE GOT BACK to Villa Pacifica, she discovered that her watch had stopped. It wasn't two-twenty, as it showed, but five-twenty. Somehow, she had spent the entire afternoon in Puerto Seco. She'd also missed the afternoon crossing to the animal shelter with Pablo, or was it Jesus? She'd have to wait till the morning.

The young receptionist-cum-waiter conveyed this to her in a low, confident voice meant to sound respectful, but the thread of mockery in it didn't escape her. He had slicked-back hair, and his slightly hooded lizard's eyes gave him a sly expression. It said, "I'll take your breakfast order no problem, but I'm also taking your measure, all you gringos who've washed up here, with your self-delusions and vanities." It didn't surprise her. They were, after all, vaguely despicable, Ute thought. Had she been him, she'd despise gringos too. In fact, she already did, a little.

His name was Héctor. He called her *señora*, which made her feel old. "My name is Ute, by the way," she said to him, and he said, "*Bueno, señora.*" She must have looked huge to him, with her practical cargo trousers and broad shoulders. But she was used to feeling this way in South America. Sometimes it even gave her a pang of dull satisfaction, a friendly giant's glee, to see the curious, alarmed looks of the locals. The worst places to be unfeminine in South America were Rio and Buenos Aires. The beauty of the women there was so commonplace that society as a whole took its absence as a public insult. Walking down the streets of Buenos Aires, Ute had actually felt the judgemental looks of passers-by, both men and women. How dare you look like that, they seemed to say. How dare you show your disfigured face, how dare you uglify our city. She had declined the offer to update the Argentina guide.

Ute went into the lounge and took a look at the furniture. It was made from a light wood, the design simple and sensitive. She already liked Oswaldo the artist. She imagined him as a silver-haired man with a suffered-in face, and wondered if she could meet him, up in his cloud forest. Héctor stood by, watching her.

"It's nice work, isn't it?" he said eventually, nodding at the tables.

"Yes, beautiful."

"It's the work of a local artist, Oswaldo Joven. This is by him as well." He pointed to a large painting in the dimmest corner of the room. Ute went closer and recognized the style of weaving words and shapes in a seasick way. It was hard to say just what it meant to depict, but the overall impression was one of rolling hills and bays, or perhaps clouds and waves. It was as if a malevolent God had run its hand through this landscape and spiritually deformed it. She managed to decipher the poem, which undulated with the landscape, but the letters were too warped, and all she could make out was: *welcome... end of the world... and the world will not... you and the world will not... you...*

"This painting used to be in a café. *Señor* Mikel bought it and put it here." Héctor explained. Ute didn't mind him so much any more.

"Are there other paintings by *Señor* Oswaldo here?" she asked.

"Yes. Many."

"Where are they?"

Héctor shook his head. "There are too many, there's not enough space for them here."

Just then, a man and a woman arrived. They were Hispanics, but from the man's clear Spanish, Ute gathered they weren't locals.

"Where can we park our car?" the man demanded, dangling a large bunch of keys. "It's a four-by-four, so we need space."

He had the imperious manner of rich Latinos speaking to those with less money, which meant most other Latinos. The woman – she was a girl, really – glanced around with studied superiority, making sure the place was up to their standards. They said a smiley, friendly "*Hola*" when they saw Ute. Héctor got on with the business of registering them. His manner had stiffened again.

The man was youngish, perhaps in his mid-thirties, but his tall frame had already slumped into the softness of a prosperous middle age. He wore a heavy gold watch, Bermuda shorts and a polo shirt with an open collar – the kind of gear affluent American men wear to signal they're outward-bound. In his earnest shorts, pulled-up socks and pristine trainers, he looked like a fat rich kid keen to join the cool kids' party. The woman was long-haired, bejewelled and tiny, with a bird's face. She looked to be in her twenties and carried a small crocodile-skin handbag. Her stick-insect figure somehow supported a pair of disproportionately large breasts in a white sleeveless top with a high polo neck. She looked like Barbie. Ute stared involuntarily. The woman smiled back blankly. Ute couldn't imagine her either loving or hating her husband.

She dragged herself back to the cabin. Back at *la tortuga*, she found Jerry lying in the hammock, asleep, the ridge of his nose marked by his glasses, which were neatly folded on his crotch, his closed laptop resting on his stomach. The door of their cabin was ajar. Ute stepped inside, anxious. What or whom did she expect to find in there, apart from mosquitoes? There was no one there, of course, though the earthy incense aroma of the previous night hung heavily in the air, like a presence. Her half-unpacked stuff was just as she'd left it that morning. After a cool shower, she felt slightly more alert.

She came out, and Jerry gave her a vivid smile from his hammock. She sat on the doorstep.

"You look very awake for someone who was dozing just five minutes ago. Nice siesta?" Ute said.

"Brilliant siesta. Possibly the best siesta I've ever had. How was Puerto Seco?"

"It's a dump. But I got us tickets for the dry-forest park tomorrow. Looks like we'll have to set the day aside for it. It's huge."

"Have you been across to the animals?"

"No, I missed the afternoon crossing."

"You're joking! You've got to see them! Stuff the dry forest."

"Yeah, I'll see them tomorrow. There's wet forest too, you know, above sea level."

She wanted to tell him about Consuelo and Oswaldo, about the painting, the sad kids on the beach, but it all seemed too complicated. She didn't have the energy.

"Ute," Jerry shifted heavily sideways in the hammock and blinked at her in that ingratiating, puppyish way he had of signalling that he wanted something. "Would you mind if we stayed here longer? Say, a week?"

"A week!"

"Yeah, I know, I know. We said only a couple of days. But I'd be happy to spend my whole break here, and you'd still have time afterwards to cover the rest of the coast. I mean, you've already covered it, this is pretty much the end of the line, as it were."

Ute shrugged. "But why?"

"There's something about this place, an energy. Last night, I didn't blink. I felt incredibly alert. All my tiredness went. I just sort of prowled around the place. I went down to the shore and I knew there were wild animals on the other side, I just knew it though only the birds were making a noise. Then I lay in the hammock and, you know, listened to the jungle, as it were. I took some notes. A lot of notes actually. To be honest, I'd like to do some writing while we're here. I've got the time off now, you know how it is. When I go back to teaching in January, my time won't be mine any more…"

"I don't mind. As long as we can stay away from that guy Max," Ute said.

"Oh God," Jerry rolled his eyes, "where did *he* come from! Big baboon. The first thing he asked me when we met, he goes," Jerry put on an exaggerated American accent, "'How much do you earn teaching lidereture at callege?'"

"What's his wife like?" Ute asked, swatting a mosquito on her arm.

"She's all right, actually. Not much to her, but at least she's not obnoxious, I suppose. God knows what she's doing with that dickhead."

"Breeding, by the sound of it," Ute got up.

"What, you heard them?" Jerry cracked a little smile.

"No," Ute said. "Max told me about it."

"A subtle operator, isn't he?" Jerry shook his head and yawned. He knew how talking about procreation made her feel. Poor Jerry – there wasn't much he could do about it, except perform dutiful sex and remain optimistic.

"There are new arrivals," Ute said. "South American couple, rich fat guy with trophy girlfriend."

"Oh good. At least that'll put some insulation between us and Max. Literally."

They smiled conspiratorially. It was nice to feel conspiratorial again. Jerry's face was lit up by the slightly euphoric light he radiated when working on something new. The change had occurred overnight, and his sudden muse, wherever it came from, had transformed the grumpy, beleaguered tourist into someone inspired, lit from within. She knew how much this transformation meant to him. This could be it, the story or novel that would be his breakthrough – finally, finally.

Three years earlier, he'd been battered by a tidal swell of rejections for a collection of stories he'd taken ten years to put together. He'd sunk into a borderline depression state after that. So all she could do was let him write when he felt like it. And he felt like it now.

She smiled at Jerry, and he leant back in his hammock and closed his eyes. She didn't understand, not really, this urge to write down made-up stories about made-up people. And she wasn't sure how good his stories were. Jerry, in turn, didn't understand the point of travel guides. He couldn't even use them. And the academic in him couldn't see the point of any text that was less than fifty years old. Guides went out of date within a couple of years.

Sitting on the steps of their hut, Ute looked at her unlacquered toenails, which she vowed to polish at the earliest opportunity. She listened to the plant sprinklers, and her mind wandered back to the morning encounter with Max. She didn't want it to, but couldn't help it. And to that horrible feeling of shaky legs and lurching innards, that readiness to run, throw a stone at something. And suddenly, without warning, she thought of the first time she'd ever felt out of control like this. It was around that time that she got her first attack of eczema.

She was seven or eight when her mother had her first nervous breakdown. They visited her in hospital. Ute held a wilted little tassel of nameless flowers that her father had bought. It was winter. It was always winter in her childhood. Her mother sat in bed and had white bandages over her wrists. Ute held out the flowers to her, and when she took them, her mother started crying. It was a noiseless, dejected crying, an apology of tears. Not an apology for what she'd tried to do, but for failing to do it well. For being there at all. It was as if she wanted all of them to cease to exist, but there she was, and there they were, and it was unbearable to be there, it was all a terrible mistake.

Ute's father placed his big, helpless hand on her head. That first time had broken her childish heart, which is why she willed herself into a numbness of the heart from then on. She numbed herself against... well, she didn't know what. At first it was against her mother's pain, of course, which even as a child Ute sensed was somehow bottomless. Then against anybody who might hurt her in the future. She didn't want this sort of pain to ever reach her again.

When, three years ago, she had walked out of the hospital after her near-fatal ectopic pregnancy, hand in hand with Jerry, she had willed herself not to feel. She could do that, she had a lifetime of practice. When she checked out of the unit, she saw that Jerry had cried. Your glasses are smudged, she said to him, and he hugged her very tight, and she felt as if she was comforting him, as if he himself had had the ordeal. She didn't shed a tear. True, her body had rejected their child. Their child was dead. But she could see no point in crying. Crying was something to avoid at all times, because once you started, you might not be able to stop at all, and who knows what might happen next.

Go away, she said, to these unwelcome memories. They were in paradise right now, weren't they? Ute breathed in the fragrance of orchids and humid earth, full of lazy naps and long afternoons. And she willed herself to feel good about it, to hope for the best.

She willed it because she was afraid here. She didn't know what exactly she was afraid of, and this was the worst kind of fear.

6

CREATIVITY HAD MADE JERRY ravenous, and Ute joined him for dinner, even if she wasn't hungry. The other guests were already there. She heard Max's loud voice and another man's high-pitched laughter before she saw them. Max and Eve were occupying a table in the centre of the veranda, and the new couple sat at a table next to them. Max was sprawled over two chairs, his legs spread out, leaning towards the new couple as he regaled them with some story in Spanish.

"Hi," Eve chimed. Ute waved hello and headed towards the far end of the veranda, away from them. But Eve wanted to chat to Jerry, and he stopped to attend to her. It was against his nature to be rude to anybody's face.

"Hey Jerry!" Max turned his attention to him and pumped his hand. "Where's your Tom?"

Eve chuckled, but it was a good-natured chuckle. She was a good-natured woman. She wasn't bad-natured anyway. The skin of her olive face was thick and sturdy – the kind of skin that sees you off into old age.

"Where you going, Uddar?"

She forced a smile. But he was moving on already.

"Jerry, this is my buddy Alejandro, and his new bride Alma. They're from Mexico City. They're on their honeymoon." He winked at Alejandro, who laughed that grating, eunuch-like laughter again.

"Call me Alex." The Mexican put out a podgy hand, and Jerry shook it.

Ute still stood on the other side of the veranda, but soon realized that she had no choice – she had to sit with them. Already Max was pulling up a chair and gesturing for Jerry to sit down.

"We met this afternoon," Ute said, smiling at the Mexicans.

"Yes, that's right."

Héctor stood by, ready to take their orders.

Jerry went for the *arroz marinero*, and Ute asked for a salad.

"One mixed salad," Héctor confirmed, and looked Ute in the eye for a second. It was just a casual look, but she sensed it was more than that.

"Give me the steak with chips," Alejandro commanded in Spanish, and snapped the menu shut. "And a beer."

"A mixed salad for me too," Alma said.

"Very well." Héctor strode off.

Ute glimpsed a broad back in a floral short-sleeved shirt, and a twitchy cracked heel in a flip-flop inside the lounge. Next to it, the furry tail of a collie twitched in agreement. Mikel and Lucía were quietly sitting inside, eating dinner, out of view.

"So," Jerry said, clearing his throat, "how come you guys speak Spanish?"

"My parents are Colombian," Max said. "I was born in the US, I have two brothers and one sister. I grew up in Miami. But I go to Colombia from time to time to keep an eye on some lands and plantations I own there. I've also got properties in Costa Rica, cos Eve's parents are from Costa Rica. My dream is to retire there by the time I'm forty-five. Play golf, live in a big house by the beach with all my concubines. And get rid of them when they're no good no more." He nudged Eve and added, "Joking, honey."

But she wasn't laughing. It looked like she wasn't even listening.

A few minutes later, Héctor brought dinner. Max and Alejandro dug into their steaks. Ute picked at the artistically arranged salad.

"And what do you do, Alejandro?" She turned to the Mexican.

"Call me Alex," he said again, a little too eagerly. "I work for a media firm in Mexico City and—"

"Alex here is wasting his time in an office, is what he does," Max cut in. "I'm telling him he should go into business."

"Yeah," Alejandro nodded, chewing his steak. "I'm workin' on it."

"And what do you do?" Jerry turned to the bride. She was wearing an open-fronted, white-linen shirt with rolled-up sleeves, beach-style.

"I? I am..." she looked at Alejandro, flustered, and asked him, "*Cómo se dice secretaria*?"

"She is a model," Alejandro translated. "Fashion model." Then, realizing that some of the other people understood Spanish, he added: "And she takes care of administration in my office..."

"Hey," Max interrupted again. "Wanna play darts after dinner? No, wait, wait, wanna go see the animals? Have you guys seen the animals?" He turned to the Mexicans. They hadn't.

"*Los animales*!" Alma chirped.

"Are we allowed to see the animals at this time?" Jerry started, but Mikel's voice boomed behind him.

"You're not allowed to see the animals, because it's going to be dark," he said. He was standing in the doorway between the veranda and the lounge. His right hand twitched at the chain on which his glasses hung. "We only allow visitors two times per day. You can go tomorrow morning. OK?"

Everybody knew this was directed at Max.

"All right," Max nodded. "No problem. I've already seen the animals, it's for these guys, I wanted to go and show them."

"No, you don't show anybody anything round here," Mikel said. "Carlos will be there tomorrow morning. He'll show them." He patted the collie, which was standing next to him now. Mikel exuded a sort of flaky authority, in his worn-out flip-flops and preposterous Hawaiian shirt. His legs were as furry as the dog's.

"That's cool with me," Max said. "You're the boss."

Mikel lit a cigarette and leant against the door frame. He looked at his guests, as if waiting to be asked a question. He *was* the boss.

"How long have you been in this place?" Alejandro asked.

"Fifteen years," Mikel exhaled.

"How you gonna sell this place one day? Who's gonna buy it?" Max asked.

"We won't sell it," Mikel said in English. "We'll stay here."

"You're kidding me," Max snorted.

"You're kidding yourself," Mikel grimaced, his eyes ironic slits. "We came here because we searched for the perfect place. We created the perfect place. We live here and we'll die here."

"But this place isn't making money," Max declared.

"We make some money."

"How much do you make, come on, what's your turnover?"

"It's not your business. We make a living."

Ute liked Mikel, despite his rants. She was prepared to like anyone who could stand up to Max.

"No no, buddy, you don't get it," Max said. "You could be making heaps out of this place. You could be running the animal refuge like a zoo – charging, say, five bucks per visitor. Bring in busloads of kids from the cities to see endangered species and all that – ecological stuff, educational visits. You rent out the cabins to school groups, pack in the kids, four per double cabin, fifteen dollars a head, ten kids per family cabin, eight dollars a head…"

"What are you talking about?" Mikel's mocking snort interrupted him. "We don't want school kids here…"

Lucía came up behind Mikel and put a calm hand on his shoulder. He visibly relaxed at her touch, took a drag on his cigarette and went quiet for a moment.

"And you need to change the name," Max rattled on. "You can't go on calling yourself Villa Pacifica, that's just… wrong, it's… neither here nor there. No buddy, you need something snappier. Like *Paradiso*, *Los Tigres*, something sexier like that."

Mikel kept shaking his head.

"Listen, pal," Max went on, "we can strike a deal here. Let's talk about it later, but here's my offer, go and think about it. If you give me fifty per cent of this place, I'll take it off your hands and turn it around. I'll get my guys to build more chalets, bigger ones, luxury ones, expand. I won't touch the animals, just make it more, you know, attractive to visitors. No school kids. Put some signs along the road. And don't get me wrong, it'll stay eco-friendly, green and clean and all that, no two ways about it, cos that's the way of the future, that's what people want these days. 'Exclusive eco-resort *Los Tigres*… See the Galápagos without leaving land…' Get the local community to make snorkelling products. Hell, get them to make ice cream. 'Organic ice cream from Puerto Seco… Flavoured with *palo santo*, for inner peace…' Yadi-yadi-ya."

"What's he on about?" Mikel turned to Lucía in Spanish. She maintained her patient smile, her hand on Mikel's shoulder. It was as if Max's words were washing over her like ambient music.

"Listen to me," Mikel said, turning again to Max. "You're welcome to stay here with your wife. You are our guests. But don't try to sell me your business plans. I've had the likes of you before. They wanted the monkey. They wanted Jorge. They wanted a swimming pool. They wanted to poison our animals. I've been offered thousands. You know what I did? I kicked them out. Simple as that. *Me entiendes*?"

"What's wrong with you people?" Max was getting heated now. "I never met anybody who don't wanna make money! Are you hippies or something?..."

"Yeah, that's exactly what I am," Mikel snapped back, pointing at Max with a burning cigarette for maximum impact. "A socialist. That bother you? I believe in treating the earth we live on well. I believe in treating people like people and not like sources of capital. Do you know how much rain we got last year in the wet season? Five days! Do you know that the tropical forest has shrunk to ten per cent of its original size because of climate change? Do you know that America has fucked its neighbours in the south with aggressive foreign policy and backing up military regimes for decades? Do you know that globalization is making the rich richer and the poor poorer?..."

The tirade went on for a while. Mikel sprayed the guests with cigarette ash until the cigarette in his shaking hand burned down to his fingers and he tossed it away. Lucía was gently clawing at him, trying to calm him down, but without success. In the end she gave up and went back inside, leaving him to exhaust himself – and everyone else. When he finally did, Jerry was the first to react.

"Absolutely," he said. He looked at Ute with mock seriousness, for confirmation.

Max had calmed down a bit in the face of Mikel's outburst.

"Look, buddy," he offered to Mikel, "I'm not in politics. But I will be soon. I'm gonna run in the local elections in a coupla years. And anyways it was the Spanish that came here with their guns and diseases and wiped out the Incas, the Mayas and all those dudes…"

"I'm not Spanish, I am Basque," Mikel announced – then, in a moment of house-keeping repentance, he bent down to pick up the fag he'd just discarded, and placed it in a table ashtray. "I haven't been to Spain since 1988, for your information."

"Goodnight," Lucía waved from inside the lounge and headed off to their bungalow.

"Goodnight," mumbled a few voices.

"OK," Mikel said abruptly, and frowned at his guests in an unsuccessful attempt to smile. "Goodnight."

Max sprang to his feet.

"All right, buddy?" he said, his hand outstretched as if about to strike a deal with him.

"I'm not your buddy," Mikel said and hesitated, but then took the offered hand for a second, withdrew quickly, and was gone down the white pebbled path. The thatched roof of the master bungalow showed above the high plants. The collie got up, shook its furry coat, and padded off behind him.

They were all quiet for a moment, sipping wine.

"So, anybody wanna swim across to the animals?" Max grinned at the company.

"Didn't you hear what he said?" Eve snapped at him.

"Sure I did."

"So," Jerry said, turning to Ute, "what was all that about? What was he saying? There was a lot of references to America in it."

"He's Basque," she summed up. "And he doesn't like the US."

"What, a retired ETA terrorist?" Jerry sniggered. "South America cracks me up. It's full of retired Nazis and weirdos."

No one responded. This was sharp language for Jerry. He seemed a bit drunk, though half a bottle of wine couldn't possibly account for it.

"All right, you losers." Max stretched lazily across his chair. "If you don't wanna play, you don't wanna play. I'm bored. What are we gonna do. Let's go have a game of darts. They have games upstairs. Alex?"

Alejandro seemed a bit lost. "All right," he said, picking himself up. "Alma, you want to play?" She did. Eve didn't. She yawned and announced she was off to bed. It wasn't even nine o'clock yet, but Ute felt shattered too, as if she'd walked through the national park all day, all twenty hectares of it.

Just then a feline roar ripped through the silence. Everyone froze and looked around. Night had fallen – a deep, equatorial night.

"Jesus," Jerry said. "That sounded close. Must be the lion cub."

"She's lonely," Max said. "She's a girl. Girls need company. Ain't that right, Alex?"

"Yeah," Alejandro chuckled uneasily and took Alma's bird-like hand in his and rubbed it.

Jerry and Ute exchanged looks. It was time to retire. They got up and bid everyone goodnight. The lion's sorrowful roar followed them down the ghostly white path all the way to *la tortuga*. The humid darkness seemed to magnify sound.

"Sounds a lot closer than it is," Ute said.

"It's not that far, really," Jerry said. "But I'm surprised the sound isn't muffled by all the vegetation."

"I'm exhausted," Ute said. "I think it's Max."

"He's unbearable. But he's a certain kind of rare specimen. Almost a parody of himself. If you put him in a book, he would seem exaggerated."

"Well, I'd rather examine the specimens of the local flora and fauna. It's more relaxing."

Jerry put an arm around her waist and kissed her eyelid. He was grateful that she'd agreed to stay longer. Everything else was peripheral. Under the mosquito canopy in their cabin, he passed a glad hand over the contours of her body, but she didn't have the energy for it. She felt disconnected from herself as well as from everyone else.

Again, she slept the sleep of the innocent. And again, her dreams were far from innocent. She dreamt of a woman statue who wasn't a statue at all. She stood in a clearing in the middle of a jungle, white, perfect-faced and naked, her breasts bursting with jungle sap. Then, out of the bushes came a hairy, olive-skinned man who stood behind her, placed his hands on her breasts and started humping her. It was Max. No, oh my God, it was Jerry. No, that was impossible. She didn't want to know. She looked away from it, and yet it was everywhere. And the statue was... It was either Alma or Eve, she couldn't tell, because the statue's identity was somehow beside the point. She was every woman, the female principle at its most basic. And as he humped her, the statue's belly started swelling. Ute felt aroused and repelled at the same time, because she knew that this primeval spectacle was put on especially for her, that they knew she was watching. That they were provoking her, trying to tell her something. She ran back into the dark forest, but straight away came onto another clearing drenched with light, and there too was an identical copulating couple. And again she turned away and ran through dense vegetation, sorrow and anger clutching at her throat, and again – a clearing where... She was surrounded.

She woke up drenched in sweat, shaken and annoyed with her dream. Jerry wasn't there.

In fact, she felt ill – not physically, just generally ill. Maybe it was the strong incense. It was as if a malevolent spirit dwelt here with them, in the heavy drugged air of the cabin, and seeped into their days and nights.

7

THERE WAS NOBODY ON the terrace or in the lounge, but the kitchen sounded busy. Ute peered inside. A squat woman in an apron was extracting juice in an industrial-sized juicer, and Héctor was pouring it into two large glass bottles. They had their backs turned to her, so she had time to look around the kitchen. It was clean and modern, with gleaming surfaces. On the wall, above the tall fridge, was a large board, which, instead of a menu, contained a single sentence in Spanish:

We cannot be sure of having something to live for unless we are willing to die for it. El Che

"Would you like some breakfast, *señora*?" Héctor had seen her and was shouting over the roaring motor of the juice extractor.

"Yes, thank you." OK, so she *was* a *señora* – what else was a married woman in her late thirties? When she first travelled to South America, thirteen years ago, she was a *señorita*.

"That's an original place to put Che Guevara," she pointed at the board.

"*Señor* Mikel is an original man," Héctor said. "Continental breakfast?"

"Yes please."

She walked around the lounge. There were shelves full of well-thumbed books. There was *The Beach*, Bruce Chatwin, *South America on a Shoestring*, Jules Verne, Alberto Moravia, a German-Italian dictionary, the poetry of Pablo Neruda, a biography of Che Guevara in Italian, *Harry Potter* in Dutch. One shelf contained several large, wood-bound, recycled-paper guest books, arranged by year. Ute opened the one from 2004 at random.

"I wanted to leave on the fourth of December. Then I aimed for the sixth. Today is the tenth," said Ben from Perth, Australia.

"This place is impossible to leave, and impossible to forget," said Saskia and Frank from Holland.

"I will be back at least one more time before I die," declared Diego from Buenos Aires.

"What juice would you like?" Héctor deposited a wicker tray laden with breakfast on the table.

"I'll have whatever you were making just now."

"Ah, that's a special preparation for *Señora* Lucía."

"Guava then, please. Are you from here?" she asked casually.

"Yes. From Puerto Seco."

"And have you been working at Villa Pacifica long?"

"Yes."

"Will you stay here?"

"Probably," he said after a moment's hesitation. She felt awkward sitting down like this and interviewing him while he stood holding a kitchen towel. He helped her out by saying "I'll bring your juice in a *momentito*" and turning on his heels.

Breakfast was crunchy muesli with yogurt, home-made multigrain bread with home-made jam and an exotic fruit salad. All served with a mug of locally produced cocoa.

When he came back with the juice, Ute asked: "So who did you vote for in the elections this year?"

"You mean last year." Héctor looked at her. "We have elections here every three years."

"But there was an election just a few months ago..." Ute smiled. "And they re-elected Gonzales."

Héctor sighed.

"Gonzales won last year, and I hope he wins again next time. I voted for him, you know. I was going to vote for the university professor, what's his name, Ramón? He seemed like a decent guy, but he's an atheist. I couldn't vote for someone who doesn't believe in God. A person without faith can't guide our nation. Where would he get his principles from?"

"Aha, that's exactly where you're wrong, my friend." Mikel's voice startled them. Mikel had a way of always being around. And here he was behind Héctor, his Hawaiian shirt unbuttoned over the grey carpet of his chest.

"Some of the biggest bigots are self-professed men of religion," Mikel was saying. "Look at that banana-baron bastard, Nortega. He stood for president, and nearly got in, that sonofabitch. Do you know what his election campaign consisted of? Going around the country in a black frock, waving the Bible around and saying he was the son of God."

Mikel had glasses perched up on his nose, a pen in one hand, and a cigarette in the other, and he was waving both of them around. Héctor stood still and expressionless.

"Have you seen his theatrics? He falls on his knees with a microphone and screams, 'I love the poor! I love you!'" Mikel spat out onto his finger a piece of tobacco leaf. "Like fuck he loves the poor. He owns seventy per cent of the banana plantations in this country. And during his election campaign, while he wooed the poor, his workers went on strike. Have you been to one of these plantations, Ute?" She had, but this was a rhetorical question. "We're talking people sleeping ten to a shack, going hungry, hungry in this country of plenty, being paid peanuts… So they go on a strike, and do you know what the banana baron and friend of the poor does? He sends in his private militia to deal with it. And they beat them to a pulp. The good Catholic that he is. So you still think a good Catholic has principles, my friend?"

Héctor was thinking about it. And so was Ute – about this strange anomaly in the elections calendar. Either these people were completely out of touch with the rest of the country, or she had well and truly got her wires crossed.

"And yet," Héctor tried, "people said they were gonna vote for Nortega because he's already so rich that he can't become corrupt."

"Ah, that's where they're wrong." Mikel raised a finger. "How do you think he got so rich in the first place, huh?"

"Well, I voted for Gonzales anyway," Héctor said, looking at the wooden board floor.

"Ah yes, Gonzales, another friend of the poor. And of Hugo Chávez. You all voted for him, and he's slapped huge taxes on us, and now he's trying to drive small businesses into the ground, nationalize everything. Great! That's exactly what this country needs. More state control, a nepotistic kleptocracy, all in the name of 'the people'… Another modern Venezuela. The Cubans must be laughing themselves sick."

"I thought you were a socialist," Ute ventured.

"Of course I'm a socialist! But this is socialism gone mad. This country is not ready for socialism of this variety. It doesn't have enough capital. It'll just become a banana republic without bananas, Cuba without Castro… Don't get me started…"

Héctor shuffled off to the kitchen.

"But Gonzales was re-elected this year, so he must be doing something right," Ute said.

"What's that?" Mikel looked at her distractedly, like he was seeing her for the first time. "The elections were last year, my dear. And I hope like hell that Gonzales doesn't get re-elected, because if that happens we're fucked. Shit, is that the time?" Mikel looked at his battered watch. "Gotta go."

"Where are you going?" Ute asked.

"Going to have a look at the mangroves down south. We own some land. The officials from the national park are trying to take over. I've gotta make sure they're not building anything there."

"Are you going by yourself ?"

"Yep. Lucía doesn't like camping down there. I'll be back tomorrow morning. Will you be here?" He was off already before she could answer.

"Yes," Ute said to his back. "We'll be here." A minute later, she heard his jeep rev out of the compound.

In the dark interior, Héctor was leaning in the kitchen doorway with an empty tray, looking at her.

"Have you seen Jerry?" She got up and walked towards him. "My husband?"

"Yes, he had breakfast early and went out."

"Did he say where?"

Héctor shrugged. "He went out that way," he pointed in the direction of the main entrance. That meant Puerto Seco.

"The American lady went with him," Héctor added.

"The American lady," Ute repeated dully.

"Yes."

Ute wasn't jealous by nature. She had never been jealous of Jerry, and he'd never given her any reason to be. He wasn't the flirtatious type, though he was very affable, and very vain – but intellectually rather than sexually. And anyway Eve was the last kind of woman Jerry would go for. But then he wasn't quite himself around here. The comments last night, his spontaneous desire to stay longer – he never had spontaneous desires, or if he did, he never acted them out spontaneously... Perhaps Eve was another such anomalous spontaneous desire?

"And have you seen Max, the American?" she asked Héctor, who was now behind the reception counter. He lifted his head.

"He went running in the forest. Like every morning."

She couldn't picture Max running. But things and people here went well beyond her imagination.

"Do you have an internet connection here?" Ute asked. She suddenly wanted to check the elections, to make sure she wasn't losing the plot.

"No," Héctor said. "We have mobile phones, but no radio, TV or internet. It's *Señor* Mikel's policy. Do you want to see the animals? I'll take you across if you like."

"Sure," she said. "But are we... allowed?"

"Sure we are, if I say so." He smiled at her, popped his head into the kitchen for a quick word with the cook, and they were off. Perhaps he was looking for diversions in his dull morning.

They walked down to the shore and got into a rowing boat moored to a small jetty. Héctor uncoiled the rope, took hold of the oars and competently rowed downstream.

"Why are we going this way?"

But she could already see why: there was a sharp, steep, rocky bank on the other side, about a metre high and with no access.

"The entrance is that way. *Señor* Mikel has talked about moving it just across from the cabins, but he likes talking and it often doesn't come to anything. Also, it's not that easy to make an entrance there, cos there's no natural shore. Very expensive."

They were gliding through the overcast day. Dull light leaked through milky ocean mist. There was a bend in the river, after which they left the tropical compound behind. The greyish mass of the Pacific was behind them too, like some somnolent beast – humming, breathing, waiting. They were now moving into a different ecosystem, and the snaking course of the river seemed to lead them into a deeper silence. The knotted trees of the dry forest along the banks had grown aridly, grimly, as if despite themselves. It was like entering a petrified forest.

"How come the animals are so quiet most of the time?" Ute asked.

"These are not ordinary animals," Héctor said. "You'll see in a *momentito*."

After a few minutes of silent rowing, Héctor asked: "Are you a journalist?"

"No. I write travel guides."

"Like the *Lonely Planet*?"

"Yes."

"I have seen them. Some tourists read them all the time. Will you write about Puerto Seco?"

"I don't know yet," Ute said.

"In my opinion, you should. And you should include Villa Pacifica. There are interesting things here." He didn't say *cosas*, things, but *cositas*, little things. Interesting little things.

"Little things like what?" Ute probed.

"Well, I'm not qualified as a guide," he said. The boat softly landed on a sandy bank, and they stepped out. She could hear the cackling of birds.

"This way." Héctor started walking inland.

The earth on this side of the river was dry and crumbly, and twisted trees grew among the animal enclosures. The beginnings of a tropical garden sprouted greenly here and there, but they were low and half-hearted. A feral, meaty smell hung in the air.

"Has this been here for long?" Ute enquired while they climbed the inclined bank.

"The animal shelter started about five years ago. I was here when they brought the first animals. And about two years ago, they started planting the tropical plants, but it's too hard to water them, there's no easy access. And it's too expensive. It's a problem. Do you want to see the display hut first?"

The display was in an open hut made from a few tree trunks and a thatched roof. It was full of patterned jaguar skins, paws, feathers, stuffed armadillos, yellow-eyed eagles in mid-flight, enormous iridescent butterflies pinned inside boxes, and tortoise shells of various sizes. A taxidermist's dream, and an animal-lover's nightmare. Ute liked animals, but not in an emotional way. This wasn't her first shelter either, she'd seen another one, much bigger, in the Galápagos a few years earlier, and two others elsewhere in South America. But not a collection like this. This here was a place of death. The violence committed against these animals was almost obscene, it made you feel ashamed.

"DO NOT BUY WILD ANIMALS! THEY ARE NOT PETS!" a sign said in Spanish. Ute wondered who this was addressed to. Those who trafficked animals wouldn't come here in the first place. Those who came here were presumably already disgusted enough. Perhaps Max's suggestion of bringing local school kids here to educate them wasn't completely crazy. Those kids were the traffickers and pet owners of tomorrow.

"These are all items that have been captured from traffickers, poachers and private individuals," Héctor said.

"You make a good guide," someone said behind them. Ute turned. It was the man in the gaucho hat she'd seen yesterday. He stood sipping maté through a metal straw from a round leather gourd. The rim of the hat cast a shadow over his Indian eyes. Héctor went quiet.

The gaucho was a slow-moving, deeply tanned and, on closer inspection, very attractive man somewhere in his late forties. He hadn't started to go to seed like overfed Alejandro or nicotine-nuked Mikel: he was still in his prime. A rough cotton shirt hung loose over his torn jeans, and he wore battered leather sandals. Every time he moved, a whiff of fresh, honest sweat escaped from him. He looked as if he'd just popped up from the Pampas for a visit.

"I look after the animals," the gaucho said, and smiled with crooked, maté-stained teeth. The etched lines and sun blotches on his face didn't dent his attractiveness one bit. Here was a well-lived-in face, which invited you to investigate.

"I'm Ute," she said. He squinted and smiled at her, and she felt a savage longing for beautiful skin. She should have worn her hat, to cover up her face. She should have at least washed her hair this morning, or polished her toenails. With Héctor and Mikel, as with most men, she could easily forget she was a woman. With Jerry too, come to think of it – they'd been together that long. But not with the gaucho.

"Carlos is from Paraguay," Héctor added.

"*Bueno*," Carlos shrugged, "everybody has to come from *somewhere*." Ute smiled unguardedly.

"Do you know that song, 'The Flowers of Paraguay'?" she asked, just for something to say.

"No. I'm a bit behind with music."

Her face was heating up under his casual gaze. And just then, with immaculate comical timing, they heard a rapid screech nearby. "*Las Malvinas son argentinas, las Malvinas son argentinas*." It meant "the Falklands belong to Argentina".

"What's that?" Ute gasped.

"That's our Enrique, a clever bird. And a patriotic bird. Even if Argentina isn't a *patria* for any of us." They stepped away from the shade of the hut and walked on.

A small ponytail stuck out at the back of Carlos's hat. Not attractive on most men, but somehow on him it was fine. So was the quickly glimpsed near-monobrow – moronic on other men, but virile on him.

Carlos didn't have the demeanour of an employee or a mere animal-feeder. He looked like he was running the show. Who was he? He was a *mestizo* – a cross of white and Indian blood; most Paraguayans were. He was also a cross between a cowboy and a preservation activist, the kind of man you might catch in any number of mutually exclusive, freebooting activities. Planting olive trees in a kibbutz, running a marijuana plantation in Morocco, teaching orphans in Cambodia, counting the tiger population of Rajasthan, or swaggering in a cigarette commercial.

But before Ute had time to investigate Carlos's life or Enrique's politics any further, she yelped in alarm because she found herself only a few steps away from a large, sand-coloured feline behind a wire cage. It stood immobile, alert, one foot inside a tyre, and fixed them with a sorrowful eye that said "life is nasty and it drags on".

"That's Melissa, our lion cub." Carlos said. "She's everybody's favourite."

"I didn't know there were lions in this country!" It was a stupid thing to say, and Carlos confirmed this with an amused look.

"There aren't," he said. "They smuggled her in from Africa. Someone thought she'd make a cute pet. Then she started growing – not so cute any more. We found her in a backyard, chained, underfed, full of parasites, and very sad. She's still subdued, you know. But it'll cost a fortune to get her back to Africa. So we're building her a pit over there, somewhere she can run. It's almost done now."

They went to take a look at it. The pit was a few metres from the lioness's cage, and the walls were all concrete. It was about three metres deep and as joyful as an empty swimming pool. Next to it, inside a separate, double-strength enclosure, lay a massive jaguar. His spotted feline face was impassive. Even in his humiliating circumstances, he exuded a supreme, ruthless confidence.

"He's only been with us a few weeks." Carlos crouched beside the haunches heaving with power. The jaguar didn't take any notice of him, obviously used to his presence. "A young adult, quite restless. We're not sure how he's lived until now. Someone brought him to us and said he'd been bought as a cub for a rich kid. But we suspect, from his feeding habits and his behaviour, that he was poached later and lived in the wild until then. We need to organize a home for him soon. His natural home is the rainforest, above eight hundred metres. Do you know, this is one of only two countries in South America that doesn't legally protect its jaguars? In parts of the country the jaguar is extinct."

"Will he use the pit too?" Ute asked. Wild animals were not her thing.

"Do you have any idea how powerful a jaguar is?" Carlos looked at her, amused. She didn't. "He'd just climb out, and you don't want that to happen, believe me. A jaguar can pull a cow up a tree. They feed on animals larger than themselves. Caimans, for example. They break their skull with a single blow. This here is the most powerful animal on the planet."

It was unnerving to be standing so close to a beast that could break your skull with a single lazy blow and lunch on your still-warm brains, and Ute was keen to move on. Héctor was tagging along, sullenly. Next, they came to the parrots.

Like his two fellow inmates, the garrulous Enrique was in a sorry state. His once coloured head had been plucked, and only the bright-green feathers below his neck revealed his natural glory. A few blue feathers had begun to sprout around his head. He looked like a cancer patient in the last stages of chemotherapy. A sign hung on his cage:

Two things amaze me: the intelligence of beasts and the bestiality of humans.

"Enrique's a clever bird – too clever," Carlos explained, and just then Enrique screeched something in Spanish that sounded like "Enrique eats *coca*. Enrique eats *coca*."

"No," Carlos shouted at him with surprising force, startling both Ute and the bird, who suddenly went quiet.

"Enrique eats *coca*," the bird screeched once more, for good measure, and went quiet again.

"What was that?" Ute asked. Carlos waved his maté gourd vaguely.

"He picked that up from someone," he said. "We had this French guy... He fed drugs to the animals. He killed a marmoset with cocaine."

"Really?" Ute gasped. "When?"

"Around the time of El Niño last year." A cloud passed over Carlos's face.

"He disappeared around Christmas," Héctor said.

"For God's sake don't say 'disappeared'," Carlos interrupted him. "For some people that word has political connotations. It's dissidents and innocents that disappear on this continent. Not that *hijo de puta*."

"*Hijo de puta, hijo de puta, hijo de puta, hijo de puta*," Enrique screeched gleefully and looked at them with a cunning round eye. Ute gave a delighted cry.

"He got that one from me," Carlos grinned crookedly and sucked on his metallic maté straw. Then he led them away from Enrique. Ute walked next to Carlos.

"We get traffickers from time to time," Carlos was saying. "Hanging about the enclave in jeeps."

"How do they get here?"

"There's a bridge. I tell them to fuck off, because *hijos de puta* is what they are, and I tell them that in no uncertain terms."

"And what about *las Malvinas son argentinas*?" Ute asked. He gave her a half-smile.

"Argentine visitors," he said. "Thing is, when Enrique first arrived, we had him over on the other side: he had a corner in the lounge where he perched and slept. One night there were some guests from Britain and Argentina, and they got into an argument about the Falklands. Enrique picked it up. It's got a beat to it. Clever bird. And here we have the monkeys."

They were standing by a large enclosure full of perches and hanging tyres to keep the five resident monkeys occupied.

"That's Alfredito the marmoset, the smallest monkey in the world."

Alfredito swayed on top of a suspended tyre and looked at them expectantly. His tiny clawed hands gripped the indentation of the rubber. He was impossibly cute with his tufty head, round eyes and expression of eternal childhood.

"They use marmosets as house pets, and you can see why. They never grow, they're pygmies. A perfect present for a spoilt brat."

"Can you not release him up in the hills? That's their natural environment, isn't it?" Ute ventured.

"Sure, but remember he's been kept in captivity since he was born." Carlos sucked on his metal straw. "He doesn't know how to survive in the wild. He'd die in a couple of days. See the howler monkeys there, behind Alfredito? Same story. Some of those rich bastards out there are so stupid they don't realize that when you get a howler monkey for a pet it's gonna burst your eardrums, cos that's what they do: they howl. But only when there's enough of them to make a din. It takes a crowd to make a party, you know. These guys in here are a bit down in the dumps. But no one's as depressed as Carolina."

Carolina next door was a scaly, soot-black iguana about a metre long. She crouched in a pit of sand and rocks, her spiked reptilian body stock-still, as if fossilized. It was hard to believe that a creature this prehistoric-looking could suffer, but its tail had been severed, and its rear end was just a stump. Ute stared at its hideous face.

"Why did they cut it off?"

"For the same reason they plucked the parrots," Carlos answered. "There's no reason for human cruelty. Anyway, you know what Darwin called the iguanas of the Galápagos?" Ute glanced at Héctor. He was sulking beside the monkey cage and interacting with Alfredito. Clearly he wasn't enjoying Carlos's one-upmanship.

"'Imps of darkness'," Carlos answered himself, and sucked on the straw contentedly, which emphasized the curious dimples in his chin and left cheek. Ute wondered how many times he'd done this spiel for the benefit of visitors. She wanted to believe that he was giving a little bit extra of himself for her – but she knew he wasn't.

"It's true," he continued, "they're ugly as hell, but they're not without emotions. We've had Carolina for three years, our longest-standing resident, and we've had to force-feed her all along. She just won't eat. I think she's trying to tell us that she wants to die, poor thing, but we won't let her."

"Who wants to die?"

His friendly paw thumped Héctor's back, almost knocking him against the mesh, face to face with the marmoset, which jumped back to safety and watched the intruder from another hanging tyre. The howler monkeys dispersed inside the cage too.

"Aha, got ya. You didn't hear me coming, did ya?" Max smiled at them. His face was a shiny red, his hair wet, and his Miami Beach Paradise T-shirt clung to his sweaty torso.

"I heard you," Carlos replied, and moved across to the monkeys to pick up some twigs that they had got caught in the mesh and were trying to pry free.

"The guard at the gate, he's armed, man," Max said to no one in particular. "Why is he armed? What's that about?" He took a gulp of water from a plastic bottle he was carrying.

"We've got to keep unwelcome guests at bay." Carlos sucked on his straw, but there was no more liquid left in the gourd. "And unwelcome guests often come armed." He whistled gently at the monkeys, and two of them bounded towards him.

"Ah, hell of a run up in the hills." Max was shaking his legs to relax them. "Went off track at the bridge, then went for a swim downstream and had a laugh trying to get out of the river. Branches and shrubs everywhere, man, it was me and the elements. Just the way I like it." He thumped his chest ape-like at the monkeys, who stared at him with their semi-human faces, unimpressed. It was true – his legs were scratched and bleeding in places.

"So, what's happening here, bit of a tour goin' on?" Max said and was ignored. Carlos beckoned to Ute with his head: "Want to see the tortoises?"

And they walked over to the giant tortoises.

In the near distance behind them, she spotted the jaguar. He had risen to his feet and was watching them quietly, unnervingly, as if storing away the information for future use.

"Jorge over here is the oldest," Carlos was saying. Max stood beside them. "Not to be confused with the oldest living Galápagos resident – also called Jorge, Solitario Jorge. He's about two hundred, I think. Our Jorge is only about seventy."

The three curved-shelled tortoises were enormous and fossilized. One of them was in the shade, underneath a high table. The sun had broken through the milky clouds. She felt the skin of her bare arms and neck heating up. Her face was flustered.

"They're boring," Max said. "They don't *do* anything."

"Jorge was found in an abandoned backyard in Guadeloupe," Carlos was saying.

"So when's the breeding season?" Max interrupted him. Carlos gave him an unblinking look from underneath his hat.

"May," he said, and turned back to Ute. "So when they found Jorge, his shell was all dried up. They can go a long time without food and water, but he was almost as good as dead." Carlos spoke calmly, almost phlegmatically, as if relishing Max's twitchy impatience.

"Come on, let's feed the jaguar." Max couldn't take the inactivity any longer. "I wanna see the jaguar eat his rabbit. You've gotta see it, Uddar. A live rabbit."

"I've fed them already," Carlos said.

"Do you actually get in the cage with them?" Ute asked.

"Yep. But with the jaguar I don't hang around, just throw in the meat and lock him up again."

"I reckon I could do it," Max declared. "It's not rocket science. Just observe the beast. I've been watching the lion cub for days. And the jaguar."

"You don't know shit about animals," Carlos said slowly in Spanish and gave Max one of his slanted looks. "You'd get yourself messed up."

"Nah, I can do it." Max winked at Ute. "All right guys," Max glanced at his watch, "I've done the guided tour already, so I'm gonna go down to the boat and hang out there. Don't make me wait too long, all right? Or I'll set off by myself." And he trotted off past the jaguar, who watched him motionlessly, and the lion cub, who lifted her head from her reclining position, then lay it down again.

"You know, the tortoises are fascinating creatures," Carlos was telling her. "They're immobile pretty much all the time, and only become animated when eating and mating. Or when threatened. But Jorge here is a bit depressed. We found him a mate, but he's just not interested. May came and went last year, this year and still nothing..."

"We have to go back." Héctor looked at his watch and then at Ute. "It's coming up to lunchtime, and I have to be there."

"OK," she said. What she meant to say was: "OK, you go. I'm staying here on this side. I'm spending the day here, I don't want to go back."

But she wasn't an impulsive person. She had planned to leave today and she always stuck to her itineraries. She thanked Carlos for the tour with a sinking heart.

"Welcome, any time." And he turned his back on them and headed for the guard's cabin, to refill his maté gourd perhaps, or have lunch, or have a siesta. Because it was already noon: time definitely passed too quickly here.

Héctor and Ute walked back the way they'd come.

"How long has Carlos been working here?" Ute asked.

"Since the beginning of the animal shelter. He and *Señor* Mikel started it together."

"Are they good friends?"

"Very good friends." Héctor flashed her a conspiratorial look. "Carlos is a... an original guy. But," Héctor knocked on his forehead with his index finger.

"What do you mean?"

"It's difficult to explain. He prefers animals to people."

"He doesn't seem antisocial, though."

"Oh no. But he prefers animals to people. Trust me."

She didn't trust him completely, because she could hear jealousy in his voice.

And there was Max again, waiting inside the boat. When they approached, Max bounced out and boxed Héctor on the shoulder.

"Come on *amigo*, let's go. I'm starving."

Héctor unmoored the boat without a word. He started rowing.

"Why are you wasting your time with these oars? Motorboats are much faster," Max said to Héctor.

"Motorboats are noisy. *Señor* Mikel and Lucía don't like noise," Héctor said.

"Fair enough," Max said. "This Carlos guy, he got a woman?"

"No," Héctor said.

"So what you are you guys up to today?" Max turned to Ute in English.

"Me?" She was startled. "Not sure yet. What about you?"

"I gotta find that lady of mine, see what she wants to do. This is her vacation, you know. Me, I'm already bored like fuck. Man, I'll be climbing the trees soon, like a monkey."

"The *señora* went into Puerto Seco this morning," Héctor said. "As did the *señora*'s husband." He nodded at Ute.

"Right. Right. That's fine by me. I'm not the jealous type," he chuckled.

He cocked his head to study her face, his thighs slackly open, exposing his crotch, dangling the empty water bottle between his fingers. Ute turned her face away. For a moment, the world went slow and quiet, as if they were under water.

"Have you, like," Max continued, staring at Ute again, "always been like this – with your face, you know, like you got what is it, psoriasis or whatever they call it, like that guy in that movie, aah, what's it called... Come on, what's that movie about the showbiz guy who got this horrible skin disease?"

"Eczema," she said in a hollow voice. "It doesn't bother me actually, I'm used to it."

"Eh, *amigo*," he thumped Héctor again. "How's it goin'? Need a hand with the oars? Small fella like yourself... you're doing a good job."

"I like rowing," Héctor said. Then, after a short, unfriendly pause, Héctor spoke again.

"The gringo, I mean the Frenchman, everybody thought that he'd left without paying. But then they found his body."

Ute blinked at him. Her face was now very hot and burning, and she felt as if a swarm of tiny flies buzzed around her head, though she couldn't see any. She took a few moments to register the meaning of Héctor's words.

"They found his *body*?" Max grimaced at Héctor in disbelief.

"Yes."

They were already touching the sandy bank of their side of the river. Héctor pulled the oars up and placed them inside the boat.

"Where?..." Ute's voice sounded dull. "Where did they find him, I mean, the body?"

"In the Agua Sagrada bay. Some fishermen saw the body... *Señora*." Héctor held out a courteous hand to help Ute out of the boat. She took his hand and stepped out on unsteady legs.

"Wait, wait, wait!" Max shouted, still sitting inside the boat. Héctor looked at him expectantly. "You're telling me that a gringo drowned here?"

"*Sí, señor*," Héctor confirmed. "In any case that was the conclusion of the police inquiry. Death by overdose and drowning. Please excuse me now, I have to rush up to the kitchen." And so he did, up the steep sandy bank.

"What do you think, Uddar?" Max continued as he jumped ashore.

"About what?" Ute started walking away from him as quickly as she could.

"About the dead gringo business. Sounds a bit weird if you ask me. Dead body floating about. Fishy."

She didn't reply and walked faster towards the main house, hoping to see Jerry there.

Eve was sitting at a table with Alma and Alejandro. All three were drinking juice and tucking into large salads. Jerry wasn't there. She exchanged quick banalities with the three. Jerry had gone to their cabin, Alejandro informed her. Max was pouncing on them already, a few seconds behind her.

"Hey guys, what's for lunch today? I'm starving. I had a great run through the forest. Take a look at this..."

Ute moved swiftly on. Two gardeners were watering the garden with hoses. Ute nodded a greeting, and they nodded back, their faces invisible under their Panama hats. Jerry was sitting on the steps of *la tortuga*, typing on his laptop. He looked up at her. His face was flushed and happy.

"Hey." He closed his laptop and flicked away his fringe in that boyish way she'd found a bit effeminate when they first met ten years ago, but quickly grown to find endearing. "How was your expedition to the zoo?"

"Kind of strange. Strange people around here."

Ute sat inside the hammock and rocked herself gently. The light breeze this created made her realize how oppressive and stuffy the morning was, how tense she felt. She was pleased to be with Jerry again, just the two of them.

"Well, this is a strange kind of place," he said.

"And how was your excursion with Eve?"

He snorted. "The delightfully vacant Eve. How did you know we came back together?"

"Well, first you *went* together, right?"

"No." He looked surprised. "I went into the village by myself. It was about nine-thirty by the time I got there. I was looking for a café by the waterside – there was only one place open, and she was already there. The café's called *End of the World*, how appropriate is that! The coffee was diabolical… but they make really good smoothies and fresh juices. So anyway I sat with her, and she told me all about her marriage, and how she can't stand Max. And how this is the first time ever they've been alone without the kids, and how she's going crazy, missing the kids, blah-blah."

"Did you meet Consuelo?" Ute said.

"Who's that?"

"The woman who runs the café."

"Oh yeah, nice woman. She's the mother of our waiter, what's his name, the small guy at reception… Hold on, when were you there?"

"Yesterday."

"You didn't tell me."

"Well, you didn't ask," Ute said. "You mean she's Héctor's mother?"

"Who? Oh yeah, Héctor. It's a small place, this, everyone's related. No wonder they all look inbred in the village. And then who do you think should turn up, in their four-by-four? Our Mexican honeymooners. They were nice enough though, they offered us a lift back, but I felt like walking, and Eve said she wanted to walk too. So I had to enjoy her company all the way back. She's not as stupid as I thought actually. She has at least three folds in her brain – one for hunger, one for thirst and one for sleep. And maybe a fourth, to hate Max with."

Ute smiled, but something distracted her. Why did Héctor tell her that Jerry and Eve had gone into town together? He had no reason to lie. After they would all leave in a week or so, he'd never see her and Jerry, or Eve and Max again. What did he care for their private passions and relationships? Or maybe he hadn't said that, maybe he'd said they'd just walked *back* together.

She was dehydrated and probably reading too much into everything. She kept rocking gently inside the hammock, too listless to get up for water.

Carlos's sun-baked neck and slanted black eyes were imprinted painfully in her mind. She tried to focus on Jerry instead. He was acting a bit strange, out of character. He had never lied to her before, as far as she knew, but what if now, here… No, she was being absurd.

"What is this fragrance?" Jerry sniffed the air. "It's like an opiate. It's everywhere."

"You mean that sweet smell? Incense, probably," Ute said. "It's a bit strong."

She could have just drifted off to sleep right there… Carlos was probably having a siesta now, breathing gently in the shade of his cabin. Long strands of his damp hair would be stirred by a fan, his high-cheeked face sculpted in repose, the feral smell of damaged animals tainting the air, but not unpleasantly. Just one quick, hushed coupling with Carlos would make her pregnant, she had no doubt about it. She discarded the dangerous dream-thought.

"Hey," Jerry rocked the hammock lightly. "Did you want to go and look at the national park or stay here?"

"Go." Her tongue felt thick, and her limbs were rubbery.

"Good," he stretched lazily. "Would be a shame to waste the tickets. Though if you ask me, I'm happy to lounge about all day. I had another sleepless night. So…"

He produced the map-sized tickets from his back pocket and waved them at her. She mustered enough energy to smile. Jerry tossed his laptop onto the bed and brushed her dry mouth with a quick kiss. He packed a small day-pack with a large bottle of water and hats. Every movement was an effort, but Ute put on her battered trainers, smeared some sunscreen onto her face, drank half a litre of water, and together they crunched down the white pebble path to the main gate.

"Mmm, we're gonna have to go past everyone," Jerry said. "Your friend Max is probably there too. Yep, I can hear him."

Héctor was carrying plates. They went into the reception area, trying not to draw attention from the people eating outside.

"Héctor," Ute said. "Could you call us a tricycle? We want to go to the park's entrance."

"No problem." He picked up the phone. "But I'll call it to the other gate, because it's closer to the main road. You'll have to walk back through the compound."

"Where is the other gate?"

"It's right behind your cabin."

He mumbled something down the phone line.

"Hey tiger, it's Daddy, how're you doing, huh?" Max was shouting into his mobile phone and pacing up and down the veranda. Max saw Ute and Jerry but didn't acknowledge them, which was a relief.

"Quick," Ute said, "let's go before he's finished."

They thanked Héctor and shuffled back out, past the bookcase and Oswaldo's painting. Ute stopped and looked at the row of guest books, a vague question stirring in her head. Last year, around Christmas, Héctor had said. That would be 2008.

"Have you seen these?" she gestured to the bookcase. She was whispering. "Guest books, loads of them."

"Hmmm," Jerry said absently. "Sorry, I need the loo, I'll catch you outside the other gate." He walked away energetically.

She looked at the shelf: the guest books went up to 2009. She picked up "2008" and opened it. There was nothing inside. She ruffled through the pages, looking for ink. The pages were blank. She put it back in, and quickly pulled another one – "2009". The same thing there. Her heart was suddenly thumping.

"Your transport will be waiting," Héctor said. He was carrying an empty tray. "Be very careful in the park. Don't get lost. You don't have much time before nightfall."

She slotted the book back, as if caught snooping. Which she was, in a way. He stopped halfway across the lounge and said:

"Everybody who leaves writes something. If you don't find their name in those books, it's because they haven't arrived." Then he added, as an afterthought: "Or they haven't left."

"Well," Ute said, dazed. "I'd better write something then."

"*Bueno*," Héctor said and disappeared into the kitchen. Ute rushed to the back gate, where Jerry was already sitting inside a tricycle taxi with his shocking-white legs and squeaky new trainers. The word gringo was invented for him, she thought. The tricycle driver was the guy from the other night, and looked just as peeved with the world now. He didn't even greet Ute.

A drowsy guard sat in a plastic chair outside the gate, a rifle between his legs. So there were armed guards at every one of the three gates of the Villa. She hadn't noticed this the first night or the first morning.

"*Buenas*," the guard nodded at her.

"*Buenas*," Ute said and hopped on, but her voice was drowned in the roar of the motorbike engine. She looked back. The guard in his chair and the gate of Villa Pacifica shimmered like a mirage in a cloud of dust and heat.

8

JERRY FELL ASLEEP AS soon as they took off. His glasses slid onto his nose from the bumpy ride, and Ute adjusted them gently. This was totally unlike him, he wasn't a napper. But then he wasn't someone prone to insomnia either. The driver kept an eye on her in his side mirror.

Ute was under the impression that the park's entrance was just around the next bend of the road. But the next bend was miles away. Weird: the park began practically at the back gate of the animal shelter, and yet here they were, circling the official entrance from a distance. She felt lost and anxious again. She never travelled without a map. It was like being half blind. You could end up anywhere, and you wouldn't know it until it was too late.

For the entire journey, which lasted about ten minutes, she saw no other vehicle on the road. At the park's entrance, there was a small kiosk with a man inside it and a large carved sign with "WELCOME TO MANTEÑO NATIONAL PARK", and a smaller sign next to it saying "Vehicles prohibited inside the park". The small parking space was empty – there was probably nobody in the entire park. Ute paid up the silent driver and nudged Jerry. He came to with a start, looked around him and wiped his cheek.

"I've dribbled," he said, and stepped off the tricycle on unsteady legs. The old man inside the kiosk looked bleary-eyed, as if he too had just woken up from a nap. They unfolded their tickets, and he nodded.

"We close at five," he said. This seemed to exhaust his duties. There was no gate or anything else to close, just a vast expanse of twigs ahead of them.

"Is there a map of the park anywhere?" Ute peeked inside the kiosk.

"No, no map. Just follow the main path. And be out by five."

"Is there another exit?"

"No, no other exit." And the man settled into his corner again.

They started walking.

"How are we getting back?" Jerry said.

"We'll hitch or something," she said, thinking of the long, empty road.

They walked along the narrow path, the only visible furrow through this soundless universe of gnarled trees, bramble and three-metre-tall cacti. The sun was an egg poached in clouds, but even so the heat rose from the parched landscape slowly, with a hiss, like some reptilian spirit. Ute crouched to pee by the side of the path, and watched the grey earth soak up her stream, leaving no trace of moisture.

Within two hours, nothing had changed, except that they had drunk most of their water. They were too dazed to speak, and anyway there was nothing to say out there. There was also nothing to see apart from the occasional darting lizard or snake. No doubt some of these species were protected, but apart from the cacti, everything blended into a beige blur. No birds either.

Ahead of them, hills began to appear. The nearest ones were covered in a sparse colourless fuzz, like the head of a vulture. Behind those hills were higher green hills and, further on, peaks lost in mist.

"That must be the beginning of the cloud forest up there," she said. "Looks appealing."

"It's three o'clock now," Jerry looked at Ute's watch when they stopped to rip into the mandarins he had thoughtfully brought along.

He'd left his own watch at home. He always did this on holiday. "The sun goes down at six, which tells me we should be heading back round about now. The old geezer said they close at five, for all that's worth. To be honest, it strikes me as a perversity to be here when we could be in our own private garden, swinging in a hammock listening to birds."

"It can't be more than thirty minutes to that first green hill," Ute said, "and then it's probably the cloud forest, but we can't see it from here. I get a feeling that place, Agua Sagrada, is up there. It would be a shame to come this far and not see it at least from a distance."

"Yes, but you forget that I've already walked a few miles today," Jerry said. "And I'm quite keen to get back before dark. We don't have a torch, and I don't know about you, but I don't fancy the company of snakes in the dark. Besides, we won't see much of it in the dark, right?"

Jerry's legs were scratched from the bramble, and he was in a scratchy mood.

"OK, I have an idea," she said. "There must be a path that leads back to the sanctuary, a shortcut. I know for sure that there's a track that starts at the back gate of the animal shelter. It must come off this main track. Let's give ourselves another half-hour, and if we don't come across it, we'll turn back." This, she hoped, would give them time to take a closer look at the alluring hills ahead.

"Why didn't we use that shortcut in the first place then?" Jerry said.

"Because we would've had to go across the river again, and you know how they only have two crossings a day." Or three, when Mikel wasn't around. "Plus I don't think that shortcut is supposed to be used at all."

Jerry sighed and looked at Ute's watch again. "All right, if you're sure we won't get caught out by the dark..."

He was making out as if he was doing her a big favour, humouring her. Ute walked on, resentful. With most couples, it was the woman who was high-maintenance, surely. Maybe Ute was too low-maintenance for her own good. She didn't make scenes, she didn't throw tantrums, she didn't complain when she was thirsty or tired, or felt crap. She did nothing when other women fawned around Jerry. He was delicately handsome, in a long-lashed, sinewy, boyish sort of way. His intellect was sharp, and his personality, at its best, was attractive. And at its worst he was a neurotic and a wimp who passively gazed at the world from his ivory tower. A man of action he wasn't. It was symptomatic that his favourite poem of all time was 'The Love Song of J. Alfred Prufrock'. Did he dare to eat a peach? Not often.

Half an hour later, they were entering a greenish, hilly forest. The air was suddenly cool. They could hear birdsong. Just then, they came to a fork. A second track led up north in the direction of civilization.

"This has got to be it," Ute said. "It's got to lead back to the Villa."

"Or to that Agua-something place if we're really unlucky. That's right, what if the main track leads all the way to the coast, and this one to the cloud forest? Didn't the guy at the entrance say there was no other exit?"

"Yeah he did, but I don't know whether to believe him. Or anyone else around here," Ute said.

"Anyway, this path leads *away* from the cloud forest, so it can't also lead *to* it."

"*Two roads diverged in a yellow wood...*" Jerry reciting was always a good sign of rising morale, or some attempt at struggle with adversity anyway. "And this is the one we'll take."

"Yep." She would come back tomorrow, with or without him. Most likely without.

The sun had gone down with alarming speed, though it was only mid-afternoon. It was at least a few miles to the sanctuary, if that's in fact where the path was taking them. They had drained the last bit of the water, and though they were thirsty, the heat had mercifully abated. Besides, they weren't under a harsh open sky any more. This wood was shady. It was almost pleasant. They no longer walked in a column like a commando unit of two, but next to each other.

"You know, Héctor told me about some gringo who died here a couple of years ago."

"Really? How?"

"Drug overdose. He drowned."

"What, he overdosed *and* drowned?" Jerry snorted.

"Yeah, he sounded like a psycho. He fed drugs to the animals, can you imagine?"

"Wow. Maybe just as well he did drown then."

"Mm," Ute said. They walked in silence for a while. "Mikel has gone into the park, till tomorrow night."

"Who's Mikel?"

"Our host."

"All right. So that means Max will terrorize the Villa tonight. Mikel is the one who keeps him in check."

"There's someone who does it even better than Mikel," Ute said defiantly.

"Who?"

"Carlos, the guy with the animals."

"That's right, the gaucho from Paraguay. He thinks he's pretty hot, doesn't he?"

"Well," she said. "He is who he is."

"A man of few words, you'd say," Jerry sneered. "And probably few brains. Anyway, does anyone actually know where Paraguay is?"

"I do," Ute said bluntly.

"Good for you. I think Eve was a bit taken with him. Primitive men attract primitive women, it's been that way since the dawn of time. She couldn't stop giggling when we went across yesterday, poor dumb potato. But he didn't give her the time of day."

"You did though, didn't you?"

"What's that?"

"You lied to me about walking back with Eve. You walked into the village with her too."

Jerry stopped and looked at her.

"For God's sake, what's got into you?" he said.

"I just don't like being taken for an idiot," Ute said, and her eyes suddenly filled with tears. But she kept walking fast, she didn't want him to see her upset.

Jerry caught up with her.

"Ute, why would I lie to you about such a thing?" he said.

"I don't know, that's what I'm wondering." Her tears were under control now.

"You're tense, and you're over-interpreting things, and..."

"Forget it. Just... let's forget it. You're right. You know" – Ute was talking fast now – "I feel like I've been here for a week."

"Me too," Jerry said, and took her hand with an affectionate squeeze. She squeezed his hand back and walked ahead, fast.

The green hills and misty clouds were now far behind them, almost out of view. The sun was gone, and it felt a lot later than it was. Soon the daylight was almost completely gone and they were moving in a wooded dusk. Sounds became amplified as the shapes of the forest blurred. The creatures of the forest were beginning to make their nocturnal noises: scratching, calling, coughing, rustling.

"This is really weird," Jerry said. They were both walking much faster now, sensing there was a lot of road to cover before they could stop. "Are the days shrinking or what? You said on the Equator they're always the same length throughout the year."

"Ah," she said, looking at her watch. It showed four-fifteen. "I know what's happening, it's my watch. It's falling behind. It did the same trick yesterday. It's probably more like six. The battery must be dying."

"And we don't have a torch."

The darkness was thickening by the minute. Forests were staggeringly black places at night. They walked some more, and it was now dark.

"God, it's like walking through Dante's Inferno," Jerry gasped behind her. "Are you all right?"

"I'm fine," Ute said. She strode on, crunching over now invisible twigs. "It's much safer to be in a place like this at night than in a place of ten million like, say, Rio – or even London. You don't get attacked by psychos in a forest."

"No, just by jaguars," Jerry snorted. He was out of breath.

"Don't worry, there aren't any large mammals in this forest. They're all up in the hills."

"Just poisonous snakes," Jerry said.

How were they going to endure all the walking ahead of them? Well, by just enduring – that was always Ute's way. Endure the fourteen-hour bus ride, and it'll be over. Endure traveller's diarrhoea, and you'll come through it a bit thinner, a bit less dignified, but fine. Endure the cold room and the thin blanket, and you'll be snuffly but alive in the morning. Endure a lonely childhood like a prison sentence in the Finnish countryside, and it will end one day. You will walk free. Very few things actually kill us, she thought.

"Fear of the dark is more a state of mind, you know," she offered.

"Every fear is a state of mind. You could argue that everything we experience is a state of mind. That doesn't make it any less real. Shit."

He was only a metre behind her, but she couldn't see him.

"Something got caught on my..." He wrestled with something that sounded like a large branch or shrub.

"Shit, shit, shit." A tearing sound and he was free again. "Some thorny shrub-thing caught my shirt. And I dropped my glasses. God I hate this. We don't even know where we're going, for fuck's sake."

"Sorry," Ute said, and crouched down beside him to feel around the thorny embankment for his glasses. It was somehow her responsibility, and therefore her fault.

"We'll get there," she said. "We'll be at the animal shelter before we know it."

"What if it's a dead end? That old git in the kiosk said there was no other way out."

Ute could hear him panting in the blackness, feeling around for his glasses. She was looking for them too.

"If it's a dead end, we'll die, I guess," she said through gritted teeth.

"For fuck's sake," Jerry said. "Whose idea was it to come here?"

"Mine, it was all *my* stupid idea, and you are just suffering the consequences, you poor thing."

"Your sarcasm is inappropriate right now," Jerry said. "Oh, found them. Thank God for that."

He exhaled, and they didn't move for a moment. Then they got back to their feet and stumbled on in bitter silence for a while.

"Why do they charge people twenty dollars to get scratched by bramble?" Jerry said in the end. "I don't get it. There are no signs, fuck all to see, and these God-awful tracks leading nowhere."

"Yeah, it's a bit strange. But then we haven't seen the whole park. There's twenty-thousand square metres of it. Or something like that."

"Oh good. That cheers me up no end. I can't wait to explore more of it."

Ute was clammy with old and new sweat. She was walking with her hands feeling in front of her, because it really was like moving through tar. Anything could be in front of you – a sheer drop into the ocean or a dead body – and you would just walk into it blindly. Except she knew – logically – that there was no such thing. It was a dull path through a dull forest.

"Do you want me to walk ahead of you?" Jerry said, pitiably.

"No, it's fine," Ute said. How different it would be walking through here with someone like Carlos. Well, not someone *like* him, but him.

The secret of a happy marriage is to know how to adjust your expectations. One of their friends had said this once at a small dinner party at their place. Everyone had been drunk on some expensive red wine Jerry's parents had brought from France, and they were talking about relationships. All three couples took turns, smug in their established coupledom, listing their three rules of thumb for a successful relationship. Rule number one, Jerry had said: stay in love if at all possible. Rule number two: no matter what, don't fuck other people. Everyone had laughed – Ute too. This was his strength. This was his brilliance. Not malarial jungles at night-time. She had fallen for his mind. Not for his courage and love of adventure. Rule number three, Jerry had said: do not become the couple, remain yourself. You never know what might happen to the couple, but you're stuck with yourself.

Slap. "Something just bit me," Jerry said. "Is there malaria here?"

"I don't think so," Ute said. "It's too dry. There are no marshes. But it's the wet season now, so I don't know. Are you taking your malaria pills?"

"Yes I am." Contracting malaria was beyond any doubt now, in his mind.

They walked a lifetime's worth of silent breathing and blackness. Ute blamed herself for this – her shitty watch, her blithe decision to go a different way, her being so cocksure about directions. It was even possible that she was showing off a bit in front of Jerry. The old South American hand. The travel professional. This way, follow me, I know where I'm going. Idiot.

"*Two shitty roads diverged in a shitty yellow wood...*" Jerry muttered at one point.

Then something – someone! – screeched ahead of them.

"Enrique!" Ute whispered.

"What's that?" Jerry croaked behind her.

"Enrique, the parrot. I think it's him."

"Hallelujah!"

"Hold on, I'm not sure yet. Might not be."

But it was. A faint light fell on the path and, a few minutes later, they were walking across a clearing towards the back gate of the animal shelter.

"My God, we're here," Jerry said. The gates were shut.

"*Hola*!" Ute shouted. Her mouth was dry and scratchy, like the rest of her. "*Hola*!"

A few moments later, the gates creaked open, and the curious face of a night-guard – Pablo, or was it Jesus – looked at them, followed by a second one.

"Where have you come from?" The guards let them in. They were carrying a gas lamp.

"From the national park," Ute said.

"Did you get lost?" the first guard said. The second one heavily sat down at the plastic table where they were playing cards and drinking.

"What do you think?" Ute said.

She wanted to lie down somewhere – anywhere would do, except next to the jaguar – and sleep. Now that they were safe again, she was ready to collapse.

"Come with me," said the first guard. "I'll see if Carlos is here, and he can take you across in the boat."

Carlos. She hadn't thought about him in the last few hundred years. No doubt she looked bedraggled and stank of sweat. They walked among various animal enclosures, and the gas-lamp was just strong enough to see shapes breathing, quietly growling, scratching and swinging gently on tyres and perches.

Carlos emerged from the guard's cabin. There was a bare light bulb swaying outside. He was barefoot, and had nothing on from the waist up. No hat this time, and strands of ash-coloured hair fell on each side of his face. His chest was surprisingly hairless. He was drinking maté again.

"What happened to you two?" His face was lit up by a gentle semi-smile. He leant in the doorway, crossing his arms. Inside his cabin it was bright, and again that strong smell of burning incense.

"We... we got a bit lost," Ute said, trying not to look at his bare torso. "My watch stopped, and we got caught out in the dark."

"Yeah, it happens easily here."

He looked at her, at them, for a quiet moment, still leaning in the doorway. It was as if he was trying to work out whether they were a good match, and she wondered what he thought.

"Do you have water?" she said with a croaking voice.

Carlos went inside and brought out a large plastic bottle.

"Is it mineral?" Jerry asked.

"Not mineral," Carlos said, in a slightly mocking way. "Filtered."

Ute filled herself with its coolness. Amazing, every time, how delicious water tasted to the parched mouth. She passed it to Jerry.

"I take you across. OK?" Carlos said.

"Thanks very much, that would be great," Jerry said cheerfully, relieved at this happy ending, "and sorry to be a nuisance."

"No problem." Carlos disappeared for a moment and then reappeared, this time with a dark T-shirt and flip-flops on, and a torch in his hand.

"Let's go," he said and walked ahead of them down to the riverbank.

Inside the boat, he gave the torch to Ute to hold while he rowed. "Shine this way," Carlos instructed her, and pointed towards the other side. Their side. His side was with the animals.

The only sound now was the gentle plopping of the oars. She was aware of his body moving, his arms, his shoulders turning in their sockets. Undemanding, uncomplaining, he was at ease with himself and his surroundings. Her foot touched his. It sent a shiver up her whole body. She withdrew it quickly.

"Do you always stay on that side?" Ute said. She swung the torch needlessly to indicate which side, and it shone into Carlos's face, blinding him for a moment. He turned his face away.

"Yes, almost always," Carlos said. "I prefer. Sometime, when I feel too lonely, I go across and talk. Before, I lived on the other side when there weren't so many visitors. But then I have to move out every time in high season, and I decide it is just better to live in the cabin on the other side. I must feed the animals two times a day. And I don't like too much visitors." He chuckled. "Sometime they are very nice, but sometime..." he drifted off.

"Sometimes they are Max," Jerry offered.

"Max is OK," Carlos said. "Too much energy and too much ego, but OK. Not dangerous."

"He's a danger to himself more than anything," Jerry said, and stretched his legs on the other side of Carlos.

"Maybe tomorrow he will make you so angry that you hit him," Carlos said to Jerry, and Ute wondered if he was mocking him.

"Maybe," Jerry said, almost amused. How quickly they had passed from a world of blackness, animal noises, and – so it had seemed – bare survival, to the civilized world of conversations and humour! Ute realized she'd been more worried about how Jerry felt than about herself.

"How long have you lived out here then?" Jerry asked. "You seem to know quite a bit about animals."

"Three years and a half."

"And what did you do before that, in Paraguay?"

"Different things."

"And how do you know... our hosts?" Jerry pressed on, a vein of irritation snaking into his voice.

"My father and his father were friends. A long time ago, at university in Spain."

Carlos moored the boat and walked with them up the sandy bank to the main house. It was dinner time, and they could hear Max's rowdy voice and Alejandro's high-pitched laughter.

"Uh-oh," Jerry warned. "He's holding court, and the court jester's there too."

"*Bueno*, good night," Carlos waved at them casually and turned down the pebbled path towards the master bungalow.

"Good night and thank you," Ute called, then added, "Carlos," and wondered if Jerry could hear the regret in her voice – or was it longing, or alarm? Something that shouldn't be there anyway.

"Hey guys," Max called out from his chair planted in the middle of the terrace. "Where you've been? We missed ya. Tom and Jerry," he chuckled.

"Hiya," Jerry said cheerily. "You'll have to excuse us, but we're bone-tired. We've walked all afternoon."

Ute waved at the four diners with a smile. A figure stirred in the periphery of her vision. It was Carlos, walking back to the shore some hundred metres away.

"Hey gaucho, how's it goin'?" Max yelled. But Carlos didn't pause or even look back. He crunched on and sank out of view.

"Shifty dude, that one," Max went on. "A dark horse. I bet you he's shagging the lioness. I wonder what *that's* like." Alejandro sniggered.

"You're not having dinner tonight?" Héctor was taking a tray outside.

"Maybe later," Ute said.

"*Bueno*." Héctor had his butler face on.

"Hey guys." It was Alejandro, out of breath from the effort, coming after them. "You don' wanna have dinner with us?" He had a beseeching look on his face. "Later, if you like? We'll be here for sure."

"Yeah, we'll come out later, we're a bit knocked out at the moment," Jerry said.

"All right, I understand. See you later, maybe." Alejandro waved and returned to the table.

Ute stripped and dived into the shower, which was pleasantly lukewarm. She soaped up her sticky neck and armpits and closed her eyes while the shower jets hit her head.

She and Jerry had honeymooned in the south of France, a pleasant honeymoon of late breakfasts and swimming in the Mediterranean. They had got married two years ago. It was almost on a whim, after eight good, seamless years together. Ute had invited her parents to the wedding and hoped at least her father would come, but in the end he didn't – her mother was having "an episode", and he couldn't be away even for two days. At the wedding, Jerry's family had seemed more numerous than ever. The men were well appointed and smug like country manors, the women dull and chirpy like a flock of geese in hats.

The main thing Ute retained from her wedding was a sense of complete and utter loneliness in the world. It had never struck her before with such devastating force. Christmases were usually spent with Jerry's family – his parents, two sisters and their bulging families. Occasionally, she went to Finland to spend a few days with her parents, but Jerry always found excuses not to go along, and she didn't blame him. Her mother wasn't easy to like, and her father was a man effaced by a lifetime of failure. A quiet, unremarkable tragedy, but since she had left home and country aged nineteen, Ute had convinced herself that it wasn't her tragedy any more. And it wasn't her country any more either. Seeing her off at Helsinki Airport all those years ago, her father had squeezed her hard against his big body and simply said, "Try and make your life over there, dearest girl." And she had.

She'd made a good life – she had friends, she had Jerry, she had an exciting job. But at her wedding she realized that all this couldn't fix the fact that she was alone in the world. She felt the absence of brothers and sisters more acutely than ever. The two potential siblings hadn't made it past the embryo stage – her mother had told her about the abortions. Her mother also told her that she hadn't wanted any kids, that Ute herself had been an accident. At least she was honest, if nothing else.

And at the wedding there was no hiding it: Ute had no next of kin who cared enough to turn up. Decent and benign as they were, Jerry's people were not her people. Even after years of knowing her, they didn't quite understand where she came from. Finland to them was a land of snow and vodka, and the odd deer. Not of people with quiet tragedies. They couldn't comprehend the emptiness, the soundless damage of dark winters that chipped away at your soul until there was nothing left. They knew only the bare facts about her parents

– German mother, mentally unstable, war orphan from the 1945 bombing in Hamburg, father a carpenter, looking after mother. And beyond these facts they sensed some gaping pit of Nordic melancholy, and knew not to go probing any further. They had welcomed her into their fold, no questions asked, and she was both grateful and resentful for their indifference.

After the ectopic pregnancy, they had stopped making enquiries into Ute and Jerry's reproductive plans. The incident had shut them up. Jerry's entire family were among those people who somehow knew how to protect themselves from unpleasantness, and they passed on this survival skill to their children.

"It's all yours," Ute called to Jerry. She stepped out and towelled herself.

Jerry bounced out of the hammock, laptop in hand. A moment later, he called out from the bathroom, "Did you remember to care about the water? *There are not many left in the world's*!" He had perked up.

Still in her towel, she lay down in the hammock and closed her eyes.

Today felt like several days rolled up into one. Something still bugged her about the morning, that distant morning on the other side of the forest crossing. The abused animals. The disturbance of Carlos's musky physicality. The strange, informal Héctor, full of insinuations. Now it came to her. *In any case*, Héctor had said. *In any case, that's what the police concluded*. And left it at that.

A mosquito was feeding on her arm. She slapped it and stirred her legs with an effort. Inside the hammock, her body felt like a bag of wet concrete. Jerry was still splashing in the shower. She dressed lethargically. She didn't know why she was doing it, instead of crawling into the mosquito net. She scribbled a lazy note for Jerry letting him know that she'd be in the lounge. She closed the thin wooden door behind her quietly, like turning a page.

9

INSECTS AND OTHER INVISIBLE creatures screeched in the tropical plants. On a whim, Ute took a different path through the compound, the one that led to the master bungalow. The windows upstairs were lit up. Standing in the middle of the path, she felt furtive and ashamed for spying like this.

She quickly walked back to the main lounge, careful to stay out of view of the diners on the veranda, which was strangely quiet.

That's because nobody was there. In the kitchen, Conchita the cook was lazily stirring a pot. Ute poked her head in.

"Is Héctor here?"

"He's down at the shore, he went after them," Conchita said grumpily, and returned her attention to the pot.

Ute went after them too. She could already hear Max's booming voice down by the water. Max had untied the spare moored boat and was pushing it into the water, helped by a hesitant Alejandro. The two women stood by. Héctor shone a torch onto the scene.

"Please," Héctor was saying in Spanish, "I already explained. You can't go across at night. *Señor* Mikel doesn't allow it." His voice was matter-of-fact. "The animals are sleeping."

"Well" – Max was seating himself inside the boat now – "*Señor* Mikel isn't around tonight, and you ain't gonna do much about it, are ya? Come on, are you coming?"

"I don't think this is a good idea," Alejandro protested. "We're..."

"Come on, stop being a pussy and jump in," said Max, switching to English. He was already getting hold of the oars.

Alejandro looked back at Alma, then stepped inside the boat heavily.

"Alex," Alma called out. "Don't go."

"I'll be back soon, *corazón*." The reluctant adventurer waved. "Don't worry, we'll just take a quick trip down the river and back."

Max pointed a victorious fist at them, and then trumpeted: "Don't cry for me, Argentina!" He had a surprisingly good baritone.

"Let's go back to the house." Eve nudged Alma, who looked distressed.

They were now walking back to the house. Héctor stood shining the torch at the gliding boat for a moment, then caught up with them, panting.

"I'll let Lucía know," he said, and turned off to the master bungalow.

"Maybe you could call Carlos on the other side?" Ute suggested.

"There's no phone on the other side," Héctor muttered. Mikel would give him hell for letting the guests across unauthorized.

Back on the veranda, Eve was tucking into a large piece of moist syrupy cake, already served at their table and waiting. She offered some to Alma, who declined and sat fingering the golden crucifix at her neck. Ute sat with them and had a piece of cake too. The women waiting back at the house keeping the fire going, while the men went hunting, that was the idea. And to confirm their ascribed gender roles, Eve and Alma picked up a woman's conversation from earlier on.

"The first one is the hardest," Eve was saying to Alma in between mouthfuls of cake, "but also the sweetest. After that, the birth gets easier. Your hips expand. Actually, it's almost kind of addictive. It's kinda sad to think that I'll only give birth and breastfeed one more time…"

Héctor was back. He was behind the reception, handling keys. Ute walked into the lounge.

"Everything OK?" she asked Héctor.

"Well" – he shrugged – "we'll see. Would you like some dinner?"

"Yes. I'd like the *arroz marinero* please, and a carrot juice."

"Fine," Héctor said. And just then, a gunshot ripped through the night. Everybody jumped in their chair.

"What was that?" Eve cried.

"Carlos. Greeting the visitors." A smile brushed Héctor's face.

"What, has he just... shot at them?" Eve said.

"Carlos would do anything to protect his animals." Héctor said, then turned around and hurried back inside. Eve rushed off down the path to the shore and, after casting an uncertain glance at Ute, Alma followed. Ute got up too and went after Héctor inside the house. He was talking to Conchita in the kitchen.

"Héctor," Ute called, and he came out. She hushed her voice. "You know how you were telling me about the gringo and all that?"

"Yes," Héctor said.

"Are you trying to tell me that he was murdered?" she whispered. Most people never get to say this sort of thing, and she was startled to hear herself utter it. "By Mikel, or Carlos?"

Héctor didn't seem shocked by the question.

"We can never be sure of anything that we don't see with our own eyes. I didn't see anything with my own eyes."

"Do you want your *arroz marinero* or not?" The cook stood at the kitchen doorway, hands on her hips.

"Yes please," Ute said.

"It's all right, Conchita," Héctor said in a conciliatory tone. "*Señor* Mikel is back tomorrow and it'll be all right."

"It better be. Cos this place is turning into a zoo. Like this whole country."

And Conchita stomped back into the kitchen. Héctor set off down the pebbled path.

Ute's carrot juice was waiting for her on the veranda, at the table next to where Eve and Alma had sat. Ute sat down and drained her juice in long, slow gulps. Its coolness spread inside her.

Conchita brought her dinner and placed it in front of her with a muttered "*buen provecho*". Ute tried to formulate a question, extract some insider information from her, but she was too hungry to think, and anyway Conchita's face didn't invite conversation. She surrendered to the fragrant mound of rice and seafood.

And now the hunting party was returning, Max's voice leading the way. He hadn't been shot.

"...And I say to him: come on, gaucho, shoot me, come on. And the sonofabitch shoots at us."

"Not at us," Alejandro piped breathlessly, "but shootin' in the air."

"I didn't see which way he was shootin', the point is he was shootin'..."

They emerged into the light of the veranda: Max striding ahead, Alma and Alejandro walking hand in hand and, last, Eve and Héctor with his torch.

"You know what? I'm gonna call the police... Hey buddy" – he turned to Héctor – "what's the number of the local police?"

Héctor didn't understand, or pretended not to.

"Don't be an ass," Eve snapped at Max. "You know that firearms are legal here. What're you gonna say? I was trespassing in the middle of the night?"

"Shut up," Max snapped back. "Women, huh" – he turned to Alejandro – "they always know better." But Alejandro was still clasping Alma's hand.

They went up the veranda stairs to where Ute was sitting.

"Hey Uddar," Max said, and plonked himself onto a nearby chair. "Hey buddy" – Max turned to Héctor – "bring me a bottle of your finest wine. The most expensive."

"We don't have—"

"I don't wanna hear what you don't have. Just do it."

Héctor stood for a moment, then went inside. Everyone else sat down.

"All I wanted to do was to play with the animals. Say hello to the lion cub. Is that a crime?" He shook his head. "This place is fucked up, man. It's a loony bin. The gaucho over there is a maniac. Mikel's got a screw loose somewhere, that's for sure. The kitchen boy here's a bit dense. And the lady of the house... What the hell's she good for?"

Nobody answered him except the creaking insects in the invisible giant plants.

"I tell you, I'm going off my fucking head here." He shook his head.

"Max, let's leave tomorrow," Eve said in a placatory tone.

Max shook his head again. "We came here for you, honey," he said. Cos you wanted a baby, remember?

Alejandro cleared his throat. "We're gonna go to bed," he said and got up. Alma followed him. Ute saw that his knee was grazed.

"What, you're going already?" Max protested. "What about a game of darts upstairs?"

"Not tonight, no." Alejandro stood his ground this time. "We're very tired."

"All right, all right," Max dismissed them with a flick of his hand. Alejandro made way courteously for his bride and, his hand on her shoulder, they walked across the veranda towards their bungalow.

Max sighed heavily, frowning with sudden introspection. He was a man alone, in a world of disappointing alliances.

"Hey *amigo*," he shouted, "where's the wine?"

Héctor emerged with a bottle in a cooling bucket, his expression inscrutable. But Ute could read him better now, and she saw the stiff neck, the clenched jaw.

"Here it is," Héctor said, and produced the chilled bottle. "Moët et Chandon."

"What, did I say champagne? No, I said wine, *vino*, *vino*. This is fizzy wine, *estúpido*."

The bottle dripped in Héctor's raised hand. For a moment, Ute thought he was going to smash it onto Max's head. But he just said:

"You say most expensive..."

Max leant back in his chair heavily. "All right, whatever, come on, we'll drink it. Uddar, you want some champagne?"

Héctor had brought glasses for everyone.

"Um," Ute cleared her throat. She felt like she hadn't spoken for ages. She loved champagne, and she didn't often drink Moët et Chandon. Even Max's presence couldn't turn her away from this. "Yes, thanks, I'll have a drop." She looked at Héctor whose eyes had gone vacant.

"A drop. A drop in the ocean," Max said, as Héctor filled their glasses.

Eve clinked glasses with him. "To the kids," she said, not making eye contact with him. "I really miss them. Let's call them now."

"I wanna speak to them first!"

Max was dialling a number on his mobile. Ute imagined a bevy of small children in a large mansion, all golden and fluffy like freshly baked pastry, with big, empty eyes. Ute drained the last bit of champagne in her glass and got up.

"Thanks for the drink," she said.

"You're welcome," Eve said absently. "Hey, Mama?" Max was saying now. "How's it goin'? Listen, Mama..."

Ute went the alternative way, via the "master" cabin. She just had to. Not that she expected to see anything, but she needed to reassure herself that someone was home. Someone who hadn't come out when the gunshot was fired. The lights were out. Ute could smell cigarette smoke.

10

"WHO'S THERE?" a hoarse voice said in Spanish.

Lucía was lying in a hammock outside the cabin, smoking. In the dingy light of the path, Ute could only just make out her skinny shape.

"Oh, I'm sorry," she said in English. "I was just… returning to our cabin. I didn't want to disturb you."

"You're not disturbing me, I'm already disturbed." Lucía snuffled a soft laugh. "Where was that from? Come and sit." She gestured towards the other empty hammock, symmetrically suspended on the other side of the door. "It's nice to have someone to talk to."

Ute went over and sat on the edge of the hammock.

"What were you looking for?" Lucía asked.

"Oh, I… wasn't looking for anything."

There was a silence in which her lie echoed long enough for both of them to make of it what they liked. Lucía offered her a cigarette, and Ute lit her second cigarette in ten years, after the first one with Mikel the day before.

"How was your walk in the park?" Lucía asked.

"Actually, we got a bit lost. Well, not lost but we got caught out by the night. We took a shortcut back to the shelter."

"You know, we've been meaning to get some maps designed, for our guests. It's ridiculous that the national park can't get their act together yet. But then again, nothing surprises me here any more…" She paused. "How did you find the shortcut?"

"I just guessed."

"That's clever of you." Lucía said.

"I don't suppose you went as far as Agua Sagrada?" Lucía continued. "It's quite far by foot, a steep climb…" Something in the way Lucía trailed off reminded Ute of Consuelo when she talked about her husband.

"No, we didn't. I wanted to," Ute said. She waited for Lucía to mention Oswaldo. Another thick silence full of insects. Even Max's voice had been turned off. Ute felt heavy-limbed, and with every second of silence she sank further into a canopy of drowsiness. Lucía's tobacco-textured voice brought her back:

"We plan things a certain way in life. But they turn out differently."

This startled Ute, and she turned it over in her sluggish mind.

"Perhaps you're too young to understand this yet. But you will."

"You have a great life here," Ute said. She was surprised by how much Lucía was talking, and how intimately.

"Yes," Lucía said. "Oh yes. Lying in a hammock all day is sweet. And eventually it kills you."

Ute didn't know what to say. "Do you and Mikel have children?" she asked in the end.

"No. I was a feminist. I didn't want nappies and suburbia. I travelled instead. I took drugs…"

"And Mikel?" Ute asked.

"He had a son." Lucía had reclined back in her hammock, and her face was out of view. "It's a sad story." Another long pause, which Ute didn't feel she could interrupt.

"You know, Mikel is an old-fashioned utopian. But, as I said, things don't always turn out the way we thought they would." Ute waited for more, but Lucía went quiet.

At one point, Ute felt a light breeze near her face: it was a very large green insect flying by.

"You'd think that in a place like this time would go very slowly," Lucía said just as Ute wondered if she'd fallen asleep. "But ten, fifteen years have gone like that. I arrived on this coast a young woman from California. I blinked, and I woke up middle-aged. Like *Sleeping Beauty* in reverse. When you come to this point in your life, it's frightening. It frightens you and pushes you to do stupid things."

Lucía lit up another cigarette and, in the quick flash of the lighter, her face looked like a skull.

Ute swallowed. Her throat was dry. "Do you ever leave... this place?"

"It's hard to find someone to manage it."

"Héctor seems onto it," Ute tried. She suddenly remembered the gunshot. "That gunshot... Did you hear it?" she said.

"Sure. It's happened before."

"What, guests of the villa crossing at night?"

"No. Traffickers. That jaguar is worth tens of thousands of dollars, and they know he's here."

The large green insect alighted on Ute's forearm and stretched its many legs.

"We're on our own out here, you know. If armed traffickers broke into the animal refuge, no one would lift a finger in Puerto Seco. If the place went up in flames tomorrow, no one would do anything to help us. The new government of President Gonzales is a pain too. They took some mangrove land we own, which we bought when we first arrived, to protect it from being turned into a shrimp farm. Cos that was the big thing in the Eighties and Nineties. Shrimp-farming. It became a huge export industry. Some officials from the Ministry of Tourism came round and basically took possession of the mangrove swamps. They refused to compensate us, and of course we refused to sign anything, but they went ahead anyway. Now they're charging visitors for guided tours there, fifty to a hundred dollars a head. And the worst thing is, there's a real danger they might want to take the animal shelter next, make it part of the national park, and start charging for it. Oh, I could go on…"

"And how come you don't get on with the locals?"

"It's not that we don't get on. We contribute hugely to the local economy. Everybody who stays here goes on the local tours, the snorkelling, the new national park. But in their heart of hearts, the people here wish bad things on us."

"I heard some kids in the village call you *la Bruja* and *el Vasco*," Ute said. She could be honest with Lucía. Lucía had been honest with her.

"That's right." Lucía uttered her mirthless laugh and exhaled smoke. "I'm a witch because I've got dogs instead of children. That's what life is about around here. Breeding, lying around in hammocks, chasing the flies, and waiting for something to happen."

But Lucía was saying this from a hammock, Ute thought. It's not as though she led a strenuous life. Ute was relishing the conversation, the first enjoyable conversation since she'd arrived.

"This fragrance," Ute said, "what is it?"

"*Palo santo*." Lucía offered Ute another cigarette, and Ute took it automatically. "A kind of tree bark. It grows in the cloud forest. It chases away bad spirits."

"Do you believe that?"

Lucía sighed, or maybe sniffed or laughed. "It's a bit late to believe it when the bad spirits have already paid you a visit," she said. "But I humour Mikel."

It seemed they'd reached the end of the conversation. Ute bid Lucía good night and walked to the *tortuga* cabin. Halfway there she remembered about food for Jerry and turned back. In the lounge,

Héctor was leaning against the reception desk, reading a newspaper. His skin had an oily shine in the dingy light.

Someone was in the games room – there were hefty footsteps upstairs. Ute asked Héctor for a piece of the lemon cake for Jerry. Héctor cut a fat slice, then put it on a small plate with a fork, covered it with a napkin and asked:

"Is he feeling unwell?"

"No, just tired. He missed out on all the excitement tonight." She reached out to take the plate. But he was holding on to it.

"Yes," he said, and walked her to the French doors, the plate in his hands. "For the time being, the situation is under control."

"What situation?"

"The situation in general. With Carlos and all the rest."

He was now walking with her down the pathway, as if he intended to deliver the cake to Jerry personally.

"By the way," Ute said out of the blue, "why has Carlos come all the way from Paraguay to live here of all places?"

"Because he got into some trouble there," Héctor said. "He plotted the murder of a politician."

"What?"

"Some vendetta. You can ask him. Though I'm not sure you will get anything out of him. *Buenas.*"

They were outside *la tortuga* now, and he handed her the plate. He looked pleased with himself. What exactly did he want from her?

"*Buenas*," she said. Héctor turned on his heels and sauntered off.

"Idiot," she said to herself. She'd forgotten to ask Lucía about the elections.

Jerry was sitting in bed, hammering on his laptop.

"Ah, you're back!" He stretched and yawned. "And with sustenance! What's the time?"

Ute looked at her watch. "Seven o'clock," she said and got into bed, with her clothes on. "Which could mean anything between ten and tomorrow."

"It feels like midnight. It's like we're in a sort of... black hole here, isn't it?" Jerry gulped a forkful of cake. "I thought I heard a gunshot earlier."

"You did," Ute said. She was already under the covers, with her back to him.

"Strange thing is, it didn't surprise me," Jerry said, but Ute didn't reply. She was sinking into a vat of sticky sleep, where bad dreams were already churning.

11

LOUD MUSIC WOKE UTE up. Jerry wasn't there. The inside of the cabin was dark day and night, because of the heavy thatched roof, and her watch showed seven-thirty. She lay for a while with her eyes closed, trying to work out where the noise was coming from. The chest-thumping loudspeakers were playing Cumbia somewhere close by. Then the music stopped, and some sort of blurred speech took over. It sounded like the fruit sellers that cruised along the sleepy streets of coastal towns here in open-topped trucks laden with fruit, shouting through megaphones, "*Un dolarito las mandarinas un dolarito los bananas...*" until you bought some, just so they would leave. But what were the fruit sellers doing here in the middle of the night?

Ute got up and stumbled outside. Her head was spinning. It was definitely the middle of the night. Barefoot, she walked in the direction of the noise. It was coming from the back gate behind their cabin. Inside the closed gate, she found two guards in plastic chairs, playing cards. Their rifles were on the ground.

"What's up, what's that noise?" she asked them.

"Supporters of Gonzales," said one.

"It's cos they know *Señor* Mikel isn't here tonight," said the other.

She listened. True: whoever they were, they weren't selling fruit. They weren't even selling a president – Gonzales was already in power. Ute caught fragments like "power to the people" and "an end to the division of wealth" and "we will implement revolutionary changes". Spotlight beams hit the gates.

"What are they doing here?" she asked. "Why don't you tell them to get lost?"

"Because we don't know who they are. They might be armed."

Someone was coming down the dimly lit path. It was Alejandro. His slow-moving body was encased in satin boxer shorts and a T-shirt that stretched across his belly.

"What's happening?" he demanded. The guards explained. Next, Max turned up.

"What's that noise, *amigos*?" he asked. The guards explained again.

"Give me that gun." Max reached out for a rifle.

"We're not opening the gate," one of the guards said. "They may be armed."

"We're armed too, goddamn it, what do you have these rifles for?"

"*Señor* Mikel—" the guard began.

"Get out of here," Max pulled the rifle from his hands and unlatched the wooden gate. The guard tried to stop him, but Max shook him off. The other guard, galvanized into action, grabbed the second rifle to back him up. Pointing the rifle upwards, Max stepped outside and yelled with powerful lungs, "*Basta yaaa*!" But the music continued, so he fired a shot in the air. Ute had never heard a gunshot so close-up. It was deafening. The obnoxious noise died down at once.

"Why the party?" Max shouted.

"Who are you?" A male voice shouted back.

"I'm the guy in charge here. What's up, *amigos*?"

No reply from the voice except an engine being started. The Cumbia came on again. The light beams moved away from the gate. Whoever they were, they were leaving. Soon, the roar of the engine died away, muffled by the forest.

The two guards sniggered and scratched themselves sheepishly. Max stayed outside the gate some more, strutting over the tyre-trodden grass, rifle in hand. Eventually, he came back inside. "Take it." He threw the gun at the guard who managed to catch it.

"See? Easy. No pussyfooting with these guys."

"True, true," the guards said.

Alejandro was full of awe. "They could've shot you," he said.

"Nah. They wouldn't dare shoot a tourist, and they saw I was a tourist. They knew they'd get into trouble."

The three of them headed back, leaving the guards to their card game.

"Where's your other half?" Max asked Ute. She was wondering the same thing.

"He's sleeping," she lied. "He doesn't mind noise."

"Sleep like a baby, huh? So what's going on," Max moved on, "why's this place got so many enemies?"

"Yes, very strange." Alejandro shook his head in agreement.

"I tell you why." Max stopped, forcing the other two to stop as well. Ute glanced at his hairy chest and looked away. "Cos they killed someone here, that's why. They killed a gringo, man, and got away with it. Why? Cos they're gringos themselves."

Alejandro didn't seem surprised. He had no doubt heard this from Max already, on the way back in the boat tonight.

"They did it man, they killed someone. The little guy in the kitchen, what's his name, he knows everything, he told me on the boat. Uddar heard it too, right?"

Ute didn't say anything, and Max continued: "This place is fucked up. I mean, you saw the gaucho tonight, with his gun—"

"You had a gun too," Ute said. "And you didn't have to use it." She started walking again.

"Well, I used it to protect us."

Ute took the *tortuga* turn-off from the main path, but Max caught up with her, grabbed her shoulder and turned her to him.

"Don't touch me," she hissed in his face.

"I was protecting *you*," he shoved a finger at her. "Cos that Jerry of yours would have left it to the women. Now you go back to your man."

"Max, for Christ's sake!" a tired voice came from the darkness behind them. It was Eve. She was standing on the dark path leading to the Whale cabin, in shorts and baggy T-shirt. Max let go of Ute, and she walked to her cabin, shaken. Jerry still wasn't there. She shut the door quickly and bolted it.

She lay in bed, her head and heart thumping. She hated the sight and sound of Max, but in his brutish way he was right. Jerry was not a man who could protect his own. He wasn't even there. Of course none of this mattered back home, where there was no need for animal instincts because their life was set up so safely that you could be a perfect coward and no one would notice. You could go through life standing for nothing, fighting for nothing, believing in nothing, and therefore leaving nothing behind you. Not even a memory. You could slip through the very same safety net that held your life together and, again, nobody would notice. Nobody would try to stop you with a single rifle shot in the night.

Jerry loved her. But his love was complacent, passive, a shadow that walked a few steps behind him. And she loved him, no doubt about that either. She had always loved him. A life without Jerry didn't bear imagining. He was her family, he was all she had. Without him, she was alone in the world. She had to love him.

She squeezed her eyes, and hot tears trickled out of them and onto the already damp pillow. Humidity must be close to ninety per cent here in the wet season. She rehearsed the facts for her new entry in the updated guide. The National Park of Manteño covers twenty-thousand square metres, with a rich wildlife above eight hundred metres, including howler monkeys.

12

UTE DREAMS THAT A woman is walking along an empty beach. The woman is either Lucía or her, it is hard to say. She can't see her face. The sea is lapping gently to one side, and sand dunes stretch on the other. She is walking towards something important, something vital, and enjoying the serene path that is taking her to it. It's a kind of extended holiday. But gradually anxiety rises in her. She has been walking for ages, and still nothing in sight. How far is it? It's too late to turn around now. She's been walking all her life. And this is not a beach. It's a desert with a sea on one side. Some beaches are like that, and both sand and water are uncrossable. She is alone and, even if she screams, no one would hear. She screams anyway. But her throat is so parched that nothing comes out except a rasping sound, a noise that an iguana with a severed tail might make. She has definitely missed the turn-off. She is doomed to wander in this desert, on this endless, pointless, barren holiday, until she grows old, and that's not so far away. She was a young woman when this journey started. And now the sand of her life has crumbled, blown away by impersonal winds. She has nothing left. She starts running, but the sand is heavy and sluggish, it's pulling her back, she's wrestling with the fabric of time itself, a hopeless battle.

Ute woke up whimpering with distress. Jerry was sleeping next to her. She took a gulp of warm water from the plastic bottle on the bedside table and lay still for a while. She could almost taste the grit of sand at the back of her throat.

She looked at Jerry's breathing face and had the unsettling feeling of seeing someone she didn't know. Someone very familiar of course, someone you saw every day, like the man at the corner shop, but, all the same, someone she didn't know. She didn't know his dreams, the contents of his laptop, what he got up to in the middle of the night.

She looked at her useless watch. Just past nine. Which could mean a.m. or p.m. She must get away today, as far from Villa Pacifica and its restless inhabitants as possible. She was still in her crumpled and damp clothes from yesterday. She ran a hand through her hair, splashed water on her face, applied some Eucerin to the inflamed patches, avoiding the mirror, brushed her teeth, put on her flip-flops and went outside. The morning was surprisingly fresh. Water sprinklers gurgled among the giant leaves. Birds chirped above her. All was well.

On the veranda, Carlos was eating an omelette. His greasy hat sat next to his plate.

"Morning," he said.

"Morning," Ute pushed her hair over her eyes. Her lips were dry, her face felt taut and scaly.

"It's very quiet. Where is everyone?" she asked.

"Nobody's up yet." Carlos's strong jaw kept chewing.

"What's the time?"

Carlos shrugged. "Probably about six-thirty." He didn't have a watch.

"Oh." Ute sat in a chair two tables away from him. She felt disoriented.

"My watch is playing up," she said.

"*Bueno*," Carlos said.

They were silent for a long time, then he said: "Conchita's not here yet. If you like muesli or something simple, I can get it for you."

"Oh, I just wanted some hot chocolate." He got up. "No, please finish your breakfast first," Ute added quickly.

"It's OK, I need to get myself some more coffee." He walked to the kitchen in his unhurried, deliberate way. She couldn't picture him being on the run from anything or anyone. She couldn't imagine him having regrets. He looked like someone who did everything for a reason, even plot somebody's assassination. He was someone she would trust to dig a well with his ropey arms and bare hands when stranded in a desert. She looked for the baby iguanas on the high plant and, amazingly, they were still there, on the same leaf, in their decorative yin-yang shape.

Perfection existed in the world of animals and plants. And perhaps even in the world of humans. Lucía and Mikel's exclusive, reclusive love was perfection of a kind. It was something worth holding on to at any cost.

Carlos returned with an espresso, a hot chocolate and an orange juice. She thanked him. It was strangely intimate, like a breakfast the morning after, but without the night before.

He stirred a spoonful of sugar into his cup, then looked at her, amused.

"You don't have to sit at the other end of the terrace. Do I smell?"

Ute's face flushed. She had always been terrible at flirting, and being in a secure relationship for so long had crushed the last stalks of womanly artfulness in her.

"No, no," she said quickly, avoiding his eyes. "I just didn't want to invade your space."

"I can look after my space all right."

Ute moved one table closer to him, spilling her chocolate a little on her trousers. She wiped the spillage with a napkin. "I heard the shot. Last night," she said.

"It scared the animals. I don't like using my gun. But it was either that or getting into a scuffle." He paused, and Ute wondered how a scuffle between him and Max might look.

"Max is bored," Carlos continued. "Occasionally we get that kind of guys. I don't know why people like that come here. I don't know what they expect to get out of this place. They always come with their families. Spoilt wives and fat kids."

"Or fat wives and spoilt kids," Ute said, but Carlos didn't smile. "Are you going to ask him to leave?"

"Oh no. It's not up to me. That's Mikel's decision. It's his business, he deals with the guests. And anyway, Max is so bored he'll want to leave soon. It doesn't worry me either way. Eventually, everyone leaves." Carlos put his hat on.

"Last night... There was somebody at the back gate..." She wanted to keep him a bit longer.

"Yes. Noise carries a long way here."

"Who are these people?"

He shrugged. "Could be Gonzales fanatics. Could be animal traffickers disguised as Gonzales fanatics."

"But why do Gonzales supporters harass a retreat like this, run by someone like Mikel? I mean, he's got Che Guevara in the kitchen!" She hoped Carlos would smile at this, and he did. He shrugged again.

"Politics don't follow logical lines here. For the Gonzales hardliners, any gringo who's making money from a business here is an imperialist. Unless he shares that money with them. You know, I came here to get away from politics. But even in the jungle, you can't get away from it. It's everywhere, it's in the air. That's why I stick with the animals." There was a short pause, then he went on:

"It could be anyone. It could be malicious folk from Puerto Seco harassing the guests with noise. We've had this sort of thing before, though it's got worse since Gonzales was elected. People have been brainwashed by his rhetoric. Let's throw the IMF out, let's throw the World Bank out, let's throw everybody out, and that's all good in my view, but he's taken it too far. Did Mikel tell you about the mangroves?"

"Lucía did."

"Yeah well, you can imagine how Mikel and Lucía feel about that."

"Can I ask you something," Ute said suddenly. "When were the last elections? You know, when Gonzales was re-elected."

"Gonzales hasn't been re-elected," came the answer, just as she'd feared. "It's his first term as President." And he looked at her hard, as if to say, "Silly gringa, you're writing a guide about this country and you can't even get the basic facts right." He got up. "Anyway, time to feed the animals. We're moving the lion cub today."

"Where to?"

"Her new pit. See you later."

Ute watched him disappear down the white path.

A voice startled her. "You're up early." Héctor stood in the lounge. Seen from the brightly lit veranda, he was a small, dark outline. He was well turned-out as always, as if he got out of bed pre-groomed. She wondered if he'd lurked in a dark corner of the lounge, listening to their conversation.

"I guess I am." Ute said.

"Shall I get you breakfast?"

"I thought Conchita..."

"She hasn't arrived yet, but I'll make it myself. Don't want our guests to go hungry." He gave a wan smile.

"Did you hear the commotion last night?"

"What commotion?"

"The music outside the gates and the gunshot."

"You mean the guards shooting?"

"No, it was Max. It was resolved pretty quickly."

"Good," Héctor said. "I'll talk to the guards."

Don't bother, Ute thought, but didn't say it. Perhaps shooting at intruders was a regular occurrence here, nothing to get excited about. Perhaps the whole thing had been a bad dream.

Héctor brought her a second hot chocolate and guava juice. He hadn't asked her what she wanted. She thanked him.

"And continental breakfast," he said. It wasn't a question, but a statement. "What are you doing today?" he then enquired.

"I haven't decided yet. My husband is still asleep." It was a lie. She wasn't waiting for Jerry in any sense. She had already decided she'd spend the day without him, exploring, moving. Physical inactivity was always bad for her, and especially here.

"Yes, he must be tired."

"What do you mean?"

"I went to bed very late, but he was still here working on his computer. Is he writing a story?"

"Yes."

"A story about Villa Pacifica?"

"I don't know." She forced a smile. "You can ask him."

"I don't like to intrude," he said, and went through to the kitchen.

And here was Eve, creaking up the veranda steps, puffy-faced. She sat at Ute's table and tied her hair into a ponytail.

"How are you?" Ute tried to sound friendly.

"I'm all right." Her voice was hoarse. "Given that Max and I almost killed each other last night."

"I'm sorry." Ute said. "What were you arguing about?"

"Oh, just *everything*, as usual! I wanna go, he wants to stay, which is ridiculous, because *I'm* enjoying myself here and he's bored like hell, which is precisely why I want to go. Cos when he's bored, he's impossible. Thank you." Héctor had brought her a milky coffee. "I want him to stop behaving like an idiot and shooting at people in the middle of the night. He does everything by force. He thinks that's the only way to get what you want. He always goes the other way to how I want it, just for the hell of it." She stopped stirring her coffee and took a sip.

"Look," Ute pointed at the baby iguanas on the plant leaf. "Baby iguanas. Have you seen them before?"

"Yeah," Eve said absently, and looked at Ute with long-lashed, sad eyes. Ute felt sorry for her for the first time. "You know what? If Max went running in the forest today and never came back, life would be so much easier."

The casual intimacies of Americans abroad always amazed Ute.

"I'm sure you don't mean that," she said.

"Sure I mean it. I don't wanna see him today. I don't wanna be here when our host – what's his name?"

"Mikel."

"Yeah, when Mikel comes back and asks Max to leave, I don't wanna be here. So, what are you two gonna do today?"

Funny, Ute thought: from the boiling hell of that marriage, Ute and Jerry's seemed blissful.

"I haven't decided yet. Jerry's working on something, so I thought I might go for a walk..." That sounded like an open invitation, so she quickly added. "But I'll talk to him first."

"Do you mind if I join you? I don't really know what's around here, I'm not a traveller, I can't find my way around new places. I'm much happier at home with the kids, where I know where everything is – you know what I mean."

"Yeah," Ute said.

Héctor brought Ute's breakfast tray and took Eve's order.

A woman in baggy trousers and a tight singlet suddenly appeared on the veranda. She had an athletic body and a horsey face, redeemed by a painterly mouth.

"Hi, I'm Liz," she said brightly. "I'll have the cooked breakfast and a hot chocolate, cheers," she said to Héctor who appeared and then disappeared without a word. Ute and Eve introduced themselves.

"We arrived late last night," Liz said. "We were so exhausted we didn't have any dinner, just hit the sack straight away. This place is awesome! I didn't realize it was all tropical plants!" She sounded South African.

"Isn't it gorgeous," Eve said, livening up.

"It's not even in our guide. Like, if someone didn't mention it on the Galápagos, we wouldn't have known about it.

Just then Max bounced up the stairs, bursting with energy.

"Morning ladies!" he shouted. "Beautiful morning."

"Hi," Liz said and gave Max a full-toothed smile.

"Max," Max said, stretching out his arm.

"Oh, I'm Liz."

"You're the folks that arrived late last night, right? I saw you from the playroom upstairs. Where're you from, you're Irish or somethin'?"

"No, we're from Australia," Liz said. "Just back from a holiday in the Galápagos.

"Did you see lots of animals there?" Eve said.

"Oh, that place is crawling with animals! We even went to something called 'swimming with the sharks'. You're in this cage, and you get really close to the sharks."

"Hey, that's what we need, a bit of shark action," Max said. "I'm sick of George here and the depressed lion. I need some adventure. Let's go there, let's leave today! Drive to the city, dump the car off and catch the first flight to the Galápagos."

"You're mad," Eve said flatly. "I'm not going anywhere."

"They're moving the lion today," Héctor said suddenly. He was standing by, waiting for Max's breakfast order.

"What what what?" Max turned to him.

"Carlos and Pablo are moving the lion to the new pit today," Héctor repeated.

"Cool! I'm gonna go help the gaucho. OK honey, we don't have to go to the Galápagos today. I'll have the cooked breakfast, *amigo*."

"You do what you wanna do," Eve said wearily and got up, propping her palms on the table. "I'm going with, hum… sorry, what's your name again?" she turned to Ute.

"Ute."

"Right. Ute and I are going walking."

"All right, fine with me," Max approved. "Liz, maybe you can join the ladies, and your man can come and help with the animals."

"He's not gonna let you across after what happened last night," Eve said, and sat back down wearily.

"Who's not gonna let me? No one's gonna stop me from doing what I want to do round here. I'm a guest – I'm paying, remember? And anyway the gaucho over there hasn't got the last word. Max's got the last word. And you know why?"

"Cos you always have to have the last word?" Eve suggested.

"That too. And cos I know something the gaucho doesn't want me to know." He allowed a dramatic pause, then leant over to the company in a hushed confidential manner. "He killed a guy. Oh yeah, he killed a gringo, and it was hushed up. Not that hard with the corrupt police round here – plus the gringo was a drifter, so it's like, who cares? But not if I get someone to look into it again. Then this place will shut down overnight, and *hasta la vista* baby. Oh yeah." Max sat back in his chair and put his feet up. "He's gonna let me play with the animals today. Anyone wanna take a bet?"

Eve sighed and shrugged. "Whatever," she said. "Who cares. I'm here for a holiday."

"I'd love to see the animals," Liz said. "Where are they?"

"Across the estuary here. You go in a boat..." Ute started saying, but just then Mikel appeared on the main path, carrying plastic bags.

"*Hola*," he yelled to his guests.

"*Hola*," answered the guests, almost in unison. Ute was glad to see him. Mikel had sweat stains on his short-sleeved shirt and two-day-old stubble that gave him a more haggard look than usual. He looked like he'd been away for ages, and it felt like ages for Ute.

"What's in those bags?" Max asked.

"Rubbish," Mikel said. "Those sons of bitches in the national park have left rubbish all over the mangroves." And he was gone in the kitchen.

"Ute, when are we gonna go?" Eve said without moving.

"In ten minutes?" Ute said.

"All right, I'll go make myself ready, then. Liz, are you gonna come with us?"

"No thanks. I'll wait for Tim."

As Ute walked down the pebble path, a man with a vaguely Asiatic face greeted her on the path. He must be Tim.

"It's *so* humid here," he said. "Have you been here long?"

"Yes," Ute said. "No," she corrected herself. "I mean, a few days. I've lost track of time a bit. I think that happens to you here."

Tim lifted an eyebrow. "Sounds exactly like the Galápagos."

It's exactly not like the Galápagos, Ute wanted to say. It's much weirder here.

"Yep," Ute said. "It is."

13

JERRY WAS FAST ASLEEP, and could carry on sleeping for hours yet. Ute made up a small day-pack, put on her walking shoes and scribbled a note: "I'm off walking." After a brief hesitation, she added: "Hope you had a productive night writing. U. xxx" and left it on the terracotta-tiled floor outside the bathroom. She glanced at her note sideways. It didn't really hope he'd had a productive night writing. It queried where the hell he'd been at three in the morning, when the music was blasting and the gunshot rang out.

At reception, she asked Héctor about the snorkelling trips. She figured, if she and Eve were underwater, that would cut down on the talking. Besides, she needed to check out all the local amenities for the guide.

"They do the boat trips most days, if there's enough people," he said. "From midday, departing in a boat from the *malecón*, about three hundred metres from Café Fin del Mundo. But I don't think there'll be enough people. I think they need at least six. This is the low season, and we've had El Niño weather... Unless" – he nodded towards the veranda – "you want to talk the others into it." She didn't.

On the veranda, there were four breakfasters – Alejandro and Alma, Tim and Liz – each pair at a different table, sipping their hot chocolates in blissful silence. Alejandro and Alma invited her for a ride with them later on. She declined politely.

"Where are Max and Eve?" Ute asked. "The American couple," she added.

"He went down that way," Liz pointed to the shore. "And she went to her cabin."

Ute retraced her steps to the far-end cabins where the Whale was. She knocked on the door. Eve opened.

"Hey," she said. "You know what, I think I'm gonna go for a drive with the Mexican guys. I'm just not much of a walker, and they were very sweet and invited me along."

"That's cool," Ute said, relieved. "Where are you going?"

"Oh, *I* don't know. Do you wanna come with us?"

"No, that's all right."

"Do you wanna come in or something?"

"No thanks." But Eve had already opened the door wide and Ute stared at the dark room. You'd think a bomb had gone off – clothes, shoes, bags, stuff everywhere.

"Oh sorry," Eve chuckled. "It's really untidy in here. We make a terrible mess when we fight." She shrugged her round shoulders and blinked at Ute.

"Oh well," Ute said. She looked around and found nothing to say. "Well, I'll see you later." She turned to go. "Maybe tomorrow we can go on the snorkelling boat trip?"

"Oh, I love snorkelling. I mean, I've never done it, but I'd love to try it."

"Sure."

Next, she was standing outside *la tortuga*, peering noiselessly through the netted window into the darkness inside. Jerry was still asleep, and she was glad that she didn't have to talk to him. So glad that it made her sad.

Ute walked along the empty beach. She strode purposefully out of habit, as if rushing to catch the last bus out of town. But there was nothing to catch here, not even fish. She was simply running away from Villa Pacifica.

The wet heat came straight off the ocean in huge, invisible waves that slapped into you. Ute was sure the heat had got denser since they arrived. Something tropical and unfriendly had been moving across the Pacific, from west to east. It had now reached this shore, and was invading the land and its creatures. All along the coast, the last few weeks had been unusually sultry. This humming, sulphurous heat was wilting plants and people. Everything was damp and mouldy – clothes, skin, the breath in her body.

When she reached the end of the estuary beach and the beginning of the *malecón*, Ute sat on the wet sand. She was already drenched in sweat and too lethargic to take off her trainers, so she let the warm water lap at her feet and observed them with a vacant stare: someone's soggy feet. Not unlike her brain in fact. Her tidy brain was succumbing to fungal growth. She didn't think with it any more, she felt with it. It was scarily unlike her. She cast her gaze over the milky water, as if to cast a net for the glittery fish of thoughts. But there was nothing there, just haze.

If someone asked her what she really wanted from life, right now and for the foreseeable future, and if she could be completely honest… No, it was better not to be completely honest. Because what she wanted was to find herself in near darkness, on a hard bed with Carlos. That was all she wanted at the moment. In his dingy cabin, to be more precise, though she wasn't fussy about the setting. To feel him, his calluses, silence and sweat, fall like a hammer on the anvil of her body. To collide with him in the feral heat, among the breathing, screeching animals, until sparks flew. To be released from herself, from her fears, from her desires.

She got up and squelched on in her wet trainers.

The football pitch was empty this time. There were no people at all along the beach or the *malecón* as far as the eye could see. The murky tide was swollen. The fish market stalls were empty. It felt like the last Sunday before the Apocalypse.

Ute tried to calculate what day it was. They arrived on Tuesday the fifteenth of December, but was it two, three or four days since then? It was hard trying to keep up with the clock. She could pretend to follow the trajectory of the sun across the sky, but the sun was invisible. Its heat filtered through cotton-wool cloud.

Café Fin del Mundo was open – and just as well, because it was where she was headed all along. There were two plastic tables outside, and a strange trio was sitting at one of them.

There was a tiny indigenous woman with a face the colour of baked earth, in a sky-blue polyester dress. She wore her hair in a long grey braid. Beside her was a young man with a ponytail, who looked like her son, and a large northern-European woman of a hippie appearance, with dreadlocks and big floral skirts. The exposed full moon of her veiny breast was plugged into a startlingly downy baby. For a second Ute thought she was going mad, because at first glance, with its tufted black hair and scrunched face, the baby looked exactly like a howler monkey.

She greeted them, and the only return greeting came from the man, who said "*Hola*" and smiled keenly with small, sharp teeth. The old woman seemed lost in thought, and the young woman in the baby. Ute almost walked on, past the café and its customers. But there was nowhere to go past the café, except further down the empty *malecón*, so she sat down at the other table and looked blankly at the menu. She already knew its contents from her previous visit, which felt like weeks ago.

"You're back." Consuelo stood in the doorway, smiling her warm shadow of a smile, notepad in hand.

"*Hola*," Ute said brightly. "How are things?"

"Fine. The weather's getting hotter, isn't it. I think there's a tropical storm on the way. I've been watching the ocean from morning to sunset every day. I can see the changes. I can feel it coming. Just like last time."

"You mean El Niño again?"

"El Niño again," Consuelo said sadly.

"I thought El Niño only strikes once every ten years or so?" Ute said. This was all she remembered about the El Niño phenomenon from her reading on the subject years ago. El Niño alternated with La Niña, whatever that was.

"I thought so too," Consuelo said. "But things are not always the way we think. A *cafecito*, like the other day? OK, guava juice it is. One *momentito*."

Consuelo went back inside. Ute must really offer to buy a painting. But she only had twenty-five dollars with her. The trio had sat silently throughout this exchange. She looked at the man, who smiled and looked at the sky as if it was a movie screen, and she followed his gaze. The sky was white and unpleasantly curved, like a blank eyeball. Only the gentle splashing of the ocean and the sucking of the bristly creature could be heard in the eerie silence. The breastfeeding woman said something in a low, thick voice. The man mumbled something and took the bundle from her.

"Are you staying here in Puerto Seco?" the man asked Ute amiably, now cradling the baby, which pursed its face as if they were feeding it lemons.

"Yes," Ute replied. "Actually, we're just outside the village, in a sort of retreat. It's called Villa Pacifica."

"I didn't know there was another hotel," the man said. "We're staying here, two hundred metres down the *malecón*. A small hotel, very cheap. How much is a room at Villa Pacifica?"

"Twenty-five dollars for a cabin," Ute said.

"For two people? A rip-off," the man shook his head disapprovingly.

The gringa was methodically eating an omelette. Black tarantulas of hair nestled in her armpits. In her boho skirts, she looked like a Bavarian farm maid. The older woman was gazing at the sea with an absent expression. Her dress front had a crumpled appliqué, and a beaded necklace was wound several times around her stubby neck.

And here, suddenly, was the fruit van again. Loud Cumbia and a puff of petrol smoke floated their way.

"*Dos dolaritos las mandarinas*!" the megaphone voice shouted over the music. "*Un dolarito las bananas*!" The van slowed down as it passed the café, but since nobody gave a sign of wanting mandarinas, bananas or anything else, it rolled on. The man with the megaphone gave Ute and the trio a funny, inert look, as if he was remembering them, rather than seeing them in flesh and blood. Was this the same van from last night? Boredom could drive you bananas here. Bananas and mandarinas.

"Well, we're off now," the man said. His name was Luis. "Helga and the baby need to rest. We'll see you around, I hope. Oh, by the way, I want to go snorkelling tomorrow, but they need at least six people. There's no one else at our hotel, and Helga can't go because she's breastfeeding. Maybe you and your friends could come along to make up numbers?"

"I'm here with my husband," Ute said. "They're not my friends."

Then she added, "I'll ask them."

"Great. Tomorrow at eleven then. The ticket kiosk is down this way" – he pointed – "it has a yellow front with some fish painted on it, you can't miss it."

Ute sat a while longer, sipping the crimson juice. Something gripped her throat the way Carlos's ropey hand must have gripped the throat of the grey-faced junkie. Perhaps she was just very tired after weeks in lumpy hotel beds and bumpy buses. Maybe she was getting a bit jaded (she didn't want to think "old") for this job. Maybe she could do less content-writing and more editing. Because those were really her only options. If she didn't want to travel any more, and she didn't want to read other people's travel compendiums, she'd be out of work and out of livelihood. What would her life amount to then? Not very much.

Even Consuelo and Lucía, two admirable women with seemingly charmed lives here by the beach, had hit on an unpalatable truth: there comes a point in your life when the choices you've made are not retractable. It's not a rehearsal any more, it's the real thing. You are so stuck with the consequences of the choices you have made that you *are* those choices. You are the relationship you're in. You are the work you do, or don't do. You are the children you have created – or haven't. You are the place where you live. Your future is not as flexible as it used to be ten years ago, or even five years ago. Your future is already invaded by large swathes of the past.

And having established this, all you can do is have a pathetic midlife crisis. A midlife crisis is exactly what was going to happen if Ute kept sitting here at the End of the World Café.

That's enough, *basta ya*! Ute scraped the plastic chair against the tiled patio and went inside the shop.

Consuelo was in a semi-dark, semi-empty room at the back of the café, uncovering canvases of various sizes stacked along the walls, presumably for Ute's sake. She flicked a switch on, and a dingy light flooded the bare room.

"I keep some of Oswaldo's work here in case someone wants to look at it. I have more at home. I don't know which ones you want to see." She started browsing through the canvases. "I don't know what sort of size you're after..."

"Maybe I could just look through them," Ute said. There was no turning back now, she had to buy something. "Actually, I haven't brought enough money with me. But I wanted to look at them and see if there's anything..."

"Yes, of course, I understand. Take your time." Consuelo withdrew and leant against a small table with her arms crossed. Feeling Consuelo's eyes on her, Ute crouched to examine the paintings.

"Oswaldo has this unique style of weaving words into images," Consuelo was saying. "Sometimes it's difficult to tell them apart. Even for me." Did she mean tell the text from the image, or tell the paintings apart from one another? Because Ute had a problem with both. Her ignorance in matters of art was to blame, no doubt.

"His triptychs are among his best works," Consuelo went on. "But all his triptychs are at home, except this one."

She pulled out a long canvas, unwrapped the brown paper from it and propped it up against the wall. It was in three parts and, unlike the others, Ute found it arresting. It stood out.

"You know," Consuelo said, "this weak light doesn't do it justice. Let's take it outside, so you can see it in the natural light."

Outside, she placed it on top of a plastic table and stood behind it, holding it up for Ute to see. Each part of the triptych was in a different range of hues, and each was larger than the previous. The first, smallest one, was metallic greys. The second was a kind of hyperreal, saturated blue. On closer inspection, there was a squiggly black hairline fracture running across, like a tear in the fabric of a dream. The third and largest was a chlorophyll green, like a rainforest.

"What's the title?" Ute asked.

"*The Three Lives of Mikel*," Consuelo said from behind the canvas. Her smile had vanished again. With her arms spread out to hold the painting, she looked like a Colonial carving of a female Jesus.

"*The Three Lives of Mikel*," Ute repeated.

"It used to hang in the reception room of Villa Pacifica. It was a present from Oswaldo to Mikel."

"And now it's here."

"Now it's here. Things change." Consuelo leant the painting against the wall and stepped beside it. She looked at it. "It's sad, but we are not friends any more. Mikel is a hot-headed person. And Oswaldo... Certain things... I'm sorry, this is of no interest to you." She waved self-dismissively. "Anyway, his triptychs are based on his vision of the three lives of a person. He believes that everybody has three lives within their single life. And the thing is, he only paints it the way it looks from our present perspective, so by definition it's skewed. For example, in our first years together, he painted a triptych of his own life. And do you know what it consisted of?"

Ute didn't.

"Three portraits of me, in different perspectives." Consuelo smiled. "I was over the moon. But then I discovered that ten years before he'd painted another triptych of his life. It was three portraits of his previous, second wife. It's just the way Oswaldo is."

"I guess that one's not for sale then," Ute said.

"No, that one's not for sale. I have it at home. To remind me of the good times." Consuelo managed a smile.

"So..." Ute examined the painting for clues. "What does this say about Mikel's life? I mean, about Oswaldo's vision of it."

"Well, the first life is his European life, before he sailed to South America. If you look very carefully, you'll see the word Gibraltar woven into the paint."

Ute scrutinized the metallic greys of what looked like a large rubbish dump seen through myopic eyes. A bleak portrait of Europe, that was for sure.

"Yes, I can see it. He wasn't very happy in Europe, if we judge from this."

"No. Otherwise he would have returned. He was an anthropologist, you know, at university. But he had some political problems, and personal ones, too. I don't like to pry. Anyway, the second part is his epic journey across the Pacific Ocean."

"The Pacific," Ute echoed.

"The Pacific. He and his young son sailed from Europe across to the west coast of South America on a small boat. Let's sit down," Consuelo suggested. "Can I get you another drink?"

"Thank you, I'm fine." They sat down in the plastic chairs, turned towards the painting as if it was a window. "How long did it take them to get here?"

"Three years. Actually, they ended up in the Galápagos. He wanted to live on an island. But..." Consuelo drifted off and shook her head.

"What happened?" Ute prompted her.

"The island of Floreana is ill-fated, you see. There were disappearances and deaths there in the last century. Some German settlers ended up there and came to a bad end, one way or another. It's still cut off from the other islands. I don't know the details. I don't know whether Mikel didn't know about all the history, or knew and wanted to find out more about the earlier settlers. Or maybe it was a strange and twisted desire to follow in their footsteps."

"And what happened with his son?"

"It's a sad story," Consuelo's smile wrinkles vanished. "His son drowned."

"Oh," Ute said. She'd expected something out of order, but not this. Consuelo shook her head again.

"Some kind of accident. They had sailed the Pacific, fished and swam every day in the open ocean... It's not as if the boy couldn't swim. It's..." – she searched for the right words – "terrible to live with such sorrow. But even worse is the guilt. You see, he must live with that guilt for the rest of his life. I feel sorry for him, even though he hasn't always been the most... I'm sorry," Consuelo waved again in that self-dismissive way. "This is of no interest to you."

Yes it is, Ute wanted to say, I don't know why but this stuff is vital to me. But she didn't want to put Consuelo on guard. After all, she was just passing through, she was just a guide-writing gringa who spoke decent Spanish and was making conversation.

"*Bueno*," Consuelo said with that kind, unsurprised smile of hers. "So that's what the black line represents in the second life. You will see that the line spells out the word Galápagos."

Ute could see nothing of the sort, but then she was too busy thinking of Mikel with his temper problems, the sudden clouds that descended over his mood, and the way Lucía hadn't wanted to tell her about his son's death – out of respect for Mikel's feelings.

"And the third one," Consuelo said, returning their attention to the painting, "you can guess."

"Villa Pacifica?" Ute asked. "It's the biggest one, so it must be the most important."

"Yes, that's how Oswaldo saw it. The last, longest, happiest life."

Something dissonant slipped into Consuelo's voice. Consuelo wanted to get rid of this painting. She must have her reasons. And perhaps she hoped that someone like Ute had her reasons to buy it.

They both looked out to the grey sea, which was hard to separate from the grey sky. Some kids were kicking a ball on the beach.

"When's the fish market on?" Ute asked. "It was closed the other day, and it's closed today."

"That's because there's no fish," Consuelo said. "The ocean is too warm. It's all gone upside down. Like last year."

"What exactly happened then?" Ute said and looked Consuelo in the eye.

"*Bueno*, as I said, we had El Niño and all the destruction."

"But what else?" Ute insisted. Consuelo sighed.

"It all happened at once. Oswaldo's illness. The elections. Oswaldo's move to Agua Sagrada. And then the falling out... El Niño."

"Was there also a... murder?" Ute ventured. "At Villa Pacifica?" Consuelo looked shocked.

"A murder," she repeated. "I don't understand."

"A junkie, a gringo... disappeared."

"Look" – Consuelo looked at her sharply – "I don't know who you've been talking to, but Mikel and Carlos are good men. No matter what happened between us, I won't have anything bad said against them." She looked hurt.

"I'm sorry," Ute said.

"Now, would you like to have a look at some others inside?" Consuelo said, quite firmly.

"Yes please." Ute followed Consuelo back inside with the painting.

The triptych for Mikel was huge, beyond her price-wise and, besides, it felt wrong to buy it. It wasn't meant for her. Ute browsed absently through the other canvases, none of which grabbed her. Whatever had happened here, the triptych carried someone else's history.

Consuelo said, "If you really like the triptych, you can have it for two-hundred-and-fifty *dolaritos*. It's worth a lot more, but I can tell you're not a *personita* of great means."

Ute got up from her crouching position in a daze, startled by the direct offer and by the price drop.

"Thank you," she said. "I'll think about it and come back tomorrow."

"For the snorkelling, you'll come back for the snorkelling," Consuelo said, without reproach, as if simply informing Ute of her own true intentions, and saw her out.

"Héctor's really nice. He's your son, right?" Ute said casually as she paid for the juice.

"Yes," Consuelo smiled. "My son."

"But Oswaldo isn't his father?" Ute asked.

"No." For the first time, Consuelo looked at her with something resembling mistrust. "Héctor's father didn't hang around. That's how men are around here. Men in the mountains don't have anywhere to run to, but men from the coast get you pregnant and – pouf! – they vanish." She said this with a forgiving smile. "That's why you see so many single women with kids around here."

"Well, thank you for showing me the paintings." Ute made to go.

"You're always welcome, any time."

Then Ute thought of something.

"What about you – did Oswaldo paint you a triptych?"

Consuelo screwed her face into a wrinkly grimace.

"No. Or, if he has, I haven't seen it. I didn't want one. I felt that as soon as my life was made into a painting in three parts, it would be over. Call it superstition, I've always been superstitious. As far as I can tell – and I'm no artist, I didn't go to university like Oswaldo, and I don't speak a foreign language like Héctor – but as far as I can tell, we only have one life."

"Yes," Ute said. "One life. Well, I'm off. *Buenas*."

"*Buenas*." Consuelo leant on the peeling blue doorway with her arms crossed.

Ute walked on along the ocean promenade to the end of the village. Just in case there was something to see, someone to meet in this ghost town. But the only traffic she saw was the fruit-seller's van driving the other way, loud music thumping away, the piles of mandarins and bananas already rotting in the heat.

From the street, Ute peered inside the dark interiors of houses perched on stilts. She glimpsed bodies lying in hammocks, and small children in scruffy T-shirts and bare bottoms shuffling in the dust, in and out of doorless doorways.

Ute walked across the beach, until her feet were in the lazy, lapping water. Even the ocean couldn't be bothered. She removed her wet shoes and lay herself down on the sand, her feet pointing out to the open sea. Pointing to the Galápagos, where in a single afternoon Mikel's life had been broken.

She wriggled her toes and spread out her limbs in a star shape. The sky exhaled its hot breath, and she closed her eyes.

Ute's three lives: how would that look? First, the glacial white of a Finnish childhood and youth. White like a snowy tundra, like a hospital corridor, like death.

Next, the world. A globe.

Jerry, home – she could paint that easily enough.

And the end of love, what does that look like? And homelessness? Not because that's how she felt. If she could paint, perhaps she might find out how she really felt.

But the idea of seeing her life on canvas – beginning, middle and end neatly framed – was oppressive. Oswaldo was assuming God-like powers. Perhaps that's why Mikel had rejected the painting. But

Mikel did say that they'd be in Villa Pacifica until the end. *We'll die here.* Mikel had already foretold his last life. And in doing so, he had foretold his death – just like Oswaldo had done with the painting.

Ute sat up and shook the sand from her hair. Her head felt full of insects. Fragments of conversations, sounds and faces from the last few days buzzed inside. She needed to cobble something together from all this.

Under every entry in a travel guide there is a short lead-in section where the writer introduces the town in a factual way, while simultaneously evoking its atmosphere, even if it didn't have any. Ute had yet to do the dry-forest national park, the cloud forest up in Agua Sagrada, the snorkelling trip... but the outline was already there. It went something like this:

> Puerto Seco is a sleepy fishing village sitting at the estuary of the Agua Sagrada River, 300 miles (500 km) south-west of the regional town of Jipilini. There is not a great deal to see or do, and tourist facilities are thin on the ground. It is however an ideal base for exploring the dry forest and cloud forest of the 20,000-square-metre Manteño National Park, which was established in 2006 and is rich in plants and wildlife. You can go snorkelling off the sandy coast of the Park with a guided boat tour from Puerto Seco. Like many coastal towns in the area, Puerto Seco was severely damaged by El Niño floods, but most of it has been rebuilt. There are two accommodation options, and a café along the *malecón*.

The unofficial story was taking shape, too, in her mind. And the more it was taking shape, the more she felt on edge.

Ute was nearing the corner of the *malecón*, where it turned inland and where the open ocean became an estuary leading back to Villa Pacifica. The coast jutted out at this point, and from there, the horizon looked curved. She was standing at the end of the human world, looking out at what was beyond.

There was nothing human beyond. The grey ocean was rising slowly like the back of a whale disturbed in its sleep, ready to spout a bitter tsunami onto the sleepy coast.

The logical thing to do now was to get out of here. Pack up, pay up, say goodbye to Mikel and Lucía, Carlos and Héctor, and leave today. Catch the first bus that passes along the dusty road, or just hitch south and go inland as soon as possible. But they weren't going to.

A solitary seagull shot down from the sky, and Ute ducked instinctively, but it wasn't coming for her. Her left cheek and eyelid were very itchy. Like the El Niño current, the eczema was spreading, and no other force of nature could stop it.

She plodded back to Villa Pacifica along the well-tended sand strip. The air was so thick with humidity, it was like moving at the bottom of a sea.

Part Two

14

THREE THINGS HAPPENED THE moment Ute crossed the gated threshold of Villa Pacifica.

First, some celestial trapdoor opened creakily high above her, and a heartbeat later the sky disgorged a deluge.

Second, she heard delighted squealing and "Oh my God!" – and her heart sank even before she glimpsed Carlos and Liz together on the veranda. Liz was standing with her arms outstretched to feel the rain, like some Antipodean earth goddess, and Carlos, in a black singlet, sat with his feet up on a chair. She was shocked at how much it hurt her to see him. And Liz's sun-struck, carefree, easy animal beauty hurt her even more. Liz took off her T-shirt and was down to her sports bra, shorts and tanned arms and legs. "I'm going to swim in the rain!" she informed all the creatures of Villa Pacifica, and ran down the veranda steps to the shore. Carlos sat a few moments longer, unaware of Ute's presence on the path, just behind the huge plant with the baby iguanas. Then he got up without rushing, the muscles of his arms moving like those of a predator sure of its prey, and walked down to the shore and out of view.

Third, a powerful lightning bolt ripped the darkened atmosphere, and Ute had a sense of foreboding – as if this was a cue for something she didn't want to happen but knew was going to happen. The unleashed elements took all responsibility away from her, from everybody. It was all up to nature now. The jaguar confirmed this with a ripe roar from across the river.

There wasn't a soul at the main house, and the garden seemed equally deserted. The Mexicans and Eve hadn't returned – their 4x4 wasn't in its usual spot outside the gate. Ute stood inside the dark reception room for a moment, distracted by cinematic images of Carlos and Liz rolling and kissing on the sand... Ute grabbed a piece of lemon cake from the tray and stuffed it into her mouth.

She then had a desperate thought and ran up the stairs to the "music and games room", stumbling as she went. She hated feeling out of control. You could say that her life until this point had been a struggle to control her emotions. But the truth was, from the large bay windows upstairs, you could see down to the shore.

"Hello!"

Reclining on the cushioned banquette along the window was Tim.

"Oh... Sorry!" Ute said, startled.

"Sorry to give you a fright," Tim smiled languidly. "I came up with my book earlier this afternoon, cos it was really quiet and there's much better light here than in the cabins, then I fell asleep and then the rain woke me up and those two downstairs chatting. Honestly, Liz is..." He rolled his eyes and exhaled in frustration. "She's a sweetie, but she's *so* on the rebound. She snapped up the cowboy before I had a chance to say 'Nice hat'."

Tim looked out to the bank. Ute looked too, the unfinished piece of cake sticky in her hand. The bank was partially obscured by plants and by the rain that fell in heavy curtains. The ground and the plants were exuding primeval vapours – any moment now, some dinosaur would poke its snout from behind a bush. She could see two blurry figures by the water, one of them rowing away, and the other one moving back towards the house and out of view. She sat down on a cushioned chair and finished eating her cake.

"Wow," Tim said. "This rain is unbelievable, listen to it." They did for a moment. It crashed onto the thatched roof like the Niagara.

"I don't know if these roofs are made to hold up in heavy rain like this," Ute said.

"I guess we'll find out." Tim picked up his tatty book. "What are you up to tonight? Going out on the town?"

"No, there's nothing to do in town," Ute said.

"I was joking." Tim smiled. "I figured Puerto Seco's a hole," he added. "So, I didn't bother checking it out today. Anyway this place is just amazing, why would you ever want to leave paradise?"

"Yes," Ute said. "I think a lot of people feel this way. Have you seen the visitors' books?"

"No, what visitors' books?"

"Oh, they're downstairs, there's a whole shelf of them. Just... guests of the Villa writing down their comments. Apparently, everybody who stays here writes something down. Those who don't, either never arrived, or never left." She tempered this with a sardonic smile.

"Oh, I like the sound of *that*," Tim said in a dreamy voice. "Never smell another reheated airplane meal again. Never have to be insulted again by drunk redneck pigs in economy class... I mean, don't get me wrong, I love my job, it's got a lot of perks, but sometimes I dream of escape. I guess everybody does."

Suddenly here was Liz, coming up the stairs.

"Oh my God, have you seen the rain?" She shook her hair.

"No I haven't," Tim said. "So how was your skinny-dipping with the gaucho?"

"Oh, you're just jealous, Tim!"

"You bet I am."

"Well, it didn't happen. He had to go across to take care of the animals. Something about the lion pit getting filled with water. I offered to go with him and help, but he wasn't interested."

"You know, I hate to disappoint you, but I think he's the lone-wolf type," Tim said.

"Bummer."

"I wish," Tim sighed.

"I better go and change. See ya later." She waved and was gone.

Ute walked to *la tortuga*, soaking up the warm rain like a moving sponge. The water was soothing on her inflamed face. Through the netted window, she saw that Jerry was sitting on the bed inside the netting, scribbling something.

She took off her sodden shoes and pushed the door open. "Hi. Are you all right? Have you been lying here all day?"

"*I'm* all right. Where have *you* been all day?" He got up, stepped out of the bed netting and put his arms around her, as if he knew that she needed soothing. She embraced him back. It felt like they hadn't touched for ages.

"Just to Puerto Seco and back," she said. "What's the time?"

He looked at his laptop. "Coming up to five."

"I don't know where the days go here. Do you?" Ute was taking her clothes off and looking for somewhere to hang them to dry. But there was nowhere dry inside or out.

"We're on holiday. That's what happens when you're relaxed and enjoying yourself," Jerry said breezily, and ducked back inside the bed netting.

"Speaking of which," Jerry continued, "why don't you come and join me in here?" He started removing his own clothes. "In this biblical deluge, we may as well get biblical."

Ute smiled. She was tired and clammy inside and out. And yes, vaguely, distantly aroused. She stepped inside the netting. Jerry was reclining on the bed, naked and white, so white he was like a glow-worm in the darkened room. His middle was slightly thickened, despite his slender boyish physique. Even boys hit forty, eventually, and became soft and doughy around the waist, and Jerry was about to hit forty. Some men – Carlos, for example – held up well and would look powerful all the way into their seventies, she suspected, but Jerry was a desk worker and wasn't going to be one of them. It wasn't that she cared much about that, but she was suddenly filled with sadness for him.

He drew her to him and she closed her eyes, feeling Carlos's hands over her breasts and back and buttocks, Carlos's hard panting body and urgent weight on her. When she reopened her eyes, the fantasy vanished. She was herself again, and for a moment she was afraid that Jerry could see the betrayal in her pupils. She listened to the impersonal rain.

Jerry's hand was stroking her back in that affectionate, therapeutic way he had. She disliked it, but had never found a way of letting him know.

She had never been unfaithful to Jerry, except for a short, drunk, non-penetrative tumble in the sheets of a dingy hotel on a starless Bolivian night. There were mitigating circumstances – namely that the Norwegian was very insistent, which was flattering; she had felt achingly lonely and far away from Jerry, and not sure whether he really loved her – and besides it was years ago, at the start of her guide career, so long ago it almost hadn't happened. She had been unfaithful in her mind before, but never like this. Still, she had no doubt that Jerry had been fantasizing for years about having sex with beautiful women – well turned-out university colleagues, young students, perhaps even random passers-by or foreign waitresses. Beautiful women were everywhere. It was only natural.

"Ute, are you crying?" Jerry propped himself up on an elbow behind her turned back and put a hand on her tense shoulder, trying to peer at her face. "Ute, what's wrong?"

"Nothing," Ute whispered, and turned her face into the pillow. She never cried in front of Jerry, why start now? She never cried full-stop. Jerry switched on the dim bedside lamp.

"It's the rain." Ute cleared her voice and pulled herself together. This was true, in a way. It was everything else *and* the rain. Jerry massaged her shoulders.

"Has someone upset you?" he said gently.

"No. It's... all this stuff, coming up to the surface. Out of nowhere."

"What stuff?"

"Just stuff. Dreams. Memories. Stuff I never think about. Like my whole life is flashing before my eyes."

He continued massaging her shoulders as she spoke, and she wished he'd stop. It made her feel like a sick dog about to be put down by a kind animal-shelter worker.

"Your parents. Childhood stuff," Jerry guessed.

"No, it's not just that." Tears made the eczema on her eyelids burn, so she dabbed her eyes dry with a corner of the top sheet.

"Maybe it's just the... I don't know, the stillness? Being still?" Jerry guessed again. "After being on the move for a few weeks, you know, you suddenly find yourself alone with your thoughts."

"Yes, I know you think I'm not introspective enough," was her brittle reply, and she sat up.

"Nonsense."

"But you do. You think I'm addicted to travel because it's a way of escaping from myself."

"Well, isn't all travel an escape in some sense?" He had stopped stroking her. They were now both propped up against the pillows.

"Isn't *writing* an escape in some sense?" she said.

"Sure. But it's an escape into a world you yourself have created."

"I don't see the difference."

"Well, maybe there isn't a difference," he said irritably. "I suppose one is more passive than the other."

"So sitting at your desk is somehow more active than taking a trip around a foreign country."

"Well, perhaps not more active, but I think it's more imaginatively involved. But so what? I don't see why we have to compare. Why are you so defensive anyway? There's nothing to be defensive about!"

"Anyway," Ute said. "I don't think it's being still. I think it's this place. Even this smell… There's something about it."

"The incense you mean?"

"Yeah, the *palo santo* bark. It's supposed to have cleansing and anaesthetic properties, but it's having the opposite effect on me."

"Really? I rather like it. It's quite… exotic. Look, if you're not happy staying here, we could just leave tomorrow. I mean… I don't mind." He did mind. He was loving it here. If they left tomorrow, he'd be sulking for the rest of the trip.

"No, no, we don't have to leave," Ute roused herself and sat on her edge of the bed, her back to him. "Besides, I haven't done my research yet. I've just been so unproductive here. I don't know what I've done with my time."

"Just relax. We've only been here three days."

"It feels like three weeks," she said, and scratched the angry eczema patch in her elbow. She wanted to tell him about Consuelo, about the paintings, her theories on this place and its inhabitants. But the moment for it had passed.

"Well, funny you say that, because I've done more writing here in three days than I normally do in three months – it's amazing. It must be the *palo*… the incense thing."

"The rain has stopped," Ute said.

15

THE RAIN HADN'T STOPPED: it had quietened down to a weak shower, invisible in the dark. Under the canopy of moisture, Villa Pacifica breathed heavily with its animals and humans, all scattered in the darkness among the dripping plants. Birds and monkeys screeched from the other side.

Along the white-pebbled paths, the lanterns came on. The main house was lit up with a warm, festive glow. Or so it must have appeared to Luis, his mother and Helga with the baby strapped at her front, who were arriving there for the first time. From the upstairs games room, Ute watched them walk in a single file.

She was upstairs because Max – and everyone else – was downstairs. Jerry was browsing through a book. The others were finishing their dinner. Lucía and Héctor were looking through ledger books at the reception bar. Mikel was out walking the collies on the beach. And Carlos was of course on the other side. The Villa Pacifica family in perfect harmony.

Ute and Jerry had managed to eat before Max entered the scene, all excited after his afternoon in the animal shelter.

"Hey, guess what! Guess what!" he'd shouted. "I fed the lion cub today, and then we moved her to the new pit. She was good as a kitten. And we fed the jaguar, two kilos of rabbit meat – boy does he eat. It wasn't a live bunny this time round..."

Ute didn't feel social tonight. She was subdued and a bit fragile. Being in constant proximity to fellow tourists she didn't like always unsettled her. It used up the precious energy she needed to stay alert and record things accurately. Still, the idea of their dingy *tortuga* with nothing to do but lie on the bed and listen to the buzzing of mosquitoes wasn't alluring either.

"Hey, hey, hey, we've got new arrivals! *Buenas*!" Max's voice carried up. There was the scraping of chairs downstairs. Jerry came up the stairs.

"New arrivals from Puerto Seco," he said. "I think they're just here for dinner. Local guy with his mother, and a sort of feral-looking woman with a baby. I thought you might want to meet them."

"I met them already," Ute said. "In the village."

"Oh, did you?" He sat next to where she was reclining, on the cushioned bank by the windows. "Are you OK?"

"Fine. Just not in the mood for Max tonight."

"Yeah, I know. Everybody's sick of him. Except the Australian woman, she finds him hilarious."

To confirm this, Liz started braying with laughter downstairs. The baby joined her with a piercing cry. Ute covered her ears. If this was their baby, it would be calling out to them, an adorable tadpole from the amoebic depths of their combined genetic pools. It would no longer be annoying. Down on the path, Mikel was returning with the two collies.

"You know that I love you, don't you?" Jerry said suddenly, and flicked his fringe. He stared at her with an imploring, puppy-like look.

Why, she wanted to ask, why do you love me, still? No other man has ever loved me, not even my father. Carlos here doesn't even notice me. Are you sure it's love and not habit?

Ute put her hand on his thigh reassuringly. Because that's what the statement signalled: *he* needed to be reassured, not she. "Of course," was her flat answer.

"I'm going to have some cheesecake and coffee. Want to join me?" Jerry said. He was visibly relieved. She felt a pang of pity – for him or for herself, she wasn't sure.

"Sure." She smiled. She felt numb, and it was better that way. Jerry never drank coffee in the evening.

Downstairs, all the diners had gathered around Mikel on the veranda. Luis nodded at Ute in friendly acknowledgement. Helga and the mother ignored her.

"...Heavy rains and storms over the next days and weeks," Mikel was saying. "Perhaps not tomorrow or the day after, but definitely some time this week. The entire coast will be affected, so I'd advise those of you who want to avoid it to leave first thing tomorrow and drive inland, away from the coast."

"What's he saying?" Liz asked Max.

"There's a storm on the way," Max translated. Eve looked relieved. Finally, there was a reason to leave.

"But we just had one now," Liz said.

"Could we leave tonight?" Alejandro asked anxiously, and looked at Alma. She blinked with heavy eyelashes and said, "Whatever you say, *corazón*, I don't mind."

"Indeed, do as you like, *corazón*," Mikel mocked good-naturedly, then got serious again. Ute caught a whiff of alcohol off him. "But you've seen the holes in the coastal road and the bad signposting. And anyway, it's coming to nine o'clock, where are you gonna spend the night? There's nowhere to stay within three hours of driving, in any direction. That's why I said, first thing tomorrow. I think the night will be calm."

Lucía and Héctor were listening from reception, their elbows propped on the carved wooden bar. With his crazy hair, glasses and Hawaiian shirt and shorts, Mikel looked like a mad zoology professor gone native in some tropical jungle, evangelizing to a loyal gathering of disciples.

Except they were neither loyal nor disciples. All they shared was the random fact of being inside Villa Pacifica tonight. Otherwise, their lives had nothing in common. Luis's mother gave no sign of interest in the world. The baby had closed its eyes, its tiny face screwed up in disgust, as if saying, "Take me back to where I came from, I don't like it here." Helga uttered something in German to Luis, but he was already addressing the group.

"I remember reading in Germany about El Niño on the coast along here – what, about three, four years ago?"

"Last year," Mikel said.

"What's happening?" Jerry asked Ute.

"There's some bad weather on the way."

"No kidding," he snorted.

"More rain and thunderstorms."

Jerry frowned. "I thought rain was good news. Didn't they want rain because of the droughts?"

"Yeah," Liz joined in. "We heard the same on the Galápagos. They've had a really dry year, and they were hoping for some rain this summer."

"*Sí*, we want rain," Mikel said. "But not El Niño."

"I don't know about you guys," Tim said in a languid way, "but I'm loving it here, So if you wanna go" – he flicked a hand at them – "then go. Liz, what do you reckon?"

"Yeah, we're gonna stick around another coupla days," Liz agreed. "We've just come face to face with sharks in the Galápagos, we're not gonna be scared by a bit of rain."

"I like your attitude," Max approved. "We're not going anywhere. I wanna see the storm too!"

"All right, you stay right here and fight it out with the elements," Eve said with controlled fury. "The children need me, and I'm going first thing tomorrow. And I'm not packing *your* things this time."

"*Bueno*," Mikel said, and lit up a cigarette. "When you've decided, let me know." Then he withdrew to his habitual table around the corner at the other end of the terrace, out of view.

"So," Luis said in Spanish, turning to Ute, "will you and your husband be staying another day? I still want to go snorkelling tomorrow, if it's not raining... I don't believe El Niño is gonna hit again. It doesn't ever happen less than five to ten years apart."

"Even if it's raining, we could still do it, it doesn't matter," Ute said to Luis.

"Perfect," Luis beamed, and explained in turn to his partner and mother that they were staying another day.

"All right folks, so who's staying for the snorkelling?" Max said, and put up a hand. "Alejandro and Alma are chickening out." Alejandro opened his mouth to say something, then shut it.

"You're not going," Max counted Eve out. She'd just taken a bite of cheesecake.

"*Mi amigo* Luis here has more guts. You're stayin', right?"

"Right," Luis said in an American accent and crossed his short, muscular arms.

"The Australians are staying, right?" Max looked at Liz.

"Yep," she chimed.

"Uddar and Jerry?" Max turned to them.

"Are you taking a census or something?" Jerry chuckled.

"OK," Luis said in English. "We need minimum six persons. How many we have now?"

"I *definitely* wanna go snorkelling," Liz said.

"What's the story with the snorkelling?" Tim asked.

"It's from the Agua Sagrada beach, on the other side," Luis explained. "We catch a boat at eleven in Puerto Seco."

"Sounds good. I mean" – Tim looked at Liz – "we snorkelled a lot in the Galápagos. I feel like I've seen every fish under the ocean – but what else are we gonna do here, eh Lizzie?" Liz agreed.

"Are we going?" Jerry asked Ute.

"I'm going. I need to check it out for the guide."

"OK, four people," Luis summed up. "With me and my mother, six. Enough." He turned happily to the pile of seafood Héctor had placed before him.

"Plus two is eight," Max yelled from the reception bar, where he was helping himself to another piece of cheesecake.

"I'm leaving tomorrow, remember?" Eve reminded him from the veranda.

"Yeah, yeah, whatever," Max shouted back.

Soft music started up inside the reception lounge. It was 'Dos Gardenias' from the Buena Vista Social Club.

"*Dos gardenias para tí*," Mikel crowed out of tune from his table round the corner... "*Te quiero, te adoro, mi viiiida...*"

Max couldn't bear to be upstaged, and snapped into action.

"*Dos gardenias para ti...*" he sang along in a loud baritone, and went down on one knee by Liz's chair, offering her the remainder of his cake. "*Un beeeso...*"

Liz giggled, took the cake, and popped it in her mouth. She was a practised party girl. Tim arched an eyebrow and looked at the seated Eve, who was busy folding a napkin into tiny pieces. Helga was breastfeeding the baby, and Luis looked at Ute, as if asking "What's going on in this madhouse?" Ute shrugged with a philosophical non-smile.

"You're way off-key, Max," Eve said, but he paid no attention.

"He thinks he's winding me up," Eve said to Ute. "But he's not. I'm way beyond that."

Ute nodded. Jerry had gone back to the bookshelves. Héctor's inscrutable face was watching from behind reception.

"So come on guys, what are we gonna do tonight?" Max said.

"We can play darts," Alejandro proposed.

"Nah, boring," Max said.

"What's the song saying?" Jerry asked.

Ute translated: "But if one afternoon the gardenias of my love die, then I'll know that you've betrayed me, that you have another love."

"Gosh, and I always thought it was a cheerful song. Do you think everything's all right between these two?" Jerry gestured in the direction of Mikel's drunken singing.

"What makes you say that?"

"I don't know what a woman like Lucía sees in that clown," Jerry went on.

"How do you mean?"

A glass smashed at their hosts' table. Ute had taken a chair closer to that end of the veranda. She heard Lucía's soft voice from a few metres away: "*Amor*, that's enough wine for tonight." One of the collies came and stood by Ute's chair with a forlorn look, like a child scared away by a violent father. She rubbed his furry flank and he settled at her feet.

"Are you guys on holiday with the little one?" Liz asked, turning to Luis and Helga.

"Yes," Helga said.

"My junior brother died some weeks ago," Luis explained in an American accent.

"Oh, I'm sorry," Liz gasped.

"Sorry to hear about it," Alejandro offered too, and translated the sad news to Alma.

"Wow, how did your brother die?" Max asked.

"We are from the *Oriente*," Luis began, "the Amazon jungle. We are *indígenas*. My tribe is the Achuar." His mother's eyes flickered into life at the familiar sound, and she gazed at her son with recognition. "You know about the Achuar?"

"A little bit," Ute said, and Luis looked at her in surprise. Ute had never written on the Amazon for the guides, and she'd only been there once.

"Ah, the Achuar Jivaro!" Mikel said with authority. "They have some things in common with the Shuar. Very interesting animistic system of beliefs... they produce the best medical plants. They have magical dreams and visions. And of course they are most famous for cooking the heads of the enemy, how do you say..."

"Head-shrinking," Ute said.

"*Sí*," Luis said quickly in Spanish, "head-shrinking is a traditional practice, especially for the Shuar. They boil the heads of enemies, usually Achuar. But it's all in the past now."

"Thank God for that," Tim said.

"So, in our culture—" Luis continued in English, but Max cut him off.

"Wait, wait, wait – what's that about shrinking heads? Sounds cool."

Luis looked annoyed, but decided to ignore him. "The Achuar tribes have many traditions. This tradition is very old. The head of the enemy is cut off, and you boil it. But it's illegal now."

"You remove the bones first," Mikel said. "Then you boil the head until it shrinks to about this size." He showed a fist. Luis stared at him.

"Shhh," said Helga, furrowing her brows.

"Gringos are always interested in shocking things, not in the truth of our culture." Luis looked disappointed.

"Ah, the word *gringo*!" Mikel had another brainwave. "You know where it comes from?"

"OK, buddy," Max said in English, leaning across his table and spreading his arms between where Luis sat and Mikel stood. "Let him continue – or you'll have your head boiling in a big pot before you know it." He chuckled, and so did Liz.

Mikel was drunk. Ute could just see Lucía, still seated at their table in front of their dinner plates, stroking the other collie, cigarette smoke curling from where she sat. What a strange woman, Lucía. She always *looked* absent. But she knew exactly what was going on.

"OK, guys," Liz said. "Just let him carry on with the story, OK?"

"So, in our culture," Luis resumed, "there are many spirits. Good spirits and bad spirits. Every community has a *wishin*, a shaman – a man who speak to the spirits. My father was a shaman. This means a very important man with three wives. My mother is his more important wife, because she gave him three sons."

"Hey, that makes me a shaman," Max leant towards Eve excitedly, "a very important man with lots of children. That's me," he chuckled. "Except where's my other wives? I should be allowed to have two more wives. See, these guys have figured it out..."

Helga shot him a dark look.

"OK, so my father was a shaman. But I don't remember him, because he died when I was three years old."

"Oh," Eve cooed.

"How did your old man die?" Max asked.

"The neighbours' tribe thought he had put a bad spell on someone there, and the bad spirits had killed him. So the other tribe, they went and killed my father."

"Wow," Liz said and licked her spoon.

"Blimey," Jerry said. "That's a bit harsh."

"The life of a shaman is dangerous. Because he has too much power."

"And because," Mikel said, "his power is subjective. His village thinks it's good power, the neighbour village thinks it's evil power. When someone dies, it's the fault of the shaman."

"Mikel was an anthropologist," Ute whispered to Jerry.

"You know about Achuar culture?" Luis asked.

"Of course. I was in the Amazon. It's not my field of speciality, but I know. It's an interesting fact that men living in a tribal society like the Achuar have a thirty per cent chance of dying a violent death. Compare with men in civilized society..."

"What about women?" Liz wanted to know.

"What is this 'civilized'?" Helga demanded. "Who is 'civilized'?"

"Ah," Mikel said, lifting a cautionary finger, "this is a very complicated question."

"I'm not civilized," Max boasted. "I'm the original caveman."

"I think the Achuar are more civilized than the slums of Mexico City," Alejandro said, and Alma nodded, as if she hung out in the slums all the time.

Luis's mother said something to him, covering her mouth as she spoke.

"Is she correcting you?" Liz asked.

"No, she wants some cake," Luis grinned. "The Achuar don't have cakes."

Héctor brought a piece of the cheesecake on a plate, and everybody's eyes were on the tiny woman, who covered her mouth as she took a first forkful of cake and then quickly spat it back out onto the plate, while her face remained impassive. She mumbled something to Luis and pushed the plate towards him.

"Sorry, it's too rich for her." Luis looked in the direction of Mikel, who had moved away from reception and sat inside, close to the veranda. “I’ll eat it.”

“*No importa*,” Mikel waved it away. “It’s a pleasure to have guests from *el Oriente*. It’s our first time. We get many gringos, but not many locals.”

Luis smiled.

“So you know where gringo comes from?” Mikel said to everyone. “From ‘green’ and ‘go’. You know why?”

“The Americans in Vietnam?” Max guessed.

“No. From the Mexican-American war, when American soldiers wore green uniforms and Mexicans shouted ‘green, go home’.”

“So what happened to your brother?” Tim asked, turning to Luis, who was cradling the baby.

“Hey,” Max butted in. “Is Luis your real name? Don’t you folks have tribal names?”

“Yes, my name in Achuar is Yánkuam. It means ‘afternoon star’.”

“That’s beautiful,” Liz said.

“My name,” Max said, “means *Homus Maximus*. The big man, basically.”

Liz giggled.

“Luis, please continue with your story,” Jerry said.

“I finished.” And he got up with the baby, who was asleep again.

Luis asked Mikel if it was OK to have a look upstairs, and Helga and his mother followed Mikel, who went ahead to show them around. Lucía had disappeared with the second collie.

The rain had stopped and the night insects had resumed their serenade on the edges of leaves. The air smelt like the inside of a rotting passion fruit. Max was inhaling loudly through his big nostrils.

“Hey, I got an idea, let’s play a sex game!” he proposed. “Lottery. Pull names out of a hat.”

"OK, I'll play on one condition," Liz declared. "If the guy from the animal shelter takes part."

"Absolutely," Tim agreed. "We've got to have the gaucho. I'm not doing it without the gaucho."

"Yeah, I agree," Eve said, and looked at Max.

Ute avoided Jerry's eyes.

"It's a joke, this game, right?" Alejandro said, looking from face to face with worry.

"*Buenas*," Mikel waved to them, as he came down the stairs.

"Hey, *amigo*, you can't walk off now! You'll miss out on the fun," Max jeered after him.

Mikel turned around and walked up to Max.

"Listen," he said in Spanish, and pushed a finger into Max's chest. "I'm getting sick of your loud voice. This is *my* place. I'll see you tomorrow morning when you settle your bill, and until then, keep your voice down. OK?"

"Well, well, well – are you trying to throw me out, *amigo*?"

"I'm not your *amigo*."

"Whatever. Anyway, we're not leaving tomorrow."

"Yes you are."

"What's happening is, we're going snorkelling tomorrow, and there's nothing you can do about it. Or are you gonna try and get rid of me like you did with that gringo? Remember, two years ago, the drowned French gringo?"

"Are you mad or what? What are you talking about?" Mikel shook his head. "You say I killed the French guy? He *drowned. Me entiendes*? He drowned in the river" – he pointed in the direction of the river – "he took cocaine and went for a swim. Bad idea."

"Yeah, sure he drowned," Max said.

Everybody watched with fascination.

"Now you say sorry." Mikel took off his glasses and pointed an angry finger at Max. His eyes looked small and vulnerable without the glasses. "Sorry for telling lies about me and Villa Pacifica."

"Yeah, whatever," Max said, and put his feet up on a chair.

Jerry cleared his throat. "Mikel, don't worry about it. Forget about what he said."

"Nobody listens to him," Eve added. "He talks garbage all the time, so just ignore him."

Just then, an eerie, fluted sound came from upstairs and silenced them.

"What's that? I wanna go and see," Liz sprang to her feet. One by one, everyone followed.

"Luis is a professional *músico*," Mikel said. "*Buenas*," and he was gone.

"You know," Jerry said to Ute, "I came across one entry in the visitors' books that says 'If you stay here longer than a week you become cracked in the head'. I think for some people it might take even less."

"How long have we been here?"

"Three days? Four to go, before we go nuts. You're not worried about that storm?"

"Not really," Ute said.

"I suppose if it rains heavily, we can just stay in our cabin all day, or play games and read here."

"Yeah. If the roof holds up."

"Oh really, does the rain get that bad here?"

The truth is, she didn't know. But she knew that if Café Fin del Mundo could be wrecked by beach waves a year ago, so could this cabin by the shore.

"*Señora.*" It was Héctor, eating spaghetti in a dark corner of the reception lounge. He dabbed his mouth with a napkin and got up.

"I'll come up in a second," Ute said to Jerry.

"You are staying on?" Héctor enquired.

"Yes."

"Good. Because, you know" – he lowered his voice to a whisper – "what Mikel said about the storms and all that, it's a bit exaggerated."

"Really? There's no storm forecast?"

"No, no, there is, there's going to be a lot of rain, but not tomorrow. Maybe not even the day after. I think Mikel just wants to see the American *señor* gone."

"I see," Ute said. "Well, I don't want to interrupt your dinner." She made for the stairs.

"No, not at all, I'm done. I hope you enjoy swimming with the fishes tomorrow."

"Swimming with the fishes," Ute repeated, and had a feeling of déjà vu.

"*Sí*, swimming with the fishes," Héctor said, smiling.

"By the way," she said, "Is there a good path from the bay that leads up to Agua Sagrada?"

"Why do you want to go to Agua Sagrada? There's not much there. Some ruins and a cloud forest. It's a long way up. Many hours of walking. And there's nowhere to stay."

"But people do go there."

"Only by special arrangement with the local community, and usually they don't walk. They hire a donkey or a horse."

"Do you ever visit" – she hesitated – "Oswaldo?"

"No. It's too far." Héctor's face darkened. "He's sick. It's very bad. Shall we go upstairs? After you."

Ute went up the stairs, and he followed. Luis was expertly blowing into a fluted, reed-like wind instrument, Helga was beating along on some skin drums with closed eyes and tantrically moving neck, while his mother's sandalled foot was tapping. When they finished, everyone clapped.

"What's that instrument you're playing?" Max asked.

"*Bueno*," Luis said, "this is a traditional Andean instrument call *zampoña*."

He said something to Helga, and they resumed their duet. Ute caught herself glancing out of the window in the futile hope that Carlos's hat might appear on the white path.

And the rain started again. Everybody instinctively looked out. Everybody except Alejandro, who was dozing in a comfortable wicker armchair, with Alma sitting on a cushion at his feet: tiny and silken-haired like an expensive puppy. Tim was reclining in his favourite spot by the windows, his eyes closed, and Liz was sprawled with her thighs open onto an armchair like some Antipodean Danae offering herself to the inseminating tropical rain of the Gods. Just as the elemental music, coupled with the rain, seemed to produce a hypnotic effect on them all, the baby started to squeal. Helga sprang up, abandoning the drums, and the musical interlude was over. Alejandro came to with a start and stroked Alma's hair.

"He's tired," Luis said. "We have to go."

The old woman shuffled to the stairs, followed by Luis and Helga.

"See you tomorrow," Luis waved to everyone, and everyone said "See you", except Max, who grabbed the *zampoña* and caught up with Luis halfway down the stairs. "Don't forget this," he said.

"So, are you a writer?" Liz turned to Jerry. "What are you writing now?"

"Well, I'm writing a story called *Villa Pacifica*," Jerry said. "It's about a bunch of strangers who are drawn together by chance in a place not too dissimilar to here."

"Am I in it?" Tim wanted to know.

"Is it funny?" Eve asked.

"What happens at the end?" Max asked. "Somebody get killed?"

"Well, goodnight," Alejandro said, and stood up. Alma was yawning.

"You guys are so *boring*." Max shook his head.

"Good night," Alma chimed, and they were gone.

"Shall we be boring and retire too?" Jerry asked Ute.

"I guess so." She was not so much exhausted, she realized, as strangely vacant, as if some nerve had been extracted from her. There was something wrong with this state of affairs, but it was better than pain.

"That's a good idea," Tim said. "I'm gonna get some sleep too, before the snorkelling expedition tomorrow. Goodnight," and he was gone down the staircase, together with the Mexicans.

"I'm also turning in," Eve announced. "Anyways, I've gotta pack." She looked at Max.

"Jesus, you're a bunch of geriatrics," Max complained. "Come on Liz, let's have a game of pool."

"OK," Liz sprang up.

Eve walked along with them in the warm rain.

"Wow," she said. "I feel like I'm in a giant shower. Do you guys believe this El Niño stuff ?"

"Yep. And the smart thing is to leave tomorrow, like you," Jerry said. "Why don't you take Max with you?"

"You're kidding me. You've seen Max. He's, like, so contrary. If I say something, he goes and does the opposite."

They continued to walk in silence, listening to the quick crunching of their own steps and the lashing of rain on the leaves.

"Why do you stay with him and have children with him if you don't" – Ute hesitated over the word – "love him?"

"You know why? Because I figured some time ago that all men are bastards. Sorry honey." She looked at Jerry. "You're a nice guy, but you're in the minority. So I figured, I might as well marry a rich bastard and stay with him. That way I've got one less thing to worry about. In my family, we were always short of money and there were always lots of mouths to feed. I swore to myself my kids'll never be like that."

Her hair was plastered to her round head, and with her rain-shiny face she looked haggard and pitiful.

"Well, that's me here," Eve said, stopping in her tracks. "I guess I'll see you tomorrow."

She waved at them and ran down the path leading to the Whale. They walked on to the Turtle. Running was pointless: they were already drenched. When they got to their cabin, Ute kicked off her flip-flops, took off her wet T-shirt and fell onto the bed in her rain-sodden dungarees.

"Amazing, that couple," Jerry said.

"Yeah. I don't get it." That initial, silly pang of jealousy for Eve and Jerry seemed weeks, months ago.

"You know what's funny and sad about them?" Jerry continued. "Max fancies himself as a successful American, but deep down he still feels like a Latino small-timer. And Eve will always be the daughter of poor Costa Rican immigrants, no matter how big their house gets. They'll never have class."

"Since when do you believe in class?" Ute said.

"I don't mean class in that way – and you know it."

"Are you really writing a story about here? Or did you just say that to get their attention."

"Both, I suppose. I don't know myself what I'm writing yet. Keeps morphing. But whatever it turns out to be, it's definitely coming out of this place. I suspect it'll be a short story. Or a novella. I want to stay till I finish it. Shouldn't be more than a couple more days. Why is it called El Niño anyway?"

"Because it always comes in December, around Christmas time. *Niño* means child, like the baby Jesus. You know" – Ute fell backwards onto the bed – "it's like this place is feeding off me."

"It's strange." Jerry swatted at a mosquito and started peeling off his clothes. "I feel the opposite – like I'm feeding off this place. You know what's funny? That chap Luis has just lost his brother, his father died when he was three, his wife is a grumpy cow with a moustache, his mother's not exactly a bag of laughs, but he's such a happy chap..."

But Ute didn't hear. She was fast approaching her first bad dream of the night.

16

IT WASN'T A BAD DREAM. It was worse.

Ute lay on her back somewhere between the floating bed and the afterworld, and knew there was a presence at the foot of the bed that wasn't Jerry. She couldn't see it, but she could sense its vegetal breath, its evil humanoid intentions. It almost touched her feet, it was almost advancing towards her face, and she wanted to scream or whimper, but her voice was paralysed like the rest of her body. There was something not quite right with the creature – it had an animal's head and a human body, or perhaps vice versa. It chuckled and hissed and gurgled, and she could almost understand it. It wanted to tell her something she didn't want to know, the answer to some essential question, the secret of life and death itself perhaps, after which nothing would be the same. It was more than Ute could bear to know, although she'd spent her life looking for it. It would give her knowledge, and it would destroy her.

Then she fell off the cliff of the bed and into the abyss of wakefulness.

"Are you all right?"

Jerry's bespectacled head was poking in through the door.

Ute was surprised to find herself on top of the bed. She hadn't moved at all. Rain battered the night roof.

"You were whimpering," Jerry said.

"What're you doing?" Her tongue felt unfamiliar.

"Just doing some writing out here in the hammock. You were out like a light."

"Something was here," Ute said.

"What *thing*?"

"I saw it."

"That would have been me." Jerry smiled. "I'm the only thing around here. I'm right here, OK? Call me if you need me." And his head disappeared again.

She got up carefully and took off her wet trousers, bra and undies. Despite the oppressive heat, her feet and legs were tomb-cold, as if she'd begun to die in her sleep from the feet up and was interrupted. She turned on the bathroom light, and the mirror reminded her that the only scary thing in the cabin was her. Two new itchy red patches blazed on her cheeks – but the good news was, the clown's muzzle around her mouth was fading. She applied some cream, combed her hair and went back to bed in her cotton boxer shorts and a long-sleeved sweatshirt to cover up her itchy arms. She closed her eyes. The only antidote to the apparition was to think about safe and ordinary things.

She couldn't think of anything safe and ordinary though. All her thoughts were dangerous. All her thoughts veered back to the creature and what it had to tell her. Eventually, she settled on her sweatshirt, which said "One Tribe, One Earth: Love It or Leave It". A Christmas present from Jerry's well-meaning parents, who'd never gone beyond the wines of France and the tapas of Spain, and thought of Ute as a professional hippie to whom words like tribe and earth would appeal.

Ah, to belong to a tribe, like Luis. It was a prison, for sure, but you could "love" it even after you "left" it. Luis had "left" it, and he still belonged to the tribe. Even after his brother's death, even with an Austrian wife and child, he was one of the tribe. Even after sixty years in Europe, he would be an Achuar. He could say we do this, we think that, even though he personally didn't.

If only she could have something akin to a tribe. Somewhere to remember, some land to return to, some thatched hut in the forest.

Something, anything... but no, she had the whole world instead. One earth, one tribe – that suited her better. That's the way she wanted it, because she was a free spirit – unchained, unburdened, unanchored, unbelonging. Un-everything.

She pictured Carlos's rough hands squeezing and moulding her body like soft clay, as if he was going to make something out of it.

She slept, and in her new dream she found herself climbing a steep, slippery hill, at the top of which she knew that everything would be resolved. But it was urgent, there wasn't much time, and she was in a rush, sweaty, scrambling among the sticky plants under the burning sun, parched with thirst and anxiety that she should get there before the sun went down.

The morning was fragrant and heavy with cloud and promise, but the Mexicans had decided to leave.

"We're too lazy. We're not into walking or snorkelling," Alma explained to Ute and Jerry over breakfast. Alejandro was writing a message in the guest book.

The monkeys across the water were arguing about something.

"And what are your plans?" He turned to Ute.

"We'll go snorkelling, if it doesn't rain," Ute said.

"Did you hear the American couple are leaving too?" Alejandro switched to English for Jerry's benefit.

"No, but I'm very glad to hear it," Jerry said.

He looked pale after another late night of writing. Pale but happy. He had the glow of creation that lights us from within and makes us feel indestructible. It's very similar to being in love, he had explained to Ute once. Anything seems possible, life explodes with flavour and meaning, something vital clicks into place and you want to hold it there for as long as possible. Ute thought she understood. Writing text for the travel guides didn't do the same for her, but travel did. Or used to anyway.

"*Hola*."

Carlos appeared with an espresso cup and a slice of buttered walnut bread. Everyone greeted him, except Alma, who didn't bother. My God, Ute thought, here is a woman who doesn't actually fancy him.

"How are things over on your side?" Jerry enquired. "Are the animals OK after all the rain last night?"

"Yes." Carlos leant against a table. He wasn't wearing his hat, and his sun-baked forehead glistened with sweat. "They're surprised because it didn't rain for a long time. We had some small problems with the lion. The... how do you call it" – he switched to Spanish – "the new pit drain didn't work, so the pit filled with water during the night. Pablo and I had to go down and try to unblock the drain. When it rains again, it will be a problem. We'll have to move her back."

"What problem?" Max said, appearing onto the veranda like a heavyweight wrestler jumping into the ring. He placed an empty plastic bottle on the Mexicans' table and clicked his fingers for Héctor, who was busy carrying trays back and forth. "Eh, *amigo*, one cooked breakfast and one *americano*! I'm starving."

He was red-faced and drenched in sweat.

"If I can feed the lioness," he went on, "I can do anything round here. You're gonna need men round here if there's a storm, to help you guys out."

Carlos sipped his coffee. He was still standing.

"I hear you're leaving today," Jerry turned to Max between mouthfuls of muesli with yogurt.

"Who told you that? Nah, we're staying. I said to my wife, 'Go ahead honey, you do what you like.' But I know her, she wouldn't go without me."

Carlos swallowed the last piece of walnut bread, his impassive Indian eyes fastened on Max, then he took his empty espresso cup to the kitchen.

"Did you hear that, honey?" Max said.

Eve was on the veranda. She wore a khaki hat with a string under the chin, colonial-style shorts full of pockets, and a too-small one-piece bathing suit.

"Hear what?" Eve said.

"Jesus, are we going tiger-hunting today or something?" Max said.

"Get out of here," Eve said, and sat down at an empty table.

"Morning." Liz came up the veranda stairs. "What's the forecast?"

"Nice weather today," Héctor said, and served Max a big plate of toast, eggs and bacon. "Maybe some rain tonight."

"Great!" Liz said.

"Bye," Carlos waved from the path.

"Oh, hi Carlos," Liz chimed and leant on the veranda balustrade, "you're not gonna join us for breakfast?"

"No, thank you." And he was gone.

"Tough luck," Max said to Liz, his mouth full of eggs. "He fucks off when he pleases." He snorted.

"Continental for me, thanks," Eve said to Héctor.

Something in the group dynamic had shifted since the day before, but Ute couldn't put her finger on it yet. Then she suddenly realized what had changed: nobody was pretending any more, those who were leaving or those who were staying.

"Guys!" Liz shouted. "It's nine a.m., it's gonna be a beautiful day, no rain, and we're going snorkelling!"

"Let's go," Ute whispered.

She and Jerry got up to go just as Tim arrived.

"It's amazing," Jerry mused on the way to the *tortuga*, "that nobody has punched Max yet."

"Give it another twenty-four hours," Ute said.

"That guy Carlos really puts his back up, I can tell."

"You don't like Carlos either though."

"Oh, I don't have anything against him. He's all right. But what's that stuff about murder that Max keeps mentioning?"

"I don't know. I mean, well, Héctor told me a bit. It wasn't a murder. It was a suicide. Or an accident. Max is just a trouble-maker."

"When's the snorkelling?" Jerry asked. Because he wanted to do some writing beforehand. He was already in the hammock, with his laptop. There was nothing left for Ute except to walk to Puerto Seco ahead of the others and hang out with Consuelo for a bit.

After the night's rain, the sand was wet and hard like concrete. She walked along the waterline barefoot. The tide was out, and the sea was its usual murky colour.

Being here already felt like a faded memory. The woman – now reaching the *malecón*, now looking out to the open sea for signs of something, anything – was a distant recollection of Ute.

But Ute wasn't seeing all this from the future. No, she couldn't picture her future at all. It's as if she was seeing herself from someone else's eyes. As if someone was watching her, some presence at the foot of the bed, some faceless shadow that came from the ocean and engulfed everything on the land.

17

A FEW PEOPLE MOOCHED ALONG the *malecón*. The kids darted about. This was the busiest she'd seen Puerto Seco. On the beach opposite Café Fin del Mundo, Luis played football with the kids from the day before and those from the day before that, or however many days had gone by.

Outside the café, Helga nursed the baby, and Luis's mother nursed something invisible, perhaps memories of happier times when her own sons were little. They both nodded at Ute without enthusiasm. Evelyn and Ricardo had spotted her and were running towards her. Their brother, the boy without a name, walked behind them. "You came back!" Evelyn said, beaming.

"Yes," Ute smiled.

"We're playing football."

"And who is winning?"

"Our team's winning." Luis came over on short, muscled legs. "Are the others coming for eleven o'clock?"

"They should be."

"I've already spoken to the guys who run the snorkelling trips. They weren't so keen on it, with the weather forecast and all, but I talked them into it. Said there's ten or so of us going."

"*Bueno*." Ute looked at the café. Consuelo must be somewhere at the back making breakfast for her two customers.

Ute felt distracted. There was something at the periphery of the visible world here. She sat down on the salt-eaten remains of a beach bench.

"I'm still trying to convince my mother though," Luis was saying. "She's scared of the ocean. She'd never seen it before. And in Achuar folklore, the ocean is where the *tsungki* live." He looked at Evelyn and her brothers, who were transfixed by the strange visitors. "The *tsungki* are beings like us, or almost like us, who live on the bottom of the ocean."

"Can we see them?" Ricardo asked.

"No, we can never see them or talk to them. Only shamans can, when they smoke special herbs. But they're not bad, they don't want to harm us. They are the lords of the fish in the sea."

"My father says the fish in the sea have died this summer," Evelyn said. "Were they eaten by the *tsungki*?" She giggled at the unfamiliar word.

"No. The *tsungki* don't eat fish. It's El Niño. El Niño brings warm water, and fish don't like warm water."

"I like warm water," Evelyn said.

"Your boyfriend is a *tsungki*," Ricardo teased, and she pushed him away.

Luis waved at the café, and his mother waved back vaguely.

"Actually, not much scares my mother," he said. "She's been through so much." He looked at Ute. "And did you sleep well?" he enquired.

Ute didn't know what to say. There was a sinister presence at the foot of my bed? As if reading her thoughts, he smiled.

"In Achuar, this is a regular greeting. How did you sleep or how were your dreams, same thing. Dreams are very important to us."

"Do the Achuar have a system of interpreting dreams?"

Evelyn, Ricardo and their depressed brother listened with their mouths open.

"Dreams influence your actions during the day. There are omens. For example, will you go hunting or not, will you leave the house or not… And then it gets more complicated when you're going on a vision quest. Then the dream is all-important."

"What is a vision quest?" Ute asked.

"It's when you go up into the mountains, drink special medicinal potions and feel compelled to go and meet the spirit world. There, you might meet the spirits of your ancestors, which sometimes appear as animals or birds. And if your quest is successful, the spirits pass on their powers to you. So when you return, you are stronger."

"And if it's not successful?"

"Then you return from the mountain with nothing. Anyway the apparitions don't always manifest themselves. But when they do, you must overcome your fear and approach them until they vanish. My younger brother, the one who died, he went on a quest, and a spirit in the form of a boa appeared to him. The boa is a very powerful animal in our mythology. But he was afraid and didn't approach the apparition. Therefore he wasn't empowered by it. My other brother had a successful quest. He became a shaman."

"Do you believe this yourself ?" Ute asked. "I mean, have you seen such… apparitions?"

"I've never been on a quest like this, if that's what you mean."

"I mean, do you believe that this is what happens? Or do you think it's hallucinations?"

"Of course it's hallucinations!" Luis smiled. "That's why you take those potions. Doesn't mean they're not real. But I understand your question. You know, I've lived in Europe for ten years, and I understand the rational mindset of Europeans. You always want to know what's real and what's not. But for us, it's not so clear-cut. I think there are things that can happen only in some places. Things you can see and know only in some places. Just as El Niño only strikes along this coast, so the spirits of our ancestors can only be glimpsed in the hills of the Amazon. Not here or in the Andes, or Paris, or Berlin."

Evelyn and Ricardo had fled back to the boys and the ball, but their brother was still listening intently.

"Do you want to see Paris and Berlin one day, son?" Luis asked him. The boy looked terrified at the prospect. "If you do, you mustn't drop out of school."

"I think they already have," Ute said quietly. The boy went and sat on the chipped steps nearby.

"See, that's exactly why I won't come back to live here." Luis shook his head. "I want my son to have a good education. I want him to have the things I didn't have in the jungle. Not material things, but riches of the mind. Knowledge."

"But isn't this knowledge somehow linked with where we come from, going back to our roots and all that?"

"That's self-knowledge. I think that takes longer, and you have to be in the right place for it. I think many gringos, like the couple from Villa Pacifica, they're nice people and everything, but they come to a place like here and expect to find something in themselves. Maybe they do, after many years. But I doubt it. I left the jungle at sixteen, and I left the country at eighteen. I joined a Peruvian band – actually there was only one Peruvian in it – and we busked our way across Europe. And it's only now that I feel I'm getting to know myself and my roots. Only now, and only because I've been away and returned."

"How old are you?"

They turned around, startled. Max was there, sitting on a chewed-up bench facing the *malecón*, back to back with their own one.

"Twenty-eight," Luis said.

Helga was gesturing for Luis's attention. He got up and walked over the road.

"Did you walk here?" Ute said.

"Yeah. I was gettin' dead bored with that bunch. Just as well we're goin' snorkellin'." He turned to the boy. "What's your name, buddy?"

"Pedro," the boy whispered, and avoided Max's gaze.

"What are your dreams, Pedro?"

Pedro glanced at Max sideways.

"You know, what do you wanna be when you grow up? Mind you, in this climate, you're already grown up at fourteen. Are you having sex yet?"

The boy flushed.

"OK, tell you what, do you wanna race me to the water? Let's see if Luis wants to join in. Hey Luis," he shouted. Luis was already returning.

"We're going to head off to the snorkelling club in a moment," Luis said. "My mother's coming after all and—"

"Hey," Max cut him off, "Pedro and I are gonna have a race. You gotta join us. Uddar, you're on for a race?" He was bouncing on the spot already.

"No, thanks," Ute said. "I'm no good at running."

"How do you know, have you ever tried running?"

"All *right*! I'll run," Ute said.

"All right," Luis shrugged. "Let's run. Where?"

"Just from here to the water," Max said. "Whoever makes a splash first, wins. Get up buddy, don't sit there like a lump, you're in the race."

Pedro obeyed, and they lined up in front of the bench.

"Clear off, kids," Max shouted at the children playing football. "We're racing."

The kids clustered in two small groups.

"*Dale* Pedro!" shouted Evelyn, and the other kids giggled. It was a mocking version of the popular presidential campaign slogan: "*Dale* Gonzales!" – Go for it, Gonzales!

"All right," Max shouted. "Ready? Steady? Go!"

Ute gave it her best and ran for the water as if there were someone drowning there. But her best wasn't good enough. Luis splashed into the shallow beach water some time before Pedro, who was followed by Max and finally Ute.

"Pedro and I win," Luis said, and put a hand on Pedro's shoulder.

"You win, man," Max said breathlessly, and punched Luis in the shoulder. "Where'd you learn to run like this? I mean, I'm fast, but you're a torpedo!"

Luis was already headed back to the *malecón*, and Ute followed him. It was a quarter to eleven on Max's watch. The kids resumed their game, and now Pedro joined them, boosted by his near win.

"Ciao," Ute waved at Evelyn, who ran over to them.

"Are you coming back?"

"Yeah, we're coming back," Max said.

"Not you, her," said the plucky girl, then ran away.

"Take care out there," Consuelo said from the doorway of her café. Her face was full of shadows today. "There's a storm on the way. I can smell it."

"Have you put your prices up like I suggested?" Max had caught up.

"No," Consuelo said. "*Bueno*, I have some work inside. Enjoy the snorkelling."

"Consuelo," Ute stopped her. She made up her mind on the spot. "I want to buy *The Three Lives of Mikel.* Can I come and get it tomorrow and bring the money?"

"Of course you can," Consuelo smiled her generous smile. "I'll be here. God willing."

"Thank you," Ute said, and strode off with Max in tow.

"No one's ever heard of this Oswaldo Joven…" Max carried on.

This reminded her that she'd made another decision that morning, and she turned back.

In the semi-darkness of the back room, Consuelo was packaging Oswaldo's canvases.

"Are you moving these?" Ute asked.

"Yes. I'm moving them tonight to my house, in case we get hit by a big storm. I couldn't bear it if something happened to them. My house is almost as close to the water as here, but I can have them upstairs. What can you do. There's nowhere else I can store them."

"What about Villa Pacifica, upstairs in the main house?"

"Oh no, that wouldn't do. I wouldn't ask… Anyway, you must go, or you'll be late, don't worry about this. Héctor is coming to help me later, he's taking time off work tonight."

"Consuelo, do you know how long it takes to climb to Agua Sagrada from the beach?"

Consuelo straightened up and pushed a black curl from her eye. "Why?"

"I want to see Agua Sagrada. Maybe meet Oswaldo." She shrugged. "If he's there."

"He's there," Consuelo said quietly. "But as I told you, he's very sick. As to the path up to Agua Sagrada, I wouldn't go. Nobody uses it except a few men when they go fishing in the bay." Her mobile was ringing on the table, and she picked it up.

"Yes? OK, well, never mind." Her voice was dull with disappointment. "Yes, come early tomorrow. OK. Bye. It was Héctor," she explained. "He can't take time off tonight, he's needed there. He said all the guests are staying, despite the storm warning. But it's OK, he'll come first thing tomorrow morning."

"Maybe I can help," Ute offered feebly.

"That's very kind." Consuelo smiled. "But don't worry about it. You better go."

"Is there a path from Agua Sagrada back to Villa Pacifica?"

"There is a path from the Manteño National Park to Villa Pacifica, but I don't think it's maintained by the park authorities. Nobody uses it. But I really don't know, I haven't been that way. I've only been up to the hills by tricycle from the main road."

Consuelo's sad, toffee-coloured eyes seemed to say: "What's eating you up, what are you looking for, my girl?" And Ute replied in the same silent language: "I don't know, I've lost my way, can you help me?"

"You'll be late for the snorkelling trip," Consuelo said.

"*Bueno*, I'll see you tomorrow." Ute waved and went on her way.

"God willing."

At the yellow kiosk with a freshly painted blue sign that said "PUERTO SECO PARADISE SNORKELLING" everybody was being fitted with lunatic-yellow lifejackets for the boat ride – everybody except Jerry.

Liz handed Ute a sealed manilla envelope from reception. It was five times bigger than the note inside it, which said:

> Decided to stay behind and get some writing done. I'm in "the zone". Afraid I'll have to miss the snorkelling. Sorry! Have fun out there with the fishes, if not with the humans, and tell me all about it later. See you in a bit. J.

The manilla envelope made the note look impersonal, like a memo from a sick workmate. Ute was surprised at how gutted she felt. A desertion, that's what it felt like.

"OK." Their guide was a young man with an acne-scarred face. "Has everybody paid?" He looked at Ute. "*Gracias*." He took her proffered twenty-dollar note. "So, please don't bend down and touch the water, because we're going fast. One American *señor* fell in the water last year, we had to fish him out before the sharks got to him." He paused, then chuckled. "Don't worry, no sharks here. Only dolphins and maybe whales. We spend one hour snorkelling, then lunch, and maybe two hours on the beach and walking. We are back here at four o'clock."

Without me, Ute thought. I'll be up in the hills by then.

"All right. Let's rock this boat, baby," Max said and jumped in. The boat shook.

"The boat's rocking all right," said Eve, stepping in. "Won't surprise me if it sinks, with you on it."

The guide helped Luis's mother on board. Ute was glad Luis was here.

When they were all seated, the driver started the engine. Now they were on the other side of the soporific morning, and heading into something less safe. Ute felt it in her guts, or maybe that was just seasickness. In a boat, the ocean is always choppier than it looks from the shore.

They rode the rest of the journey in silence because of the engine noise. Max had positioned himself next to the skipper, where he observed closely with the evident intention of becoming an expert.

The land was rocky and inhospitable along the shore, and further inland its green tops rose high into steam and cloud. The harsh sunlight fell at a ninety-degree angle today, like a stern finger from Heaven. You down there, it said, and you, and especially you, all of you will feel what's coming to you, sooner or later. But in the meantime, enjoy the sparkling waters of El Niño, where fishes get fried, and gringos warm their cold bones, and dead bodies get washed up.

Ute applied some sunscreen to her face, neck and bare arms and pulled her cap low over her face. "Good idea," Eve shouted, and asked to borrow the lotion. After twenty minutes or so, the engine was turned off. They were close to the rocky face of the coast. Then, just round the corner, they came into a deep, dreamy bay.

"OK." Paco, the guide, got up and removed his yellow vest. "We are near the bay of Agua Sagrada. We stop here for snorkelling. Ladies, you can go downstairs for changing if you want."

"I already changed before we left," Eve announced.

"Over there" – he pointed at the rocky coast they'd just passed – "are some underwater caves. You can swim up to that point, but do *not* swim inside the caves. Not safe. OK? So, we have very warm weather this month, El Niño weather. This means that maybe you don't see so much fish."

Paco took a bunch of diving masks and snorkels and distributed them around.

"*Señora*?" he handed one to Luis's mother. She shook her head.

"She won't be swimming," Luis said, and dived into the water, soon followed by Max, Liz and Tim.

"I've never done this before." Eve was fussing with her mask. "How do you breathe with this thing?"

"You breathe through the tube," Ute said. "There's nothing to it."

"Do I keep my eyes open?" Eve said nasally through the tube.

"Yes," Ute said. "That's the whole point."

Eve sat at the edge of the boat, her legs testing the water. The guide and the skipper were busy preparing sandwiches from a couple of big chilly boxes. As soon as Eve plopped in, Paco collapsed into laughter. "'Do I keep my eyes open,' she says!" and the skipper joined in. Luis's mother had something resembling enjoyment on her face, and her eyes momentarily met Ute's behind the snorkelling mask.

Ute jumped in. The water felt like warm champagne gone off, fermented and golden with light. Masked bodies hovered at the surface like roots. Their algae-like limbs stirred. It was a blissfully soundless universe. Up there, in the light, was the blue blur of Luis's mother.

Ute pulled herself deeper. How deep did she have to go to reach the underworld of the *tsungki*? She'd read somewhere, once, that the *tsungki* wear crabs for watches, fish for hats, and sit on giant turtles and caimans. There were some fishes darting about down here, and she could now see the sandy bottom, where nameless things scuttled about. She swam around, pretending to be one of them.

She was surprised how far from the boat she popped up. She was in fact closer to the rocky shore than to the boat. There must be a current drifting northwards. She swam closer and looked under. No fish, lots of algae. It was deeper over here. She went a bit further along, feeling the sharp rock with her right foot. And here were the caves in question. The entrance was comfortable enough even for a boat their size to go through. Ute went through. This was only the first of several chambers. The underwater rock was deeply fissured.

The water in here was different – darker and cooler. The reddish rock plunged underwater like an abyss. Time to get out.

She turned around – and just then something gripped her ankle. And like in her nightmare, her choked scream was voiceless. Her reflex was to wrestle her ankle free, but she realized that what was clasped around it was not some tentacular creature of the depths, but a human hand. It was Max's hand.

She held her breath, which was difficult, because she already had very little left of it from the shock. The snorkel didn't allow for long periods far from the surface. It was one of his "jokes", no doubt. He now pressed against her belly as his legs pulled her in closer.

She fought him off, and his legs disengaged as they went up. They burst through the water together and scrambled to remove their snorkels. For a while, there was just frantic breathing.

"Gave you a fright?" Max gasped.

"Fuck off," Ute gasped back.

"Yeah, you know how it is. I came to have a look and I see a hot babe. Synchronicity." He chuckled.

"Bullshit." And she swam away from him, catching her snorkel in one hand, swallowing water.

She scrambled up to the boat, where she found Eve and Tim sitting on towels and munching on sandwiches, bananas and *mandarinas*.

Standing on unsteady legs, she dried herself with her weightless travel towel and sat down to eat. Soon they were joined by Luis, whom Ute caught with a corner of her eye glancing at her, and Liz.

The skipper started the boat, and soon they could see the bay of Agua Sagrada. The horseshoe-shaped beach stretched for at least a couple of kilometres, and a dry tropical forest rose straight up from it, like a thorny crown sat atop a gigantic, faceless forehead.

They passed Max and waved to him. He stopped swimming and waved back, squinting in the hazy light of early afternoon.

The skipper stopped the engine to see if he wanted to get on. "I'll catch up," Max shouted.

Tim and Liz hid behind huge, face-shielding sunglasses, and Luis's mother squinted at the swimmer. Luis looked at Ute with his amused, crow-footed Indian eyes, identical to his mother's. Ute shifted her gaze. For a moment, the boat was suspended in the bay, and the world was so perfectly still and noiseless that they could be inside one of Oswaldo's triptychs of someone's life.

When they hit shallow waters, the skipper switched off the motor, and they all waded across to the beach carrying their shoes and daypacks. A warm, soundless spray floated in the air. A sweetly putrid smell of seaweed and gathering tropical storm had come to brood here.

"Uh-oh, is that rain?" Eve said.

"Just warm spritz," Luis said.

The skipper was still on the boat, tidying up and keeping a look out for the errant swimmer. The group dispersed. Liz went for a walk along the water's edge. Tim lay belly-down on his towel with his book. Paco started texting someone on his mobile. Eve waded back into the water and splashed her rounded shoulders. Luis's mother headed to the shrubs on the edge of the beach.

"She needs the bathroom." Luis sat down on the sand, and Ute joined him there. She should go and investigate the start of the path leading up to Agua Sagrada, but she needed a moment of stillness. She was still shaken by the cave encounter. They turned their faces to the fine mist in the air for a while. Ute closed her eyes.

"Do you think there'll be a storm today?" Ute asked.

"Yes, I think there will be," Luis said. "I can smell it."

"Me too."

"I'm thinking of going to Villa Pacifica tonight, away from the beach, but I don't think my mother will agree."

"Why not?"

"She thinks there are bad spirits there."

"Like Max?"

"No." Luis laughed his breezy laughter. "Not Max. We can see Max. But we can't see those spirits. They're like... Energy. Bad energy. She felt it last night."

"Did *you* feel it?" Ute asked.

"I'm not so much in touch with the spirit world. Are you?" He looked at Ute.

"No, not at all."

It's possible that I'm not even wholly in touch with the human world, she thought. That I'm living somewhere in between.

"Always competing, that one," Luis said, looking out to sea. "Trying to prove something to someone. He must be an unhappy man."

"Oh, I think he's happy," Ute said.

"Are *you* happy?"

"Me?" Ute searched for an answer. "Sometimes."

"And now, are you happy now?"

"Right now?"

"Yes, today. This week." His smile was playful.

"I don't know." She could be honest with him, like with Consuelo. In fact, she could be nothing but honest with him. He would know it otherwise. "It's been a strange week. I guess I haven't been all that happy."

"Your relationship is not very happy," Luis said. That was wounding to hear, because it came from a stranger, and it wasn't even a question.

"Oh, we have a very good marriage actually. It's just that at the moment, Jerry is writing something, and I have some work to do as well..."

"I understand. You can't always be together," Luis said.

"No. Yes." After a short silence, she asked: "And you, are you happy? Are you and Helga happy?"

"We have many differences, but also things that keep us together. Music is the most important."

Ute noticed Luis's mother who was sitting right behind them on the sand, her skirt drawn modestly around her shins. Luis said something to her in Achuar, a joke perhaps, because her face cracked into a smile. Her teeth were oddly blunt, as if filed back. Then she looked at Ute and said something. Luis translated.

"My mother says that illness is a sign of bad energy that must be cleansed. Your face, has it always been like that – if you don't mind me asking?"

"Yes." Strangely enough, she didn't mind Luis or his mother asking. "And where does the bad energy come from then?"

Luis looked at the sea. "Usually from the past. It can be an ancestral spirit."

"I don't have any ancestors."

"You are disconnected from your past," Luis said. "Like many Europeans."

"From my ancestors' past, you mean."

"Same thing. You know, our past doesn't begin neatly from the moment we are born. It's not that straightforward. If you were in the Amazon, my mother would arrange for you to have a seance with a shaman. Take some herbs, vomit, see the past, and understand yourself better. Your skin would clear up along with your spirit."

"Too bad we're not in the Amazon. Excuse me," Ute said, and got up to talk to Paco, who was passing by.

"I'm not coming with you on the walk," she said.

"How come?"

"I want to visit the community of Agua Sagrada today," she pointed to the invisible hilltop behind them. "I'm updating a travel guide, and would like to include the different points of interest in the national park."

"It's out of the question," Paco frowned. "We can't let you walk there alone. You don't know the way. You need a guide. The walk there is three, four hours, perhaps more."

"I have four hours. I don't need a guide."

"We'll get you a guide for tomorrow, you can go there tomorrow," Paco said. "I don't even know if we have time to get to the top of the hill. Look." He pointed at the horizon, which was darkening by the minute. The fine spray had turned to a drizzle.

"Tomorrow might be too late." She put resolve in her voice. "And we're leaving soon."

"But I can't do anything about the weather. Those hill paths, when there's a storm, they're not safe. Trees snap. There are mudslides. Ah, thank God, there he is."

Max emerged from the shallow water. Behind him came the skipper, carrying a pack with small plastic water bottles, which he handed to Paco. Liz was returning from her walk and Tim was deep in his book. Eve was swimming.

"Hey guys!" Max saluted with a wave. Nobody paid any attention except the relieved Paco.

"You're a good swimmer." He shook his hand. "Very good."

"I like to keep fit," Max said.

"OK everyone, we're going to head up in a few minutes," Paco shouted. "Go and get the *señora*," he gestured to the skipper.

"I'm not comin' on the walk," Max declared, and cleared his left ear of water. "I'm gonna hang down here while you guys are sweating up the hill."

"OK," Paco said. He looked like a man with a headache. "If you don't want to come walking, that's OK. But where are you going to go? Agua Sagrada is too far, you're not permitted to—"

"Who said anything about Agua Sagrada?" Max was towelling himself energetically.

"I don't know, the *señora* here was talking about going by herself." Paco looked at Ute.

"No way, we won't let this *señora* go nowhere by herself," Max said, and his eyes met Ute's.

"I'm not going." She shook her head.

"Right," Paco said. "Ah, there she is. We're ready to go." He glanced at his watch nervously.

Eve was changing under a huge towel, her back to the group. Max went up to her and reached under the towel playfully. "Hey, honey."

"Keep your hands off me."

"Jesus Christ." Max opened his arms to the heavens.

"OK everybody," Paco shouted. "We have about two hours before the storm. Let's go."

The skipper waved at the group and waded back to the boat.

They headed for the northern tip of the bay. Max was lying spread-eagled on the sand like a hefty starfish.

Soon, they were climbing a sandy path. Luis and his mother wore identical Jesus sandals with Velcro straps. Everybody wore shorts, except Luis's mother and Ute, who had long cotton trousers on for the scratchy forest she wasn't going to traverse after all. She felt cheated and robbed of her afternoon and of her dream. She'd had an auspicious dream, and now the toad had butted in and poisoned it with his secretions.

The dry forest was heated like an oven. All moisture was gone.

Ute trudged up the hill and pictured a bored Max swimming out to the caves to take another look, going deeper and deeper into the fissured rock underneath the cliff path they were treading now, and vanishing for ever in the *chambers of the sea*, as in that T.S. Eliot poem. No, she must stop quoting Jerry's stuff to herself, as if he were there. It was pathetic. She didn't really want him there. She didn't want to be there herself. She wanted to be on that path at the other end of the bay, striding to the top of the misty hill, to the realm of cloud forest and Oswaldo Joven's lucid, Cyclopean eye of a dying giant. There everything would become clear, one way or another.

Down by the ocean, in the sulphur-pongy air pregnant with storm, nothing could ever be clear. She crunched along the scorched white path, last in line behind Luis.

Thorns, branches and giant cacti all around. The cacti, gnarled and bulbous, were twice a human's size.

"...Blue-footed boobies are not afraid of humans," Paco was saying to the group. They'd stopped to look at a nonplussed booby, which sat hatching eggs in the middle of an explosion of excrement from above.

"This tree here is *algarrobo blanco*, Latin name is *Prosopis alba*." Paco moved up the path to a pale-barked tree with a large crown of tiny leaves.

"In Europe it is called carob. This tree doesn't have problems with heat and dryness. This is why it is green now."

"But it's not dry, it was raining just before – sort of," Eve pointed out from underneath her safari hat.

"Raining now, raining last night, but not for many months," Paco said in a patient voice. "This is our dry season – usually finishes in January." And they walked on.

The ocean was a thin strip of blue glanced here and there through the gaps in the pale trees. The further they climbed, the wider the blue strip grew. Ute took big gulps from her two-litre water bottle. She had cleverly prepared for a major trek, but had she been really clever, she would have made her escape from the beach in time, instead of chatting to Luis. Now she'd have to hire a tricycle the following day and bribe the sleepy old man at the entrance kiosk to let her through all the way to Agua Sagrada. She really had no time to see everything on foot. And how else could she justify a week of her travel schedule spent here?

"Check this out," Liz was saying. It was a thick tree with a green trunk covered in spikes.

"Wow, it looks unreal," Tim said.

"Young *Ceiba trichastandra*. The ceiba tree is green because it does photosynthesis with its bark." Paco glanced at his watch.

"What are the spikes for?" Eve touched one.

"Spikes protect the tree from animals when it's young and still growing. When it's older, it grows very large roots." And on they went on their hurried expedition. Luis's mother was saying something to him in her muted voice.

"You know" – Luis turned to Ute and evened his step with hers – "the ceiba tree was the tree of life for the Mayans. They believed that the long roots hanging from its branches connect the living with the souls of the dead above." Ute stopped and scribbled this in her notebook.

After a couple more stops, they reached the top. Here, the dry-forest fuzz receded to reveal the plucked, rocky nape of the hill. The ocean rushed into the picture from all sides. Part of it was under the sky's dirty carpet, which kept rolling out their way. The bay was out of view behind them, but on the other side of the hill Puerto Seco's huts squatted behind the estuary of the river, which lay fat and sluggish like a replete boa. Segments of it could stir any moment. Ute recognized the inlet where the entrance to the animal shelter was. Beyond, it became lost from view in the dry forest.

"How long does the river go inland?" she asked Paco.

"About five kilometres after the bend. Then the mangroves begin, and the river Mapuyo." Paco led them briskly to a rocky outcrop right on the edge of the cliff. It was covered in birds and guano.

"Please don't go close to the edge, OK?" Paco warned. "If you fall from here, I am not coming after you." They all laughed feebly with what remaining breath they had from the steep climb. All except

Luis's mother, who hadn't understood. She shuffled to the very edge of the jutting rock and stood there, squat and penguin-like.

"For Chrissake, tell your mom not to stand there – she's freaking me out," Eve said.

Luis pulled his mother back from the edge. She said something and pointed down at the tiny beach. Luis quickly stepped into the space she'd just left and looked down at the bay.

"The boat." He turned to Paco. "It's not there."

"What do you mean, not there?" Paco said, and stepped over to have a better look. "Why the hell's he moved it?" he muttered, dialling his mobile phone, his ashen face glistening with sweat. "Jesus?"

Jesus answered. The boat had in fact been moved, but not by him. He'd been woken up from his nap by the roar of the motor. Max was at the helm. They were now two bays further to the south. Max took over the phone. The familiar loud voice was enough to pull the others around Paco.

"We don't have time for silly games," Paco was shouting into his mobile, the sweat pouring from his face and onto his T-shirt, which said, in faded letters, "I LOVE NY". "The storm is about to hit us. You are putting everyone at risk..."

Max shouted something in reply.

Paco handed the phone to Ute. "He wants to talk to you."

"To me?" Ute said.

And just then, a massive bolt of lightning ripped sky and ocean, blinding everyone for a second.

"Max," Ute shouted. "What's up?"

His reply was deafened by a loud thunder crash.

"What?" Ute shouted.

"I'll talk to him," Eve said, extending her arm. "Pass him over."

"What does he want?" Liz asked.

"I'll talk to him," Luis said. "Max!" He listened for a few seconds. "What?" he shouted in Spanish. "Are you mad? That's suicide." He translated for everyone. "He want us to jump in the water from here, and they come and collect us in the boat. He's out of his mind."

There was a collective gasp of disbelief.

"We can walk back through the park," Ute said. "There's a path that leads to Villa Pacifica."

"Yes," Paco said. "But it is far away." He wrenched the phone from Luis's hand and shouted, "Jesus, put Jesus on."

But Jesus and Max were gone. The connection was cut off. Paco redialled angrily. Sweat poured down his pitted face. The ocean went very dark. It looked as if it was rising.

"There's no signal," Paco shouted in Spanish through the noisy rain, shaking his mobile. "I'm not getting any signal. It's the storm. Anyone got a mobile phone?" Nobody did.

"One of his pranks," Liz said. "But this one's gone too far."

"Let's go!" Luis said.

"But how're we gonna get back?" Eve said, panic in her voice.

"We're not walking *all* the way back to Villa Pacifica. You've got to be kidding!" Tim wiped the water pouring down his face. "Are we?"

"Walking back is better than swimming back," Liz said, and set off behind Luis.

"Hey," Eve shouted, running behind them, frantic. "Let's get back to the beach. He'll be there, it must be just one of his stupid jokes."

Paco shook his head. "But maybe he isn't there. We can't take a risk."

"Why is he doing this to me?" Eve moaned – but they were all walking fast now, and she had no choice but to keep up. The dry forest wasn't a great shelter from the downpour, but they felt less exposed. Luis quickly summed up the situation to his mother, and she nodded in her matter-of-fact way. They were all adapting to survival with surprising speed.

"OK," Paco shouted, and moved to the front of the column. "Soon we take another path. Don't separate from the group. Follow me."

"I swear it must be one of Max's jokes," Eve was saying to Ute, and Liz and Luis, her safari hat drooping with water. "If we go down to the beach, I'm sure—"

"Move on, Eve," Liz cut her off. "Jesus, this is like Judgement Day."

Lizards darted about in the roots and twigs, and birds fluttered in the trees. The cracked earth of the path quickly turned to mud. Water poured down everyone's head and body: it got into their eyes and noses, and when they opened their mouths to speak, water filled it.

"Great." Tim's face was screwed up with distaste. "Can we do it again tomorrow, please?"

The rain pushed them downhill, as if on a waterslide. Every few minutes, someone slid into the mud and cursed. Their backs dripped with sludge.

"OK," Paco yelled eventually. After trying his phone several times on the way, he'd given up. There was a narrow path turning inland. "Here we start the walk to Villa Pacifica."

He stopped to count them and rounded off the column. They continued to glide downhill. It was hard to say how long they spent squelching and sliding in silence. The rain interfered with human time. Huge thunderbolts ripped the forest from time to time, and made everyone duck instinctively. Ute turned and saw that Eve was crying. Luis and his mother were keeping a lively pace at the front, their Jesus sandals invisible under the mud.

The forest had come to life. Ute could hear the moisture-starved trees breathing, swelling with hope, growing leaves and moss, humming with new, verdant thoughts. The path evened out as they hit the grounds of the park, and it was now possible to walk without falling. No one dared ask how long it was going to take. Ute's estimate was at least four hours.

It seemed impossible that the rain could get any worse, but it did. It wasn't rain any more. It was a solid wall of water. They were now walking through the Niagara Falls in slow, incredulous motion, blinded and gagging in the deafening thunder of water.

"Jesus Christ!" someone gagged, and those were the last words anybody managed for a long time. In the tangled curtains of water, it was hard to see who was who. They all looked like watery holograms that could vanish in the space of a blink. Ute feared for Luis's tiny mother. She could be swallowed whole by the water beast.

It was hard to breathe. The air had darkened, and the steaming forest looked evil and endless in every direction. Pushing against the rain wall, Ute felt she'd be covered in bruises later. The water kept slowing down and accelerating, slowing down and accelerating, like a pulse. They kept moving in a dumb daze of survival through this chthonic water world.

After an eternity, they finally reached Villa Pacifica. In the grey mist it was hard to tell whether it was night or day. The back gate was open: they were expected. Carlos, wearing a plastic hooded raincoat, greeted them with no comment. Paco seemed on the point of grateful tears, like a man whose death sentence had just been waived. Birds twittered from all sides, excited by the rain.

"*Las Malvinas son argentinas*, *las Malvinas son argentinas*," Enrique rattled off by way of a greeting, but nobody laughed. The rain kept falling at a steady, thoughtful pace. It didn't bother Ute any more. She felt at one with it. In fact, it was now hard to imagine a world without rain.

The animal and bird enclosures were covered with large plastic sheets. The lion cub was back in her cage, lying dejectedly. The jaguar lay in a corner of his enclosure, breathing heavily, as if the humidity was inside his lungs.

Carlos and Pedro ferried the bedraggled crew across the river in the two boats. The river was swollen. In his black plastic hood, Carlos looked like Charon transporting shadows across the Styx back to the world of the living.

18

"I MUST GO GET HELGA and the baby," Luis said to Carlos as they all scrambled up the already flooded bank of the estuary towards the main house. "It's not safe along the *malecón* any more."

"It isn't safe here either," Carlos said. "See how the water has already risen? If it doesn't stop raining, it'll keep rising. Last time we were completely flooded, half of the cabins came under water."

The tropical plants were half hidden in a mist of rain. On the veranda, also half hidden in vapours and cigarette smoke, were Jerry, Mikel, Lucía and Héctor, plus the two dogs.

"You poor devils!" Mikel said in Spanish, and patted Luis on the back with good cheer. "You made it after all. We've been going off our heads here."

"Are you OK?" Jerry reached out to Ute and gave her a hug – a slightly guarded hug as if protecting himself from something so saturated.

"Yeah," she said. "Fine."

"I'd normally say 'have a shower', but I'm not sure that's what you need this time." Jerry was trying to be light-hearted.

She did need a shower. She looked down at her feet and legs, which were aching with fatigue. She was covered in mud and bits of plants to the waist, like some mythical beast – half human, half vegetable.

"*Señora*?" Héctor held a tray laden with steaming mugs of hot chocolate. Ute took one.

Most of the expedition group were already plonked in chairs – shapeless, speechless and stunned to be back in the familiar world of furniture and hot drinks. Liz sat on the veranda steps, the rain falling on her legs. Tim and Eve had gone straight for the lavatories, first removing their mud-covered shoes. Even so, they left muddy traces across the polished boards of the lounge. Luis, Mikel and Paco were already setting off in the rain.

"Going to fetch his wife," Mikel called to them, and said to Lucía: "*Amor*, show the *señora* to the Monkey, it's got a single bed." Lucía nodded and exchanged some words with Carlos, who flipped back his black rain-hood, removed his gumboots and went through to the kitchen with her. Luis's mother sat in a chair, her dress fetched to her knees and exposing her scratched and bleeding legs. Behind her, the two baby iguanas faithfully guarded their leaf, though their pattern was now disturbed and no longer formed a yin yang. They were now like two quotation marks without a sentence. Sitting on top of a table, Ute sipped her hot chocolate. It was heavenly. Jerry stood beside her, his arm around her.

"So what happened?" he asked.

"I don't feel like talking," Ute said.

Nobody else did either. Mikel's engine started up. Ute felt on the verge of tears. She glimpsed Héctor inside the lounge. He stood propped behind the reception bar, looking at them.

Carlos was drinking black coffee from a mug.

"Coffee at this hour?" Liz turned to face him. She had removed her soaked T-shirt and was down to a white sports bra again.

"Yes," he said, and looked at her breasts. "I'm drinking coffee now because I may be staying up tonight."

"Oh, really! Why?"

"Because there may be a storm during the night."

"See you later." Tim was back from the bathroom and off to his cabin. "I need to decrust, I feel gross."

"God, I can't believe we made it." Eve was back from the bathroom too, her mouth stuffed full of cake that she'd grabbed along the way.

"And I can't believe that Max could be such a cunt," Liz said.

Jerry sniggered. Ute suddenly felt like hitting him. Why wasn't he out in the forest looking for her? Why was he – the only person whose other half was out in the storm, possibly dying for all he knew – waiting here tamely with everyone else? Was there in fact anything more important in the world than his laptop, his own needs, his self-regard?

"What?" Jerry said. "Why are you looking at me like that?"

"Like what?" Ute said hoarsely.

What would you do if I didn't return? How much do you love me? Questions that could never be asked – or answered.

One of the dogs followed Lucía as she walked silently away from the main house, and presumably to her cabin. Lucía was clearly unable to deal with crises.

"Want to go?" Jerry asked Ute. She shrugged her shoulders. She didn't care. "Want to eat something?"

She shook her head.

"Well, what do you want to do?" Jerry insisted.

"Nothing." Ute looked at him with a blank expression.

"Fine," he said. "Fine."

He stood there, propped against the table, then he went inside. She heard him creaking about the lounge, perhaps looking at the books. Another mindless silence set in, and nobody moved a limb. It was as if they were all too exhausted to go a few steps further to their cabins. The rain was like a spell that paralysed all free will. While the rain fell, nothing could be decided, nothing could be undertaken.

You had two options in this rain: to move and merge with it, or to stand still and hear it. There was no middle ground.

Eventually, there was a noise: a tricycle arrived outside the gate.

"Ah, and here's the c–u–n–t in question." Jerry poked his head from inside the lounge.

"I didn't think you guys would make it before me," Max shouted. "Hey, baby!" He went over to Eve, who had just sat down on the floor after finishing her cake.

"Keep your hands off me!" Eve squirmed.

"Just fuck off, Max," Liz said from the veranda stairs.

"I think you better not show your face round here. You're not very popular right now," Jerry echoed.

Carlos gave Max a circumspect look, but not a muscle moved on his face.

"All right, let's get this straight, guys!" Max stood, his legs spread out. "Little bit of rain hasn't killed anyone yet. And anyway, it was a joke! All right? A *joke*."

The jaguar answered with a lazy roar from across the ditch. Carlos smiled crookedly to himself.

"At least you have a friend on the other side," Eve said.

"Or an enemy," Carlos said, and disappeared into the kitchen again.

"What the hell were you thinking about?" Liz turned to Max.

"I told you, it was just a joke. You should have known it was a joke. I'm not out of my fucking mind. I was just having a bit of fun! I was bored, man, all by myself on that beach. Just me and Jesus..."

Pacing up and down the veranda, he tripped over Eve's leg. She looked up at him with hatred.

"OK, let's go," Jerry said to Ute. She nodded, but didn't budge. Héctor was looking through ledger books again.

"Don't forget to sign the guest book before you go," he said to them, and his voice was like an echo from a past life.

"Yeah," Jerry said. "We'll do it later."

Along the path came, with heavy steps, Helga and baby, followed by Mikel and Luis. She handed the baby to Luis, stomped up the veranda steps, and went straight over to Max.

Without a word, she grabbed him by the front of his T-shirt and tossed him against the wooden railing, which went a bit slack under his weight, and stopped just short of tipping him over. He hit the plant behind, and Ute saw the baby iguanas fall off their leaf.

"Bastard!" Helga spat. "Bastard!" Max tried to steady himself, too surprised to react, but Helga continued shoving him back against the edge with strong arms.

Nobody moved, not even Luis, who was holding the baby anyway. Mikel came into the lounge and spoke to Héctor in quick Spanish – something about where Carlos was. Héctor indicated out the back.

"Let's go," Jerry took her arm, but Ute couldn't move. She was transfixed by the scene. Max was now defending himself by pushing Helga back with some energy. They looked like two oversized kids in a schoolyard fight during lunch break. The baby gave out a shriek of protestation.

"OK, *basta ya*!" Mikel yelled and stepped in, pulling Helga away. His face, just like Helga's, was purple.

"Get this woman off my back!" Max said. "Fucking hippie nutter!"

"OK! Please." Mikel was visibly making an effort to remain calm. He gave the out-of-breath Helga a conciliatory nod to leave this to him. "Max, I'm asking you to leave tomorrow morning. Tomorrow morning, OK?"

Carlos popped up from behind a giant leaf. He just stood there, his arms crossed in the rain.

"Oh yeah?" Max said to Mikel. "You're gonna force me to leave? You tried that before, buddy, remember? Didn't work. What're you gonna do, huh, call the police? Have me killed and toss me in the sea? Huh?" He looked around at his audience, to garner support.

"That's not a bad idea," Liz said.

"You will leave with your wife tomorrow morning," Mikel repeated, this time in Spanish. "Or Carlos and I will make sure you do."

Eve looked from one face to the next with a perplexed face, in a dilemma of loyalties.

Max suddenly started to laugh – a forced, cracked laughter – and raised his hands in a peace-brokering gesture.

"OK," Helga said bluntly, and turned to Mikel. "Please, we want to go to our cabin now." She was again holding the baby, who had gone quiet.

"Right," Mikel said with impatience, then called out, "Héctor!"

"*Sí.*"

"Show the *señora* and the family to their cabins."

"The Monkey and the Boa?"

"Yes."

Luis's mother got up and silently followed the young couple, who went with Héctor to the reception area. Max stepped to the side to make room for them to pass.

"OK," Max started again. "Let's get this straight. Goes like this. I called these guys from the boat just for a laugh, cos it was funny to make them sweat a bit."

"You didn't call us, it was Paco who called you!" Eve said.

"All right, all right. It was a joke, stupid! It was a joke, but I didn't know the phone was gonna cut off and… and this is not how I planned it! All right?"

"It's not all right." Mikel shook his head and lit a cigarette. "It's not all right to make jokes when there is storm and rain, and..."

"Jesus and I, we waited for ages, like hours, we went up the hill as well, shouting your names like idiots. We waited for you, and you won't even thank me for it! I've had enough of it – that's it, I'm leaving tomorrow."

"Right, right." Eve said. "I wanna go too. I miss the kids real bad." And she started crying.

"Oh, honey," Max squatted next to her. She let herself be consoled.

Carlos had vanished again.

"Here's what." Max got up and looked at Mikel with a conciliatory face. "I wanna do my bit for this place. I'm gonna donate two thousand dollars for the animals and to offset any damage you guys sustain if El Niño strikes again. I know you think I'm an asshole, but I wanna prove you wrong. I like you and what you've done here, and I wanna help. All right?"

There was a silence. It was hard to say whether the listeners were stunned or too exhausted to care.

Mikel blinked a few times at Max, then he announced: "Dinner tonight is simple, because Conchita is not here. Salad and rice and... *Qué más*?" he turned to Héctor, who shook his head.

"Just salad and rice," Mikel concluded.

Max was momentarily thrown by the indifference, then he said to Mikel: "Well, I'm gonna bring my chequebook. Don't go anywhere."

Mikel didn't respond. Max ran off to his cabin.

"Come on," Jerry whispered to Ute, and he pulled her along on their way. She followed automatically. They walked along the path. The rain seemed to fall in slow motion now, and Ute could see individual raindrops.

"The baby iguanas fell off," Ute said in a phlegmatic voice. The rain seemed to have seeped into her vocal chords.

"What?"

She shook her head.

"Do you want to leave tomorrow?" Jerry stopped, and looked at her. There was something insincere in the way he put this.

"I don't care," Ute said, and meant it.

"Are you OK?" They were outside their hut now, and Jerry was unlocking the door.

"Just tired."

She stood under the cool shower, which felt very different from the rain, even if it was the same temperature. She tried to still her mind, because she was scared of what she would find there.

She didn't exchange any more words with Jerry before collapsing on her side of the bed. He was outside in the hammock, anyway. The rain had stopped as suddenly as night had fallen.

And next, the creature was here again. Except it wasn't standing at the foot of the bed, but at the door. She could see it with her peripheral vision, though her eyes were closed. Even in her terror, she could perceive that it was short, a kind of dreadful homunculus. Short but powerful. She wanted to scream and, just like before, she couldn't. She tried to reason with herself, so she could somehow stop this nightmare. The creature was at the door because it wanted to show her something. If only she would look at it, she would know exactly what it wanted to tell her. And it was important, very important. But she couldn't look at the thing. Peripheral vision was all she could bear, and even this was too much. She thought she could feel her blood vessels hardening with terror, her heart turning to stone. Until she woke up from the cold. She lay there, not daring to look at the door.

When she did, the creature wasn't there. The door was closed, she could tell from the fact that no garden lights were filtering in at all. It was pitch-black. Jerry wasn't there either. She felt his side of the bed. It was made: he hadn't even been to bed. She was numb with cold and fear. But she knew that something had shifted. The creature wanted her to go outside. It wanted her to know something about this place. It was terrifying, and she didn't have the courage to follow it. But staying still and closing her eyes again and having another vision like this was even more terrifying. Because in the waking world, there is always someone else within earshot. But in the world of visions, it's just you and the *tsungki*. It's just you and those subterranean souls who held the keys to your life and death, and the life and death of everybody you cared for. The creature had appeared to her – and no one else – for a reason. She couldn't continue to ignore it, whether it was on her side or not. Ignoring it might come with too high a price.

She threw off the sheet and groped in the darkness for the nearest piece of clothing on the floor – shorts – and put it on. She already had a sleeveless top on. Her body was frozen. She couldn't find her flip-flops or any other shoes, so she walked out barefoot. She could hardly feel her feet anyway. Her face felt strangely calm and cool, as if the chill of the horrible vision had frozen her eczema together with her feet and her soul.

It was unnaturally black outside. The garden lights had gone off. The only hint of light came from the cloud-veiled moon, enough for her to see the vague shapes of giant plants all around as she crunched along the path towards the main house. A warm drizzle tickled the plants. Her heart was thumping hard. She almost expected the homunculus to jump out of a plant and bar her way. Because, clearly, Villa Pacifica was its home. It lived somewhere here, among the plants and cabins, the insects and baby iguanas.

On shaky legs, her feet suddenly hurting on the sharp pebbles, she made it to the main house. No light there either. Just the looming bulky outline of the two-storey building. She went in. Nobody inside, at least no shape she could make out in the darkness. It felt as if everyone had left while she slept. Everyone had left, and it was now just down to Ute and whatever dwelt in the garden.

She stood in the reception lounge for a moment, then suddenly remembered Héctor suggesting that Carlos had been out at the back. She walked carefully through the kitchen and out of the kitchen exit. She'd never been that way, because she didn't know there was anything here. But there was.

There was something that looked like a small cabin or shack. She approached, her heart in her throat, because she thought she heard something creaking. At first, she thought it was crickets in the plants. But there was another noise too, animal or human. It was like panting. She stood next to the cabin, her cheek glued to the wall, her heartbeat now choking her and making her sick.

Even though she couldn't hear distinct voices, just the panting, she knew exactly who they were. It was finally happening. She stood there for a while, paralysed with pain and curiosity. They were still going when she noiselessly padded away.

Back inside the lounge, she leant on a wicker chair, dazed. There was nowhere else for her to go. At first she thought of the couple, to keep thoughts of the creature at bay. But it was worse. She couldn't bear to contemplate any images of Carlos and Liz fucking. The creature was terrifying, but at least it hadn't hurt her – yet. Those two had.

She smelt the air: there was a whiff of something resembling pot. It wasn't *palo santo*, or any other incense. She got up, as if she could follow the smell. She walked around the lounge, bumping into chairs and tables, and the floorboards creaking underneath her. She went into the kitchen, but the smell wasn't coming from there. She headed towards the stairs to the music room, her heart in her mouth. She had an awful feeling the smell – or rather the smoke, it was definitely smoke – was wafting down from up there. Someone or something was lurking upstairs, waiting. She couldn't face it. But at the same time, now that she knew about it, she had no choice but to face it.

The music room was better lit because of the moonlight streaming through the panoramic windows. The smell was very strong here. It made her dizzy, but not for long because, next, she saw the creature. It was huddled in a corner, beside a large African drum. Ute's scream froze in her throat, just like in the dream, and for a moment she couldn't move.

But then she scrambled down the stairs, taking two at a time. It was a miracle she didn't fall or pass out from terror. She ran down the main path to their bungalow – or she hoped so: there was no time to think about directions, and she had to trust her instinct.

The door to the *Tortuga* was ajar. Jerry was back.

"Jerry," she called out. Her voice rang hollow and desperate in the dark. There was no answer.

"Jerry!" The silence shocked her.

The key was inside the door, and she locked it with frantic hands.

She sat heavily on the bed, accidentally pulling the entire mosquito net down from the ceiling. She sat shaking in the mess of mosquito netting. Sleeping was out of the question. And so was leaving the cabin.

It felt very much as if everyone had left Villa Pacifica – except Carlos and Liz, and the creature, which was now wandering about freely. She sat in a frozen stupor and lost track of time. Perhaps she even fell asleep.

Someone pushed down on the door handle outside. Ute jumped up, then crouched instinctively on the floor, out of view. A loud knock followed. She stopped breathing. Then another knock.

"Ute?" It was Jerry. There was a beam of torchlight.

She got up and unlocked the door, shielding her eyes from the sudden harsh light.

"Sorry to wake you up," he said, and stepped in, shining the torch away from her face.

"Where have you been?"

"The lights went out after you went to bed. I couldn't write and couldn't sleep. So I went out for a wander. To see what was happening."

He turned the torch off and fumbled in the dark.

"What are you doing?" Ute asked.

"Taking off my trousers."

"What happened to the lights?" she asked. "The lights went out."

"It was the rain, I think. And the storm."

She felt him creep into bed. They lay quietly for a while, not touching.

"There are things here," Ute said. "Inside the Villa. I saw something. Someone."

And immediately she had a ghastly feeling that she had betrayed something. That implicit in the creature's appearance on the edge of her reality was an absolute prohibition of sharing that knowledge with another. That the creature and its secrets should not be invoked in words. And she had done just that. Jerry snorted.

"Ute, of course you saw someone. There are lots of people staying here!"

No there aren't, everyone's gone, she wanted to say, but instead she just said: "Yeah, I know." She wasn't going to insist. It was enough that she'd mentioned it. Perhaps there was still hope of retaining the secret that the creature was trying to convey to her, to her and nobody else. Because clearly no one else here could perceive it.

"You know, it's funny. I thought I was the fiction writer and you were the traveller, the facts-and-figures person."

They were lying next to each other, still without touching. Not even their hands. So this was the fate of all marriages, eventually: to lie down in the dark with an invisible wall between, just breathing minimally, as if rehearsing for the grave.

"Maybe you've underestimated me," Ute said. And overestimated yourself, she thought, but she didn't say it. "What are you writing about?"

"This place. Or some version of it."

"How far along are you?"

"I still need an ending."

Ute relished this normal conversation after the abnormal encounters earlier. But she knew that the longer she talked, the further away she was moving from the moment of truth that the creature was bringing. But she was only mortal. She could only deal with mortal things. She didn't want to handle the creature's secrets, she only wanted the secrets of her own life, her own future. And she wanted to regain control of things. She'd lost it these last few days. She was mapless and adrift and filled with dread.

Jerry was now snoring gently. The door was locked, she was safe again. Except she knew she wasn't. She found Jerry's warm, reassuring forearm and gripped it. She slept fitfully. She was woken up by the sound of heavy rain hitting the thatched roof. She was alone again.

19

BREAKFAST WASN'T SERVED. THERE was still no power, no Conchita and no Héctor. And no one else either except Mikel, who was making coffee in the kitchen on a gas camping stove. Ute crouched by the dog, which was lying on the veranda, and stroked it.

"Morning," Mikel said.

"Has everyone left? It's very quiet."

Héctor had borrowed his car and gone to the village, Mikel said absent-mindedly. That's what bugged Ute about Mikel and Lucía: their obliviousness. Here they were, living in their self-made paradise, and yet they seemed permanently absent from it. It was as if they weren't here, only their shadows.

Ute sat down with a glass of mandarin juice that Mikel offered her. Mikel hovered around, looking like a dark cloud about to burst its lining. Lucía wasn't up. Jerry had gone for a walk earlier. Where, Mikel didn't know. On the table was a basket of stale buns and some jam. Ute smelt the air. The faint whiff of pot still hung in the air, but it was mixed with the sweet rot of humid plants.

"The baby iguanas, they're gone." Ute pointed at the empty residential leaf. But Mikel wasn't listening. He was counting money in the reception till. She went up to him. He was snuffling, as if he had a cold.

"Did Max really write out a cheque for two thousand dollars?" she asked.

Mikel looked up at her. "Yes, he did, it's in here," he tapped on a drawer Ute couldn't see, and continued counting the money.

"Use it," Ute said. But something else was on her mind right now. "Mikel," she said, "was the French guy really short?"

Mikel frowned in confusion.

"What French guy?"

"The French guy who drowned here last year."

Mikel thought for a moment. "Was he short?" he said.

"Yes."

"I can't remember his height. He was skinny, like all junkies." He looked at her with amused curiosity, his eye twitching in that unnerving way he had. "What a funny question. All your questions are funny."

"Mikel, can I ask you a personal question?"

He looked at her again in surprise and lit a cigarette. "Go on. Ask another funny question."

"Why aren't you friends with Oswaldo and Consuelo any more?"

"Who told you that we aren't friends any more?" He frowned. "Consuelo? You've been to her café of course."

"Yes," Ute said. "She seems a very kind woman."

"She is. And we are still friendly, but we don't spend time together any more. Oswaldo is dying of cancer in Agua Sagrada and doesn't want to see anyone. He's a fine artist, you know, some of the paintings here are by him." Mikel swept a vague hand towards the lounge. But he was still preoccupied elsewhere.

"And you don't visit him?" Ute felt bad about insisting like this, but she had to.

"Even Consuelo doesn't visit him."

There was something utterly shipwrecked about this man. Ute couldn't help but like him. She said:

"You know, I am buying that painting of Oswaldo's, *The Three Lives of Mikel.*"

Mikel stared at her and chased another fly. Smoke came out of his nostrils.

"I really like it. And you don't seem to want it..." Ute added. Mikel stared at her again and inhaled from his cigarette butt. Rain-water was dripping from the roof and onto Ute's head where she was sitting. She didn't feel like moving. The collie was sitting up now, looking imploringly at Ute, as if waiting for her to remember something.

"Can I have a cigarette?" she asked. He handed her the packet and gave her a light.

"I thought your husband was the writer," Mikel said.

"He is," Ute smiled. "I'm just a travel-guide writer: facts and attractions."

"Ah, but people's lives are an attraction to you, right?" Mikel said.

"Not at all," Ute said, "I'm just... I was bored. And I liked talking to Consuelo."

"Consuelo is a good woman. We miss her."

"And Oswaldo, you must miss him too?"

Mikel looked at her under a frown, stubbed out his cigarette on the sole of his flip-flop and shrugged his shoulders. "Oswaldo was a good friend for many years. But what good are friends who be-tray your trust? Who can you trust in this fucked-up world where nothing beautiful lasts and you lose the people you love one by one, and everything has a price? Who can you trust, if not your friends? Tell me."

"The person closest to you. The one you love," she tried. She trusted Jerry more than she trusted herself. He wasn't like other men – he had chosen her.

"Sure, the one you love," Mikel said, and she wasn't sure if he said it in earnest or mockingly. "You have to trust the one you love even against your better judgement. You better trust them, or you may as well shoot yourself in the head."

"Yes," she said.

"Though that too might be a solution." Mikel broke into a cracked laugh. Ute wanted to console him, say it'll be all right, you don't have to shoot yourself in the head, but she sensed that whatever had caused Mikel to be like this could never be put right.

"So," Mikel said with sudden brightness. "What are your plans for today? Are you staying on?"

"Is Max leaving?"

"I hope so. Haven't seen them yet, but I'll make sure he leaves. I've got enough on my hands without him."

"Morning, guys!" Liz said. "Forecasts of doom and gloom were wrong after all. We're all still here, no storms in the night..."

She sat down in a chair, then realized something wasn't quite right: no Héctor, no breakfast, no lights inside. But Ute wasn't going to explain the situation. She finished nibbling on a dry bun and scraped her chair as she got up. Mikel had vanished. Even with all the doors open, the place looked shut, almost abandoned. Ute and Liz were like the last laggards in an expired paradise.

"Where's everyone else?" Liz asked.

"Gone. It's just us and the resident malevolent spirits," Ute said.

"You make it sound creepy," Liz chuckled. "Are you and Jerry gonna leave today, do you think?"

"Don't know. Don't think so. You?" Ute went down the veranda steps.

"Well, Tim and I don't mind. We're kind of tired of travelling. There's not much to do here, but we don't mind the place really. But we'll go in a couple of days, for sure."

Ute was already walking towards the riverbank. The estuary had risen more overnight, and was now lapping up almost all the way up the bank. The monkeys called despondently from the other side. There was something odd and muted about the day: it didn't feel like day at all. It felt more like dusk. Instead of light, there was rain.

A boat had just turned the sharp bend in the river, and was gliding towards her. It was Carlos. As he approached, his bare arms and neck glistened with rain. She stood motionless for a while, in surprise. He should have been on this side, in the cabin at the back of the main house. It was logical. Why was he on the other side? It was hard to follow logic in this place, increasingly hard.

She waded into the swollen water, which quickly came up to her waist. She shook her hair and had a sharp, dizzying sense of unreality. As if anything was possible now. Anything at all could happen now, and it wouldn't matter very much.

"I wouldn't go for a swim right now," Carlos shouted. He was pulling up near the mooring place.

"Why not?" Ute said breezily, and felt like laughing. Perhaps she did laugh. Then she peeled off her T-shirt and left it to float or sink in the water. She was naked underneath.

"What are you doing?" Carlos shouted. The water was deep, and she was swimming – not towards the steep shore across, but out towards the open ocean.

"Come and get me," Ute gurgled, choking on some water. It was quite funny. Why did she have to take things so seriously? She'd taken all of life too seriously up until now. In fact, it was all a laugh. It was all a gamble. Nothing was terribly important, she saw that now. The water was lifeless as the rain hit it, as if the rain itself was gurgling: "After me, the deluge." Ute wondered if she could swim all the way to the *malecón* in Puerto Seco. She wasn't a great swimmer, but there were no waves and no currents there.

"There's an undertow, come back!" Carlos was shouting. There was no undertow, the water was dead. It even smelt of decay.

Carlos had caught up with her in the boat. He was leaning over into the water and saying:

"Are you mad? Where are you going?"

"I'm swimming."

"Get in the boat." He didn't seem in a mood for jokes. "The water is contaminated, you'll get sick."

"I won't drown, don't worry," Ute said, and swallowed some water again.

The rain started hitting the water harder, like thousands of pebbles to her head and face. Carlos was now reaching down from the boat to get her. She gripped his arm, and he started lifting her out of the water. He was phenomenally strong. It was hurting her arm, but she didn't mind. She stepped over the boat's rim and sat next to him, shaking the water from her hair and smiling. Carlos let the oars dangle for a moment and looked at her. She stared at him hard. He took in her bare breasts, but didn't linger on them before he started rowing without a word. Curtains of rain fell over them. Ute kept quiet.

"El Niño drives people a bit mad," Carlos said while he moored the boat.

"Like last time?" Ute said. She had to shout to be heard over the clamour of rain.

"Yes, people went mad."

"Which people?"

"Everyone, the whole village."

"And here as well?"

He gave her that slightly condescending look which she found so intriguing and so exasperating at the same time. Actually, she found everything about him both intriguing and exasperating. Intriguing because she couldn't get close to him, and exasperating because he seemed to have an answer for her – if only she could get close enough to him.

"Where's your T-shirt?" Carlos shouted, scanning the water. His hair was plastered to his head and his face looked blurry in the violent rain. Everything looked blurry. The T-shirt was nowhere in sight.

"Don't worry," Ute shouted back, and stepped over the boat rim and waded waist-deep into the water.

"Another day of rain and the water will cover up the shore," Carlos said.

"How long before it reaches the cabins?"

"Not long. And you don't want to be here for it."

"You don't want to be here for it either," she said flippantly.

"You can go home any time you want. We have nowhere else to go."

"And Paraguay?"

"Paraguay's Paraguay. Screwed up for all eternity."

They reached dry land. He took off his black singlet, wrung it out and handed it to her. She put it on. This took a moment, and standing like this, blurred and muffled by rain, with nothing but water on their naked skin, was delicious. She wanted to prolong it.

"If something happened to this place," she shouted, "where would Lucía and Mikel go?"

"Nowhere," Mikel said. She walked behind him. It was like the day before all over again: moving slowly in the heavy, slippery soil, your body crushed by rain. His singlet clung to her. She would follow him anywhere now, anywhere. To any dingy cabin, any ends of the earth. Except they already were at the ends of the earth. On the porch of the main house, a clump of people huddled together, nibbling dry buns and sipping yesterday's juices. Neither Jerry nor Max were there. But Luis and his family were. Ute could swear the baby was shrinking from day to day inside its bundle, as if time was going backwards for it.

Nobody was in the mood for greetings – not even Luis. They all just sat there with dull complexions and listened to the waterfall thundering around them. Except Liz, who openly ogled Carlos as soon as he turned up. But he quickly disappeared from view as usual. Then Ute heard unhappy male voices inside the main house – something about phone lines being down and about getting help. Ute sat down at Luis and Helga's table. Luis looked at her. His usual friendliness was gone, and he looked preoccupied.

"How were your dreams?" Ute tried. Luis smiled faintly.

"I didn't have any. A good thing too. My mother said if you have dreams here, they will be bad ones, and you will be doomed to fulfil them. She refused to sleep in her cabin. She spent the night upstairs in the music room. She's convinced there are bad spirits here and wants us to leave immediately."

Ute felt herself blush, but no one seemed to take notice, except Luis's mother, who was looking at her with kind, mustard-yellow eyes. She'd seen her upstairs – seen her bolt like a lunatic, running for her life in the black night, running from a kind old woman who was quietly smoking a joint, minding her own business.

Suddenly, she felt the same as in the water just moments ago, and she saw that this whole thing was unreal. The place, the people gathered here, even the stupid weather was a joke. And life itself, all their lives were a joke, a divine practical joke. Ute laughed a nervous little laugh and drew a few surprised eyes, but she didn't care.

"So what are we gonna do today, guys?" Liz asked.

"Drown, by the looks of it," Tim said.

"Leave," Eve said. "I wanna leave. I can't take it any longer. I wanna see my kids."

"Yes, we must leave." Helga said, and looked at Luis.

But somehow leaving didn't seem possible any more. Leaving was a topic of conversation, nothing else.

"Liz, I know what *you* can do today," Ute heard herself say.

Liz looked at her, surprised, friendly.

"You can continue your little shag parties with Carlos, no one will hear you in this rain. Don't let us stop you."

There was a stunned silence. Liz blinked at Ute a few times, then she suddenly looked at Eve. Eve's eyes widened.

"Lizzie, is that true?" Tim said, his voice hurt, as if she'd personally betrayed him with Carlos.

Liz slowly got up, went up to Eve and slapped her on the face. Both women were in shock, then Eve jumped up, holding the side of her face.

"You bitch! What are you doing that for?" she cried, her face turning red. "What's wrong with you people? Can't you see I've had enough! I just wanna go home."

She turned on her heels and stumbled down the terrace steps. But instead of storming off, she just sat at the bottom of the steps and sobbed loudly in the rain like a lost child. Ute knew she should feel sorry for her, but she couldn't feel anything right now.

"Jesus, girls, get a grip on yourselves! Liz, for Chrissakes!" Tim got up, went to Liz and took her by the wrist. She was crying now too, but silently, big tears streaming down her face. Again, Ute felt oddly unsympathetic.

"What's happening with you today?" Tim turned to Ute. "What was that about?"

Ute shook her head and closed her eyes. Something had possessed her. Since the night before, she had felt disconnected.

"I'm sorry," she said – but she wasn't sorry. She wasn't anything. Liz was walking away, fighting the curtain of rain as she went, and Tim followed.

Helga, Luis and his mother were staring at Ute like a three-headed Sphinx.

She wished Jerry was there: he would find something clever to say at least. Then Luis's mother spoke, her eyes still on Ute, and Luis translated for Ute's sake into Spanish:

"Humans, animals and plants have a stable core. It's called *wakan*. It is expressed in their physical appearance, their emotions, their vitality. It doesn't change. But the *arutam*, the spirit or the soul, is in constant flux. It is impacted by energies and spirits. My mother believes that in this place there is spiritual interference, the *wakan* becomes confused with the *arutam*. This can have a destructive impact on all living beings."

Ute couldn't follow. Luis repeated: "It's best to leave. If you stay, you must remain in a state of contemplation, because every action you undertake will be untrue."

Ute giggled.

"Some people are more susceptible to interferences than others," Luis added. "And the animals add to the disharmony of the spirit world because they are damaged."

"Where are all the men?" Mikel wanted to know. "We need a hand or two. There's trees fallen over the road, we need to remove them."

"OK" – Luis got up – "I'll give you a hand." He spoke to Helga in German, and she nodded. "Ute" – Luis turned to her – "make sure my mother doesn't wander off. Can you keep an eye on her?"

Ute shrugged. "Sure."

The three men disappeared and, as if on cue, Max appeared.

"Hey, hey, hey," he said, "what's up today? Where's breakfast?"

"Self-service," Ute said.

"The others go to the road," Helga said to Max. "Now. You go too."

"Yeah," Ute joined in, "they went to remove some fallen trees from the road. I'm sure they could do with your help."

"Right." He considered it for a second. "Right. I better grab some breakfast first."

Ute got up. The baby started crying. Max went into the kitchen to forage for food. She glimpsed him from the lounge – in the grey daylight he looked like a giant rat rummaging in a rubbish tip, his rump moving.

He was done quickly and then, to Ute's surprise, he went off to help the other men.

Then she thought of the Mexicans and their farewell note, and went straight to the guest book shelf. She looked at them again and counted them: 1999, 2000, 2001, 2002, 2003, 2004, 2005, 2006, 2007, 2008, 2009. She pulled out 2009 and opened it. It was blank, untouched. She tossed it on a chair and picked up the next one down – 2008. Blank, again. 2007 – blank. They were filled in from 2006 backwards.

There was some vast, inexplicable mistake here. An anomaly. She tried to fit it all together, but her mind was brittle and she couldn't do the maths. Instead, she just kept turning the blank pages, still looking for some sign of life. Time was out of joint. She looked up and around. Luis's mother was still sitting out on the veranda, motionless and totemic in her blue dress.

"Hey!" Max was back. His face was all red, and he was soaked in rain. There was a gash along his thigh.

"Wanna come feed the jaguar with me?" he said.

Ute clearly saw herself standing there, a woman at the end of her thirties and at the end of – what year was it really? – standing among these guest books, as if they contained an answer to all her sorrows.

"Max," she said, and held the 2009 book open. "What do you see in here?"

She flicked the empty pages.

"It's empty, man," Max said.

"OK." Ute flicked through the empty pages of 2008. "What do you see in here?"

"Nothing, *nada*," Max cried. "What are you showing me these empty books for?"

"And here?" Ute flicked through 2007.

"Oh man, everyone's losing the plot. Are you coming with me or not?"

"All right," Ute said, and clapped the book shut.

"Cool, cool," Max said, and stepped out onto the terrace, then turned around.

"Hey, by the way," he said, "I'm real sorry about yesterday. I was an asshole. I don't know what came over me in those caves. Just wanted to say sorry, that's all. Long as we're still friends."

Ute stared at him, blankly. "Yeah, whatever. What happened?" she pointed to his thigh.

"Ah, just a scratch. We moved all the trees though. The road's clear now."

"What, in just five minutes?"

Max looked at his watch. "More like an hour, Uddar. Are you all right? You look a bit… wonky."

Ute blinked. An hour. Time *was* a nonsense here.

"Let's go," Max urged her, "before everyone gets back."

Then she saw that the Achuar woman had got up and was gesturing to her. Ute followed her to her cabin. The woman gave her a bunch of leaves and mimed that she should chew them. She was trying to mime something else too, pointing at herself, but Ute couldn't make sense of it. She thanked the woman and put the leaves in her pocket. She'd give them a try later.

Ute didn't know how it happened, but when they waded into the swollen waters and got into Carlos's boat, there were three of them. Luis's mother was there too. Well, Ute had promised to keep an eye on her, and here she was.

And then Max was rowing to the other side. The water carried them fast, he hardly needed to row. The current was going inland. Ute was sure that the current had been going the opposite way when she swam that morning. But there was no point trying to make sense of things any more.

Max was talking about rabbits and the jaguar, and investment, and El Niño, but Ute couldn't concentrate – and, anyway, the combined noise of rain and rushing river muted everything. Max's thigh was still bleeding, the old blood caked and dark around the wound, but he didn't take any notice of it. Luis's mother sat motionless as always in her polyester dress, now plastered to her drooping breasts, her hands in her lap, looking at nothing visible to anyone else. What was it – the past, the future, someone present but not visible with the naked eye? For the first time, Ute wished she could talk to the old woman. Ask her what year it was. But this woman lived by some clock of her own anyway.

Then they were mooring the boat on the other side, and walking among screeching birds and agitated monkeys.

"*Enrique eat coca, Enrique eat coca,*" Enrique shrieked in his garbled voice when he saw them. The lioness stood up under her black plastic awning. She looked damp and bedraggled. The jaguar looked at them with a circumspect, mean face. He was huge, as if he'd grown in the last few days. Then Max said something and disappeared. Luis's mother started shuffling away, back towards the boat, battered by the rain, which hadn't let up. She didn't want to be here.

"Wait," Ute shouted, and went after her. The woman broke into a hobbled trot. Ute caught up with her and grabbed her by the arm. The woman shook her head and pointed to the shore. Her eyes were slits in the rain. They were now at the open hut with the animal-skin display.

Just then Max reappeared, carrying an inert-looking rabbit.

"What are you doing?" Ute shouted. Then she wondered the same about herself. What was she doing there? The rain battered her, and all she wanted was for all this to stop.

For the spell to lift and this brutish joke to be over.

For things to be restored to their natural state.

For Mikel and Lucía to have their paradise back.

For El Niño and corrupt officials to stop plaguing them.

Ute and Jerry could love each other again, like they used to – purely, unquestioningly. They could be their better selves again.

And standing in the rain here, in Carlos's flooded beastly realm, Ute realized that she didn't hate Max any more. He was OK. He was just a fallible human dripping with rain, like all of them there.

And immediately she realized something else too, something much more important. All her earlier turmoil hadn't been about Carlos at all. It had been about Jerry.

She held the frail Amazon woman by the arm and stared at the empty armadillo shells, the pinned butterflies, the snake skins. And in a horrible lurch, what she already knew hit her with full force. It wasn't Carlos and Liz in that cabin last night, or Carlos and Eve. It was Jerry and Eve. She had recognized Jerry's moans of pleasure, but her brain had rejected the truth.

"No," she cried, and tried to pull Luis's mother back. "You can't go back yet."

But the woman wasn't budging. She fought back, and Ute gave up. She didn't have the strength for this. Max was now opening the jaguar's cage and stepping inside.

"What are you doing?" Ute shouted, and the rain entered her mouth. Max threw the rabbit at the jaguar's feet and watched it. The animal didn't seem interested in the meat, though. His ears were drawn back, and he kept his unblinking eyes on Max. Ute ran to the cage.

Just as she got there, the semi-open door of the cage swung shut by itself. It had an automatic lock. There was a key in the lock, which served to open the latch. But Ute didn't turn it.

"He's not eating it cos it's dead," Max was saying. "Should've given him a live bunny."

After a few moments of silent staring and heavy breathing, Max went for the door of the cage. The jaguar twitched, his eyes still on the intruder.

"All right, you can let me out now," he said coolly, and shook the door, which rattled.

Ute just stared at him, transfixed. She couldn't move. Max told her to open the fucking gate, but his voice was quickly lost in the roar of the jaguar. Max stopped yelling and focused back on the animal, which had now risen. It was a very small space, now that two bulky animals occupied it, and Max didn't have anywhere to go.

"Open the door *now*," he said to Ute quietly, his eyes on the jaguar. He had presence of mind. But Ute didn't. She found herself unable to move, as if she was paralysed.

Then things happened very fast. So fast she couldn't have possibly done anything about it even if she'd tried.

Max tried to stare the jaguar down.

"Easy now, boy," he was saying. "We're gonna be friends."

He stood with his feet planted wide apart, arms stretched out defensively, the same stance he took when he was being a nice guy, reasoning with a world full of idiots.

"You know me, I'm a friend. I brought you food yesterday. Friend. *Amigo*."

But the jaguar wasn't interested in his friendship. He was approaching now, supremely sure of himself, supremely enraged – and with dreadful, effortless grace, he swiped at Max. Max yelled and pulled back.

"Open the gate!" he implored. This annoyed the jaguar even more: he growled and swiped harder, and tipped Max over. Max fell heavily on his back, and the animal was over him at once.

Max uttered a high-pitched, horrible scream – a scream of primal protest. The scream that comes out of us when we know the nightmare is real.

The scream jerked Ute out of her trance. Slowly, she reached to unlock the door. Just to stop the screaming. She turned the key in the latch with a numb hand. The gate was now unlocked. Max could push it open and come out if he wanted to. But it was too late. He now had the angry jaguar on top of him, and his screams went on in the thundering rain. Then they stopped. There was a snapping sound. Ute turned away.

She turned and saw the old woman standing in the display shelter. She was gesturing to her, but she couldn't tell if the woman was beckoning to her or sending her away – saying, "Go, go, gringa, go to the forest, because there is no way back for you now."

Ute turned and headed for the back gate. The woman was shouting something, but Ute couldn't make sense of it – and, anyway, all this was already slipping into the past. She pushed the gate, and it opened soundlessly.

It was darker, and the rain felt colder. A chill began to enter her blood, and as she stumbled on in the mud, blind and deaf with rain and shock, the cursed forest embraced her.

Part Three

20

THE RAIN WAS INVISIBLE, inhuman, like time itself. It had obliterated everything, even the night and the day.

Ute scrambled in the swamped forest like an animal, whimpering and breathing hard, and her heart was a wounded bird inside her chest. The dripping branches scratched her face, reached for her eyes, her mouth, her nostrils. Somewhere far ahead, she could hear the sea, or maybe it was more rain.

Everything you do would be untrue, the Achuar woman had said.

And now, the world was being washed away, and she had to keep moving. *I can't go on, I will go on*, Jerry would quote Beckett if he were there. But he wasn't there. He would never be there again. He didn't love her, and it was over for them. Everything was over now, suddenly and brutally. Max. Jerry. Villa Pacifica. Ute's future.

She stumbled on, willing her body to become an empty shell, until the atmosphere darkened and the rain eased off. Animal noises rose from the sodden forest. The path, or what had been the path, became steeper.

She walked for an immeasurable time, until she noticed that something had changed. She was climbing a green hill, the rain had stopped, there were trees, and she saw vapour rising ahead. She was entering the cloud forest. Then it was suddenly night, and in the bloodless moonlight all she could see was cloud. Her singlet was in shreds, and she didn't care to investigate how the rest of her was.

At the top of the hill was either Agua Sagrada or hell itself. Hell is what she deserved, because she was unlovable, iguana-ugly, barren, stupid, a murderer, and a destroyer of everything she loved. Oh how she loved her life now that it was destroyed. She even loved Max now.

Somewhere among the animal screeches and the invisible shrubs, she had to stop. She lay on the warm ground, feverish, weak, and waiting for some wild animal to come and eat her. Just as the jaguar… No, she couldn't think about that.

Ute wailed like a coyote under the ragged moon. Nobody heard, or at least nobody replied, not even the animals. The world of humans was far behind her, she no longer belonged to it. She shivered in the blackness, still alive in a graveyard of time.

Then it was dawn, and a couple of humans were standing over her. Birds and frogs chattered loudly, and white cloud was caught in the tops of the trees. The air smelt fresh as if nothing bad had ever happened.

The women were saying something. There was a horse too, which sniffed around her and spluttered. Ute was parched.

"*Agua*," she whispered. Her throat was scratched raw and her mouth tasted like manure.

"*Sí*," a woman said in a heavy coastal drawl, "Agua Sagrada. You need help, my girl. Where have you come from?"

"Villa Pacifica," Ute sat up and felt like vomiting.

"What?" the other woman said. Now she saw that there was a local man with them. He was standing a few feet away, looking on with his mouth agape.

"I walked from Villa Pacifica," Ute said in her clearest Spanish. Foreign languages came in handy even in the afterworld.

"Villa Pacifica." One of the women turned to the other, perplexed.

"Poor thing," the other one said.

"She's got fever. José!"

José came over, and together they hoisted her up onto the horse, which wasn't a horse but a donkey. The man's T-shirt said in faded English letters "JESUS IS A COCK". She wanted to laugh, but instead dry-retched. Her guts were on fire.

One of the women undid the threadbare shawl that was wrapped around her shoulders and handed it to Ute. Ute's singlet, which was Carlos's singlet, was in tatters. Her sandals and feet were caked in mud – she hoped it was mud anyway, and not her own excrement. They trudged in silence higher and higher up the steamy green hill, the donkey sneezing from time to time, until they reached a wooden gate that said "Comunidad artesanal Agua Sagrada".

The settlement consisted of a few huts. A few people came out to see the donkey's strange load. There was confusion about what to do with her now. Ute asked for water again, and someone brought out a grimy plastic bottle, which she drained in one go. Normally she wouldn't, but nothing was normal any more. Besides, she'd obviously contracted something from swimming in the estuary yesterday. Yesterday was another world that was now lost for ever. Carlos had warned her about the water with good reason. He did everything with good reason, and she had destroyed his only home.

Eventually, she was deposited in one of the huts. A woman was washing something in a tub outside the hut. Ute's rescuers explained to the woman that Ute was sick and needed somewhere to rest. The woman nodded, and the other three disappeared back down the dirt road with their donkey. Ute sat on a tree stump and thanked the woman, who looked at her with dull eyes and continued with her washing. It was semi-dark inside the hut, and three hammocks hung from the ceiling. In one of them something small – perhaps a child – was sleeping. Then she suddenly remembered.

"Oswaldo Joven," she said feebly. "Does he live here?"

The woman stopped washing and gave her a veiled look. Her nails were bitten down and raw.

"Where have you come from?" she asked. Her face was broad, but her delicate features were all bunched in the middle. It was hard to tell her age – she could be anything between twenty and forty.

"From Villa Pacifica. I walked through the forest."

The woman stared at Ute.

"Villa Pacifica," she said with suspicion. "What were you doing there?"

"We were staying there... Holidaying." She sounded to herself like an idiot. And her guts were churning again.

The woman had a slight squint, which was disconcerting, as if she was looking simultaneously at you and someone invisible next to you. She suddenly looked familiar to Ute.

"When?" the woman asked.

"Yesterday."

How meaningless the notion of yesterday was. The woman seemed to think the same, because she scoffed as if Ute had just told her a mildly funny joke.

"Are you on your own?" she asked.

"Yes," Ute said.

"So you want to see Oswaldo," the woman went on. She now seemed less interested in her washing and more interested in the strange gringa. Ute nodded. She was feeling weak, and speaking was becoming an effort.

"How did you know about him?"

"From Consuelo. His wife."

The woman jerked up as if stung by a scorpion, and went inside the hut. The sleeping mass was now awake, and it stepped out in the bright morning light like an apparition. It was a girl with coffee-coloured eyes, perhaps five years old. It was an inappropriate greeting, but Ute heaved, and the water she'd just drunk came out in a yellowish jet. The little girl watched with fascination. When she recovered, Ute smelt the familiar scent of *palo santo*. The woman had lit some of the stuff inside the hut. Perhaps she thought Ute was a bad spirit.

"*Señora*," the woman enquired as she came out. "Did someone send you here?"

Then, seeing Ute's blank expression, she seemed to take pity on her and said in a sad voice, as if about to break bad news: "*Bueno*, if you like, I'll take you to Oswaldo now."

Ute got up on shaky legs, and they walked through the settlement.

The little girl held her mother's hand. They passed a few people who were going about their business – a pottery workshop, a few domestic animals – until they came to the outskirts of the settlement. They continued walking along the dirt road. Birds screeched in the lush forest. At one point, a fat toucan with a yellow beak waddled out onto the road and looked at them suspiciously, before waddling back into the bush.

Soon, they reached a rocky lookout point. From here, she saw the bay of Agua Sagrada and the open ocean, which was sparkling blue, like the sky. There was no trace of the storm. El Niño had vanished overnight.

Then Ute realized this was a small cemetery with simple gravestones. The girl ran up to a gravestone and stood beside it, looking pleased. Ute's head and stomach throbbed with confusion.

Clearly, Oswaldo had died in the last few days, and nobody at Villa Pacifica had heard the news. Not even Consuelo. Ute was the first beyond this little community to learn the sad news. Now she would never meet the intriguing Oswaldo.

"This is where Oswaldo is," the woman said in her resigned voice. "He asked for this inscription. We did it his way." Ute read the inscription:

On earth a prisoner
of fear and desire,
death will set me free
OSWALDO JOVEN 1949–2007

Ute read the whole thing several times.

"He died in 2007," she said, and her voice sounded the way she felt – hollow.

"Yes," the woman said. "April 2007."

Ute could hear the buzzing of a fly somewhere near her head, or possibly inside her head.

"Are you an admirer of his work?" the woman asked. The girl was now picking wild flowers among the sparse graves.

Ute swallowed with difficulty. The white glare of the sun was blinding.

"How come... How is it possible that nobody in Puerto Seco knows about his death? Not even his wife."

The woman looked at her with something resembling pity.

"His wife has been dead for three years," she said.

"You mean his ex-wife, not his current wife. Consuelo lives in Puerto Seco."

The woman opened her mouth, closed it again, and said slowly, as if explaining to a child:

"After El Niño destroyed her café and Oswaldo's paintings in December 2006, Consuelo hanged herself in the café. January 2007." She shook her head. "Very sad."

The woman looked at the gravestone for a while.

"Who are you?" Ute said in a small voice.

"María. I was Oswaldo's... Well, we weren't married, but we lived together after he moved up here."

"Is the child his?"

"No, I had Luz with someone else. He left. Oswaldo was only here for a year."

"You got together up here while he was dying," Ute said.

"Oswaldo was a... special man. A great artist. Not everybody liked him, but..."

Ute had to throw up again, and only just managed to hobble away from Oswaldo's grave.

"Sorry," she said afterwards.

"Don't worry." María's smile was fleeting. "Let's go back."

Back to the future? Ute wondered. She nodded.

"Was there a storm here yesterday?" she asked. "And the day before?"

"No," María shook her head. "The last time we had storms was during the El Niño disaster in 2006. It devastated the coast..."

"Yes!" Ute cut her off, "and severely damaged Puerto Seco and Villa Pacifica, and... and..."

"That's right," the woman said gently. "After the floods, Villa Pacifica closed down. They couldn't afford to repair the houses after one of their staff ran off with all their savings. They also had some personal problems, I heard at the time. Oswaldo had an affair with the *señora* before he moved here, and her husband, he went a bit crazy after that. Oh yes, and during the storms, traffickers broke in and stole some animals."

Ute realized that they were walking on, beyond the graveyard. Luz ran ahead, clutching a sprig of flowers.

"Which of the staff ?" Ute asked. Her head was spinning in a sick vertigo.

"I don't know his name. But he was Consuelo's son."

Of course!

"Where did he go?"

"No idea."

They had reached a hut. It was overgrown and looked derelict.

"This is where Oswaldo lived. I walked here every day, to visit him. He wouldn't see anyone else. The *señora* from Villa Pacifica came a few times with supplies and medication. She wanted to see him, but he refused. You see, he didn't love her any more, or Consuelo. He loved me. Then he died on me. But such is life."

Ute looked at María. *Such is life*, Consuelo had said. Oswaldo had fallen in love with the same woman over and over again: small-boned, curly-haired, gentle, but strangely tough. Consuelo, María, Lucía, they were essentially the same woman. Only their race was different – Consuelo was coastal black, María was an *indígena*, Lucía was white. And they had all loved him.

Ute squatted shakily on the ground outside the hut.

"Are you OK?" María was saying. "Do you want to go inside?" She pushed the door, and it opened with a creak. "Oswaldo's things are still in here. I don't know what to do with them. I don't lock it, because nobody comes here."

"And Carlos?" Ute implored her.

"Carlos?"

"The guy in the animal shelter. The Paraguayan."

"Ah yes. They say he went to work in another animal shelter, up north. Come in."

Inside the dark hut, it smelt of *palo santo* – and oblivion. Luz was already clambering inside a low, sagging hammock hanging from a beam in the ceiling. There was a single bed with a worn blanket carefully folded at one end of the stained mattress. Ute sat on it, limp and dumb like a rag doll.

"How long are you staying?" María asked, as if Ute was checking into a hotel.

Ute looked around the cabin for clues, for anything to help her out. It was bare and unlovely, nothing like their *tortuga* hut, which now belonged to another life. The wooden floor was stained with oil paint.

"I don't know," Ute said. "I killed someone."

María was standing in the doorway, a dark outline framed by the dazzling light of morning. She didn't say anything. She wasn't easy to shock.

"At Villa Pacifica," Ute added.

María laughed dryly. Luz stopped rocking in the hammock.

"I don't know you, and I don't know where you've come from," María said in a conciliatory voice. "But there is nobody at Villa Pacifica. It's overgrown, nobody lives there. There are no animals. There was a jaguar before, but it got taken by the traffickers. Some animals were taken to other shelters. You have fever, and you need to rest. I'll leave you here to rest for a *momentito*. And I'll come back later."

Ute felt like shouting or laughing, but either was too much effort. She lay back on the musty mattress and pulled the grimy blanket over her legs with an effort. It was cold inside. She just needed to put her head down, close her eyes, and everything would fall back into place again. It had to.

Then she sat up. "What will happen with Mikel and Lucía?" she asked.

"*Bueno*," María frowned, confused by the question. "I don't know… Mikel went a bit mad. They say he was always a bit mad… But I don't know where they went."

María retrieved Luz, and when she shut the door with "See you later", Ute was plunged in a grubby darkness. She listened to the birds and tried to imagine staying here for good. Just move into Oswaldo's hut, and look at the ocean from the graveyard every morning, and become someone without a past. Just as Villa Pacifica seemed to have nothing *but* a past.

But she had just been there, she had just been inside its present. She had met those people. She had liked, desired, disliked, hated and killed some of them. She hadn't imagined all that. Had she? Jerry had been there with her.

She ached in strange places – in her throat, in her guts, in her loins. Perhaps those were the fragments left of her heart after it had broken. Because it had broken at some point. She couldn't say at which point but, ever since, she had lived with the shards of it hurting her in unexpected places. She knew this now, and it was the only thing she knew.

No, she knew something else too: Villa Pacifica was already a broken paradise when Ute and Jerry had arrived. But *when* had they arrived? Perhaps María was insane. She closed her eyes and drifted off.

She shivered in her sleep, and when she woke up, the rough texture of the blanket shocked her skin. There was a skinny boy there, and the door was open. Sunshine was pouring in. She sat up in the bed. She felt as if lead had been poured into her head while she slept.

"*Hola*," the boy said shyly, and didn't look at her. "María said to bring you this."

There was a plastic tub of boiled rice and a bottle of water on the table. The boy was dark-skinned and looked familiar.

"What's your name?" she asked.

"Pedro." He was already leaving.

"Pedro," Ute said. "Evelyn's brother."

"Yes," Pedro stopped in the doorway.

"Don't you remember me? We met at the beach, I talked to you and Evelyn and your brother Ricardo, and you raced with Luis and… the American gringo. On the beach. Just the other day, remember?" Ute sounded the way she felt – cracked.

"No." Pedro shook his head.

"In Puerto Seco," Ute insisted. But there was no point insisting. She changed tack. "Where do you live?"

"Here," Pedro said. He was keen to leave.

"In Agua Sagrada?"

"Yes."

"When did you come to live here?"

The boy frowned and thought for a bit. "In 2006."

"And what about Evelyn and… the others, where are they?"

"In Puerto Seco. I ran away."

"You ran away from home?"

"Yes. I walked here from Puerto Seco. I didn't tell anybody." He scratched his thin neck.

"And what do you do here? Is there a school?"

"No. I work in the kiln."

"Did you know Oswaldo?"

Pedro nodded, then shook his head.

"When did Oswaldo die?" Ute pressed on.

"I don't know."

"Does María look after you?"

He shook his head again. It was definitely Pedro, the same boy, the same timid body language, as if he didn't want to be there, as if he hadn't asked to be born at all.

"Nobody looks after me. I look after myself," he said defiantly.

"Of course. You're almost a man now." But he wasn't. He was a twelve-year-old boy who also existed in some parallel life down on the beach. In that life, he doesn't run away from home and become a potter. In that life, he slowly rots away in Puerto Seco and eventually turns to crime.

But it was impossible. There is only one life for all of us. Only one chance to get it right, to win some love for yourself. Or screw up beyond redemption.

Ute got up and walked over to Pedro. She reached out and grabbed his arm, to check that he was real, that any of this was solid. He pulled away, scared by the mad gringa with tattered clothes and a crusty face, and ran off down the path.

Ute sat on the steps of the hut and listened to the birds in the bright light. It felt like morning again. Perhaps it was always morning here.

She felt inside her trouser pockets. There was a leaky chapstick, which she applied to her scabby lips with greed. The chapstick was the only item she had brought with her from her previous life, like a memento from a lost civilization. That, and the leaves from the old woman. She took them out and rubbed them in her fingers. They didn't smell of anything. She put them back in her pocket.

Later, she drank some water and ate some of the rice, and threw up all of it immediately in the tall grass outside. She then dragged herself to the graveyard, to look at Oswaldo's grave again and check the dates. They hadn't changed. He was still two-and-a-half years dead. The ocean was still a scintillating blue, with sweet nothing between here and the Galápagos.

Max had definitely existed. You couldn't make him up. And the jaguar had definitely pounced on him, she had seen it and heard it all. She could doubt her dreams, but not her waking life.

It was this place that was unreal, some afterworld of punishment after the crime. Yes, she had killed Max, but her original crime was being unlovable, which is why Jerry had finally betrayed her. And the punishment was madness.

Ute slowly walked down the path to the last huts of the community. She walked into what looked like a workshop. A few people were making pottery inside. They didn't seem surprised to see her. She greeted them and asked the time. It was just before noon. She asked after María.

"Ah, there you are," María greeted her without enthusiasm outside her house. "You slept since yesterday morning. We checked up on you. Feeling better?"

"Yes, thanks," Ute lied. She felt like death warmed up – one of Jerry's expressions.

And suddenly Jerry's absence pierced her with such force she almost doubled up with pain. She had always had Jerry to return to. She wondered where he was, what he was doing in that other reality of El Niño – betrayal, death by jaguar, and other things that didn't bear thinking about.

"You can get back to Puerto Seco whenever you like, we'll get someone to take you down on horseback," María said. She was smoking a cigarette a few metres away, and looked at Ute through a cloud of smoke. They too wanted to get rid of her. There was nothing for her there. Oswaldo was dead, and these people were complete strangers.

She had to go, now. But where? She was running out of realities.

"Didn't Oswaldo leave any notebooks, anything… written?" Ute asked.

María shook her head. "He left his paintings. But he asked to have them sent to a private collection, so we did. We needed the money too." María went into the hut and came out with a T-shirt and a pair of cotton shorts. "Take these, you need a change of clothes."

She went into the dimly lit hut. Luz was inside, sitting at a table, drawing on a huge sheet of brown paper with crayons.

"What are you drawing?" Ute asked while she changed into the shorts.

"My mum," Luz said.

"Can I see?"

Her drawing showed a stick figure in a dress with an outsized, long-haired head. Big teardrops fell from the eyes and formed a trail that went all the way to the far corner of the sheet, to a small house against a blue background, with smoke coming out of it.

"Who lives in that house?"

"Oswaldo," Luz said. "His house is on top of the sea."

"But I can't see him."

"That's because he isn't there. That's why mum is crying."

"And where are you?"

Luz looked perplexed.

"Shall we put you in the picture too?" Ute suggested. Luz nodded.

"Here, for example, next to your mum," Ute pointed at a spot next to the crying woman. "You can be standing next to your mum, and that way, she won't be crying any more because she has you."

"OK, I have to paint another picture then." Luz pulled a fresh brown sheet over the old one.

"Yes, you'll have to paint another picture," Ute said, and tears rose from her throat into her voice, and then out of her eyes.

"Why are you crying?" Luz looked up at her.

"Because sometimes," Ute said, "I cry for no reason."

"Me too, sometimes I cry for no reason," Luz said.

María stood in the doorway. She looked familiar again, in a distant way.

"Do the clothes fit?" she enquired.

"Yes, thank you." Ute quickly wiped her nose and her cheeks. The T-shirt was too short, and the shorts were too baggy.

"*Señora*," María said, "we can't offer you much hospitality here, there's no hotel, nowhere for you to stay. But we can organize transport in a *momentito*."

"*Bueno*," Ute said. The message was crystal-clear.

"I'm ready to go. But I need to go back to Villa Pacifica, the way I came."

María gave her a look that said "You really are as crazy as I thought".

"Well, you can discuss that with the *personita* who accompanies you."

"That boy, Pedro, when did he come to live with you?"

"Three years ago. He ran away from home."

"I met him on the beach a few days ago," Ute tried one last time. "I met Pedro in Puerto Seco. He was with his sister Evelyn, his brother Ricardo, and their baby sister. They were on the beach."

María busied herself putting some clean laundry on a clothesline stretched between two trees. Ute stood on the doorsteps of the hut and watched her dumbly. She was out of place and out of time here. Then María said:

"Oswaldo used to take these potions. They were hallucinogenic. He had them sent by a friend in the Amazon who was a shaman. They induced vomiting and cleansed the system, and he believed that was slowing down the growth of his cancer. Maybe it was. I don't know. But when he took those, he had visions. He saw things that nobody else could see."

"What things?" Ute said.

"I don't know. People. Dead people. Animals. He called it the spirit world. I don't really understand those things." She looked at Ute. "He believed there was some sort of special energy here in the Manteño cloud forest. You know, an ancient civilization lived in these forests. That's why he moved up here. He called it a hot spot. He said there are only a few hot spots in the world."

Ute sat down on the half-rotten wooden steps of the hut.

"Did he wander off into the park?" she asked.

"He was too sick." María sat down on the steps next to Ute and rolled up a joint with some mossy-looking substance from a cloth pouch. María offered her the rolled joint, and she gratefully accepted.

"*Yerba*," María said vaguely. Grass. Ute lit up. It tasted like sweet rot.

"Oswaldo was looking for a home all his life," María said. "He lived in Europe, he lived in the big cities, he came from a big city. But he said he didn't like civilization. He said he felt 'out of time', and that he didn't belong anywhere."

"I can understand that," Ute said.

They smoked in silence for a while.

"Once he said he saw his dead mother. Another time, he saw the dead son of *Señor* Mikel, the one who drowned in the Galápagos. He said, 'We can never get too far from those we have wronged.'"

Ute's head was beginning to feel pleasantly light.

"But he himself was trying to get as far as possible from those he'd wronged," she ventured. María looked at her with incomprehension.

"Consuelo, for example."

María was quiet for a while, then she said: "Oswaldo never set out to hurt anyone."

Neither did I, Ute thought.

"And you, where are you from?" Ute asked.

"From Jipilini. My mother died in a bus crash when I was little, and my father remarried and gave me to my aunt. She lived in Puerto Seco, she had a shop there where I worked, but she passed away and I came up here with a cousin. I hated Puerto Seco. But to me, this is not a magic place. I always wanted to do something with my life. Go somewhere, even if it's just to the big city. I don't want to make pottery all my life. But now I have Luz to take care of."

"How old are you?" Close-up, María looked older and somehow even more familiar. And with a shock, Ute realized where she had met her. She looked at the bitten-down nails and it all came back to her.

"Twenty-four," María said, her squint magnified in close-up. "And you?"

"Thirty-nine."

"Oh," María said. It was her turn to be shocked now.

"Your aunt..." Ute said with a shaky voice, "her shop... where was it?"

"In Puerto Seco."

"Where?" Ute almost shouted. "Where in Puerto Seco? Which street?"

"At the corner of Moreno and Bolívar, one block behind the *malecón*. Why?"

"I was there," Ute said quietly. "I bought a bottle of water there. And you sold it to me. And you were breastfeeding a boy."

María looked bewildered.

"Oh my God," Ute said.

"I don't understand." María shook her head.

There was no point trying to explain to María what Ute herself couldn't grasp.

"You know, it's funny." Ute suddenly felt talkative and full of energy and light. "I met the brother of the shaman too, and his mother. They were in Villa Pacifica. I know you don't believe me, but I did. He told me about this thing called the 'vision quest'. Young Achuar men do it, to find themselves. That's what we call it, 'finding yourself'. But for us gringos, the vision quest is travelling. The Achuar lives in ignorance of the world outside. This is his blessing. This enables him to embrace tradition and harness the power of his ancestral spirits. Then he returns home stronger. What do gringos do? We embrace sunstroke and diarrhoea, and mistake it for self-knowledge. Then we return home more confused than ever."

María stubbed out her joint on the steps.

"Yes, but I have neither," she said. "I am not living in the Amazon, and I can't travel. I am stuck here."

Luz appeared behind them in the doorway, holding a sheet of paper.

"I painted another picture," she said, and held out the sheet to Ute. In the new drawing, the woman was smiling, there was a small stick figure next to her holding her stick hand, and inside the little house in the corner there was a little stick Oswaldo.

"That's very nice," Ute said. "It's much better now, and nobody has to cry any more."

"Yes," Luz looked pleased. María hugged her, and the child went back inside the hut.

"You don't have children?" María asked.

Ute shook her head and put out the joint. She got up to use the latrine behind the hut. Outside it hung a shard of mirror. Ute glimpsed a face in it. It was her face, but there was something wrong with it. She took a closer look. The eczema was gone, only faint blotches of past inflammation remained on her eyelids and cheeks and around her mouth. She couldn't remember the last time she'd seen her face like this. She touched her face to make sure it was real, and she smiled. She was an ordinary woman now, an ordinary good-looking woman.

María and Ute sat in the harsh midday sun, among the birdsong and the noise coming from the kilns. They rolled another joint and smoked in silence for a while.

"So where are you going next?" María asked at one point.

"I don't know." Ute shook her head. It felt very light.

"*Bueno*," María said in a gentle way that reminded her of Consuelo.

Later, they ate roasted plantain. Sitting in the dim light outside the hut with Luz and María, with the screeching insects, heavy *palo santo* smell and another spiff of the potent mossy stuff, Ute felt closer to peace of mind than she had been for a long time.

She slept in María's hut, in the spare hammock. Or rather she didn't sleep in the spare hammock. She remembered the leaves the Achuar woman had given her, and chewed some of them outside with a bit of filtered water. They were bitter, and soon she began to shiver and retch.

She started walking, past some other darkened huts. Then, suddenly and violently, she puked her guts out. She had never vomited like this before. It was good to empty herself so comprehensively. She slumped down next to a tree and leant on its trunk.

It was as if she was acquiring a new pair of eyes. She began to distinguish shapes in the pitch-black community, and in the outlaying forest. There was a boy there among the trees. She kept losing him from sight, and then he would appear again. At first she thought it was Pedro – he was about his size – then she saw his face, even though there was no moon. It was the face of a white boy. He seemed to want to tell her something, and she was strangely unafraid. But she was also unable to speak or move, and eventually the boy disappeared.

Then she saw a small old woman. At first she thought it was the Achuar woman, but then realized it was her own mother. It was clearly her mother. Her mother was looking at Ute and smiling. Her mother was *noticing* her, watching over her, telling her that everything was going to be OK. Ute felt the warm trails of tears on her face, but they were happy tears. Things were falling into place, finally. Time was not out of joint any more.

And at some point in the night, Ute knew exactly what she needed to do next. It was blindingly obvious. She felt light and free. She could take off any minute now, up to the blue sky of the new day, where birds and clouds lived and from where everything looked small and connected, and made sense, in a distant sort of way.

She was floating in a light-filled sky, looking down on Puerto Seco, Villa Pacifica and Agua Sagrada. In her bird's-eye view, the topography of the whole area was mapped out with luminous clarity. She could see the paths criss-crossing the dry forest at the foot of the Agua Sagrada cloud reserve. They were like blazing trails, they were many, and they all led somewhere. This was the map of her life, and she would take control of it, finally. She would be smiling if her face wasn't paralysed.

In the insect-thick night, she lay and listened to the whispering in her mind – or was it in the forest?

Two roads diverged in a yellow wood…

At one point, she may have heard a roar somewhere far off in the forest. It was the jaguar, but she was not afraid. Everything was clear now. Everyone was safe.

21

IN THE JAGUAR'S CAGE they found half a rabbit, Max's limp body, and no jaguar. Ute had disappeared too. The only witness to the accident was the old woman. Jerry was convinced she was a witch as soon as she confessed to giving Ute some leaves. Her son translated as she explained how Ute had gone off "for a walk in the woods" as soon as they crossed in the boat, leaving the old woman with Max and his jaguar-feeding obsession, which had brought about his grisly end. But the old woman was distressed about something, and it wasn't just Max's death. The leaves had to be ingested in a special way, with supervision, she explained. If you took them alone, you could fall prey to the spirit world and die a psychic death. Whatever that meant.

"Then why did you give them to her and then let her go off by herself?" Jerry wanted to know.

The old woman rocked disconsolately. She didn't know. She was having a bad time herself. She had a strange way of crying: her face suddenly became wet, but Jerry didn't see any tears in her eyes. Then she left with her son, Helga and the baby.

Jerry spent two weeks discovering the meaning of hell. Hell was waiting. Jerry had never had to wait for anything in his life.

First, he waited for Ute to come back after a walk in the storm – after all, it wasn't *completely* unlike her to go off walking in extreme conditions: she was moody, she braved the elements in that slightly loony Scandinavian way, and she was a weathered traveller who could find her way in and out of most places.

Then, he waited for her to come back after forgiving him. People told him how strangely she'd behaved that morning. She must have figured out his betrayal, and this had tipped her over the edge and into the flooded woods. Already she had not been quite herself since their arrival. Or perhaps – not a nice thought, but he had it anyway – she had been too much herself since they arrived: cold, distant, unhappy.

Finally, he waited for the search party to bring her back. But the search party returned prematurely, because the only car access to the interior of the national park was via a bridge that was flooded, and nobody was going to walk – they were slobs down to the last man. Admittedly, the paths *had* been washed away. Jerry asked about a helicopter, and got sniggers from the local police. They had more urgent things to worry about than a missing gringa. An American mangled by a missing jaguar, for example. Then came the tidal wave, and they forgot about the American too.

After the tidal wave, and drinking himself to sleep night after night in the only open watering hole in Puerto Seco, Jerry waited for Ute's body to be washed out on the wrecked *malecón*. It seemed to be the way in this cursed place: people went missing, and the sea spat them out later. This was what had happened with Consuelo.

A few days after Ute disappeared, a small tidal wave wrecked half of Puerto Seco – the half closer to the ocean. Consuelo's café was among the first to go, along with her house and all of Oswaldo Joven's paintings. Miraculously, nobody died in the calamity, except a few mangy dogs, but Consuelo went missing. It was several days before kids found her on the beach, like a mermaid tangled in big clumps of leathery, flesh-coloured seaweed nobody here had seen before. Someone said it came all the way from New Zealand. It was the kind of thing El Niño brings, the locals said. There were also sightings of flying fish.

The entire village went to Consuelo's funeral, which was modest and hasty among the wreckage. Héctor was ashen and stony-faced. Lucía was even more absent-minded than usual, as if she had always been preparing to live in an afterworld. Jerry hated her now. Mikel cried like a child, clutching his big fists, his big tears falling into the open grave. This sight shook the already unsettled Jerry to the core. It was amazing how quickly one's life could unravel to its barest threads, leaving you a sudden pauper.

With the tidal wave, the estuary rose monstrously, and Villa Pacifica was flooded down to the last hut. Jerry and Ute's *tortuga* hut was at the back, so their luggage – packed by Jerry and ready to go as soon as Ute appeared – only got sodden. But the foundations of the huts were under water, and most of them would rot and eventually collapse. This is when Mikel stopped noticing Jerry. His livelihood was suddenly destroyed along with his dream. Lucía never talked to Jerry, before or after the wave.

Héctor was nowhere to be found, and neither was the safe that contained all their takings for the past three months, and all the guests' passports. The animal refuge was spared because of its raised shore, but the animal sanctuary couldn't be sustained without the human sanctuary – even Carlos grimly agreed. He took Enrique out of his cage, and the bird now followed him everywhere, perched on his shoulder and screeching in garbled distress, "*Las Malvinas son argentinas*, *las Malvinas son argentinas*, *las Malvinas son argentinas*" – the only sentence he seemed to remember from his repertoire.

Carlos stuck with Jerry until the end, sat with him almost every night, although he didn't drink, and offered moral support. But he couldn't offer much hope about finding Ute. He came to check up on Jerry every day, first in his *tortuga* cabin, and then in the village. He was the one who said to Jerry, "Hell is waiting." His brother had been among the "disappeared" under Paraguay's fascist dictator. His family had waited for twenty years to know for sure that he was dead. "And the bastards who murdered him are living in air-conditioned houses in Rio and Buenos Aires. That's why I came here," Carlos told Jerry, who could find no response to this except to get drunk on *aguardiente* yet again.

In the wake of the disaster, Jerry moved to a bare room with a single hammock in one of the undamaged houses in Puerto Seco, where a family offered him a very cheap rate and the benefit of their complete indifference. By then, the guests of Villa Pacifica had long gone – Tim and Liz had left soon after Luis and his family. They had all testified at the local police station, and been driven in a special police vehicle to Guadeloupe, to get replacement passports. No buses were going anyway.

And of course there was the suddenly widowed Eve. She went into a hysterical fit when Max was found, and never recovered from it. She screamed and thrashed about until her face looked the colour of a cooked lobster, and then she screamed some more. In the end, they had to call a doctor, who administered an injection. Eve's grief made him wonder what is a better measure of our love for another: the way we are when they are alive, or the way we are when they are dead.

Eve left in a police vehicle two days later, clutching only her handbag and looking like a mental patient. She left behind a cabin full of scattered clothes and shoes. Her last words to Mikel and Lucía, delivered as she was getting into the clapped-out police car, were "I'm gonna sue you!" Fair enough, Jerry thought. Perhaps he should sue them too. But that wouldn't give him anything he needed, because all he needed was for Ute to be found alive.

During the day there was nothing to do but hang out at the wrecked beach. He sat in the sand, the dull thud of the ocean like blood in his ears. He thought about Ute and their life together. Often, Jerry had felt that she was like that boy Kai in the Andersen story *The Snow Queen*. A shard of the evil troll's mirror had lodged itself in her eye and in her heart, some time in her childhood – perhaps at birth – and she saw the ugliness in everything and everyone. Especially in herself. It took the tears of childhood sweetheart Gerda – that was Jerry – to melt the icy kingdom and dislodge the shards from Ute's eyes and heart.

Because that's where she'd gone now, to the ultimate destination that you couldn't find in any of her guides: the evil kingdom of the Snow Queen, where there are no other humans, just bad dreams. In the story, Gerda goes all the way to this kind of underworld. But desperate as he felt, Jerry couldn't bring himself to go into the woods looking for Ute. Carlos said the jaguar, Max's killer, was out there in the hills. The paths had been washed away, they said. Ute could be anywhere by now, the police said in their lethargic coastal drawl. Even Carlos advised against going, and Carlos was fearless. So Jerry waited in his safe hell, and with each passing day, more of his self-respect drained away.

One afternoon, in a bout of despair, he waded into the murky sea waist-deep and flung his laptop as far as he could. It made a heavy plopping noise. This way the stupid, mediocre novella he'd been writing in his week-long delusion was flushed out by the retreating tidal wave along with his ambitions, his marriage and his self-respect.

Then, one morning, Mikel and Lucía left. They came to say goodbye. They were in their jeep, piled up with luggage. They were going scouting for a new place to live, Mikel said. They were also broke. Mikel shook Jerry's hand distractedly, and Lucía waved from inside the car with her impenetrable smile, which had seemed enigmatic before but was chilling now. She gazed at Jerry sideways, as if she barely knew him, as if they hadn't spent several sweaty nights making love in the noisy rain.

He had felt a fatal attraction to this woman from the moment he saw her dreamy face behind a cloud of smoke. He had risked his marriage for a few nights of sex with her – it had been heaven, and now she meant nothing to him. Clearly, the indifference was mutual. Jerry wanted to forget all this on the spot, along with the image of the gored, limp-bodied Max in the jaguar cage.

With these two gone and only Carlos left to look after the animals, Jerry felt as if the last hope of finding Ute was fading away. He was considering contacting the British Embassy when Ute suddenly appeared.

She was picked up by some locals in a truck. She was walking along the main road. He was in his darkened room, lying in his hammock in a vacant state.

She looked distracted, as if she was on her way somewhere else and was only stopping by to say hello. She had wasted away so much, she looked like an apparition. Her face, feet and what was left of her clothes were blackened as if she'd been climbing through chimneys. Her clothes were hanging off her bony frame like a scarecrow's rags. Her hair was matted, her nails were filled with dirt, and her eyes had a messianic glow that dislodged Jerry's jubilation and replaced it with dread. He put his arms around her. She was limp and smelt foul. He squeezed her tight. Involuntary sobs came out of his throat.

"I'm so sorry," he howled in her feral hair. "I'm so sorry."

She finally put her arms around him and patted him on the back reassuringly. He gave her a drink from a large bottle of Coke he'd just bought. She drained it all in big gulps and handed him back the empty bottle.

"Where have you been?" Jerry said. "I've been going out of my mind."

"I've been looking for something. It's hard in the forest, because the paths are flooded. But I figured it out."

"You figured out what? I thought you were dead, Ute!" Jerry realized he was shouting, and stopped. The family he was staying with had come out of their hammocks to see what was happening and were gathered at the doorway to his room.

"I need to go back to Villa Pacifica," Ute was saying. "Then exit again through the back gate of the animal shelter, and there's a path there which..."

"Ute, for God's sake, we need to get out of here immediately. Max is dead. Consuelo's dead. Everyone's gone. The Villa's closed down. Mikel and Lucía..."

Ute flinched, then said "Don't shout at me" in her new, flat voice, her eyes fixing him in a dreadful, unfamiliar gaze.

"I know. I killed Max. Consuelo hanged herself. I know what's going to happen here, because it's already happened, you see. I've figured it out. We're in a time loop." She sat inside the hammock. "A time-trap where things happen over and over, but in different versions of themselves," she continued. "We all have different versions of our lives. At first I thought it was the past. Then I thought it was the future. Then I realized it's neither. It's a turn in the road, a time warp. We can set it straight. We can undo it. You don't have to be sorry. I don't have to kill Max. Even El Niño... Villa Pacifica goes on..."

A new kind of despair gripped Jerry. She had lost her mind. Just like her mother. It was in their genes. It was what he'd always feared. Her hardness was just a front, he'd always known it. Underneath it, she'd always been fragile. It was his fault for not being more caring, more careful, a better husband, a better writer, a better man.

"I need to retrace my steps." Her words were getting garbled with fatigue now. "I need to go back to the Villa and the forest, and find an alternative path. I have to…"

"Please, darling, just lie down for a while, you're exhausted." Jerry squatted by the hammock and put his hands around her shins and his head on her emaciated thighs. He lifted her sandalled feet and placed them in the hammock. She didn't protest. He put a blanket over her. She shivered, closed her eyes and muttered something.

Jerry sat on the floor by the hammock and signalled to the family at the doorway to leave. They shuffled away. He looked inside the small canvas shoulder bag she'd been carrying. He hadn't seen it before. It had three empty plastic bottles in it. Who had given her this?

She slept the fathomless sleep of lost souls. He sat there for a while, relishing her new-found aliveness. She was here, they were together again, and all would be fine, eventually. He just had to get them out of here fast. There was no time to call a doctor. He would do that once they were back in Britain. He would make it up to her. He would set everything straight.

Some local buses had resumed services as the roads were being cleared up. He carefully removed the rags from her upper body and put a new T-shirt over her head, one of his. He carried her from the hammock to a taxi, and then from the taxi to the bus. There was no time to say goodbye to Carlos, and he didn't want Ute to get agitated any further. By the time they were on the bus, with their bedraggled luggage and the weird painting Consuelo had sent for Ute via Héctor before the flood, Jerry felt exhausted. Sleeping was out of the question though, with the music blaring out of speakers a few seats away. Ute woke up just as darkness fell.

"Where are we?" she asked, her eyes unfocused from sleep.

"We're on our way to Guadeloupe to get emergency passports, and then we're going home. How are you feeling?"

Ute grabbed him by the front of his T-shirt and shook him with surprising force. "We have to go back! Jerry, we have to go back!" she shouted. Heads turned to look at the sorry gringos.

"Darling, we can't go back, there's nothing there." He tried to contain her, but she was suddenly very awake and struggling violently.

"You don't get it, do you?" she was saying. "We can't just leave, we have to go back. It's all wrong, it all happened the wrong way around, we have to fix it."

She wrenched herself away from him and stumbled out of her seat. He held her back.

"Let me go," she cried, and pulled away from him. She was heading for the front of the bus. He caught her before she reached the driver.

"Ute, for God's sake!" He put his arms around her, like a psychiatric nurse containing a patient.

She screamed, "Let me go! I have to go back! I have to go back," then broke down sobbing. She was saying something Jerry couldn't make out, and it didn't really matter what it was. The main thing was to contain her now, to stop her from harming herself or disrupting the bus journey. The bus was full. She collapsed on the floor. People offered help, but there was nothing they could do except help take her back to her seat and mutter sympathetic words – not that Jerry could understand what they were saying.

She cried in his arms. Saliva came out of her mouth, and her hot tears burnt his face and hands like acid. Jerry knew that everything until now had been a mere rehearsal for this moment of naked truth. Nothing would be the same again.

At one point, a travelling salesman got on. Jerry could swear it was the guy from last time. He was wearing the same pink shirt. Jerry couldn't understand what he was saying, but the man was handing out tiny ginseng bottles.

"Hey, *amigo*!" Jerry called out to him. "Do you remember us? From a few weeks back?"

The guy looked at them warily, but made no sign of recognizing them or understanding what Jerry was saying.

"It's the guy with the ginseng bottles," Jerry nudged Ute. "Talk to him, ask him..."

"I know," she said placidly, looking at the seller. She had calmed down. "I told you, we're in a time loop. But you don't believe me. You don't believe me."

Later, in their hotel in Guadeloupe, he called an English-speaking doctor, who gave Ute some mild sedatives and advised a few days of "physical and emotional rest", while they waited for their emergency passports to be issued by the British Embassy.

The sedatives worked. They worked too well. Ute went quiet, and only spoke on the second day. She tried, once again, to tell Jerry about Agua Sagrada, about diverging realities, about the time loop.

"I don't know what to think," Jerry said after listening to her. They were sitting up in bed. "It's completely mad. I mean, you were quite sick when you got to Agua Sagrada, you can't be sure of your judgement of events and dates."

"I saw his grave. And I spent two days with María. She told me..."

"Yeah, you told me all this. But Ute, thinking that you can rearrange your own life is crazy enough already. Thinking you can do that with other people's lives is delusional mania. I mean, do you think people and places just appear out of thin air, just so that you and I can play out our neuroses?"

"OK, let's go back to the facts. How do you explain, for instance, that you thought I was gone for two weeks, when in fact I was gone for only a few days? Three days in Agua Sagrada, and maximum two days wandering in the forest. I wouldn't have survived any longer. I didn't have food or water for more than—"

"Ute, I didn't *think* it was two weeks, it *was* two weeks. A lot happened in those two weeks while you were gone. People died. People left."

"Exactly. This proves that there's a time discrepancy, a divergence of realities where—"

"Ute, this is the stuff of fiction." Jerry knew he should indulge her more, but if he agreed with her version of events, she would then insist on going back, and that was impossible.

"No," Ute said bitterly. "It's the stuff of hope. Because if we don't go back, there is no hope for anyone. Consuelo is dead. It didn't have to be that way."

"Ute." Jerry sighed deeply and took her hand. His chest felt as if a ton of cement was sitting inside it. "To fix everything, we'd have to go back all the way to the womb. We can't do that. It's not possible. I'm sorry. I'm so sorry that I, that I..."

"No, I don't want to know," Ute said, and got up. She stood at the window in her undies, her long legs ethereal in the late afternoon light that streamed in from the port dotted with ships' masts. Soon, they would be leaving too.

They were silent for a long time, Ute turned towards the port, Jerry sitting miserably in bed.

"I promise we'll come back one day," Jerry said in the end.

Ute didn't say a word for the next few days, and not much more over the following months. The fevered look in her eyes was extinguished, and a flat, unmoving gaze replaced it.

* * *

Ute and Jerry did return six years later. They pretended to each other that it was a "family holiday", but the only one who believed it was their five-year-old daughter Amber. Amber had been miraculously conceived at Villa Pacifica, born eight weeks prematurely. She had the intent, intelligent grey eyes of her mother.

After the events in Puerto Seco, Ute had carried out her pregnancy quietly and stoically, and soon tumbled into post-natal depression. On their return she had also given up her job for good. She would never write another semi-true line about a place again, she said. Travel is meaningless, she said, unless you arrive in some place that changes you radically and therefore makes all further travel futile. In the end, she didn't include Puerto Seco or even the Manteño National Park in the updated guide. She didn't want anyone else to go there, and left it at that.

It had taken her two years to recover, two years that were a blur of sleepless nights and survival for Jerry. He nursed her back to relative wellness, while also nursing the baby. He felt he was atoning for his crime that way, but part of him wondered. He wanted to talk to Ute about Max, and what exactly had happened by the jaguar's cage, but she had imposed an embargo of silence on all Villa Pacifica matters.

Now they would visit Puerto Seco. They didn't even have to say it: they knew it was the only way to lay those ghosts to rest.

They walked along the littered beach to the familiar gates. It was so overgrown, the carved wooden sign "VILLA PACIFICA" was hardly visible. They walked among the collapsed remains of the huts, and even found what looked like their *tortuga* cabin. A baby iguana was sunning itself on the collapsed steps. Amber crouched beside it and poked it with a stick. "Dad," she cried. "It's dead."

She picked it up gingerly with two fingers and placed it on her palm. It was dried out.

"Leave it where you found it," Jerry said. But Amber was like her mother – fearless, and rarely listening to anyone, especially not her father. "It doesn't weigh anything," she said, and carried it with her hand held out ceremonially. "I will take it home and bury it in the garden."

The main house was full of weeds that had broken through the collapsed wooden floor and were growing inside the shell of the building like in a surrealist painting.

"Careful," Jerry called out, "there will be snakes in there."

Ute walked across to the visitors' ledgers, which were amazingly still there on the shelves. She picked up the one which said "2006". It fell apart in her hands, and then into the undergrowth, dispersing the invisible reptiles, which hissed and darted this way and that.

The shore of the estuary was much wider than they remembered it – either memory was playing tricks on them, which was likely, or the water had retreated, which was also possible. Anything was likely here, as they already knew, so they tried to take in the place without undue excitement. They found nothing to say to each other, except "watch out" and "look at this". This was a place where words lost all meaning.

Back in Puerto Seco, they asked around. Nobody knew where Carlos, Mikel and Lucía had gone, though some said Carlos had gone to work in another animal shelter. Nobody remembered Ute and Jerry from five years ago. The locals couldn't agree which year Villa Pacifica had fallen into abeyance.

"And Agua Sagrada?" Ute asked.

Someone had stumbled across stunning artefacts from an ancient civilization, and the community had been flooded by archaeological teams. The authorities were keen to turn it into a national tourist attraction and were financing the excavations. This had put the pottery community out of work, and many people had left. Neither Jerry nor Ute mentioned going to Agua Sagrada.

Jerry was relieved to get on the day's last bus out of town. On the way back to Guadeloupe, Amber dozed between them, her mouth open, still clutching the dead baby iguana in her hand.

Jerry reached over Amber and squeezed Ute's cold fingers. They were always cold these days. Her face looked serene and distant in the grubby dusk. Her eczema had cleared with the pregnancy and never returned. But she took little pleasure in her new-found beauty. It was as if some essential part of her had departed with the eczema.

"Remember when I promised you we'd come back?" Jerry said.

Ute was looking out of the window at the shrimp farms along the road.

"These were once virgin mangroves," she said. "Mikel and Lucía's land must have long been turned into shrimp farms too."

Jerry squeezed her hand again.

"I remember," Ute said, her eyes on the road.

And at this point Jerry understood what he had always feared: we can never really know other people. Especially those we are close to, especially those we treat as if they are part of us. They are not. We are alone. Even with the longed-for child firmly wedged between us, we are always alone.

"I remember everything," Ute said again, so quietly that he almost didn't hear her.

Postscript

THE AWFUL THING IS not that what we love will eventually be taken from us. No, the awful thing is that nobody warns us. We are unprepared. We assume that what we love will always be there. I remain unprepared, six years later, and yet I've somehow managed to live with it since the day we found Max's body in the jaguar's cage. Max's neck was broken and one side of his head was pulped. The jaguar was crouching in a corner looking a bit sheepish, if you can imagine that. The cage door was unlocked. Either of them could have simply pushed it open and walked out, but it seemed that neither of them had wanted to.

It quickly became clear to me that if I didn't go looking for Ute, nobody was going to do it. So I walked through the cursed forest all the way up to Agua Sagrada, with Carlos, who was willing to abandon his animals to save a human being, proving that vile little Héctor wrong. We walked for hell knows how long in liquid mud. It was as if the forest was sweating blood and bile. I'd given up on keeping track of time there, and Carlos never wore a watch.

At Agua Sagrada, we met the squinting María and her precocious child. She told us about Ute's visit, about her confusion, about her distraught talk of murder, of not having a place to return to, about how she'd asked to go back down to the forest and gone off with a local man and a local woman, and two horses. She had been very sick with vomiting on the morning she left, but she'd seemed happy, and no one could stop her from going.

They had dropped her off, at her insistence, at the foot of the cloud forest. She had been hell-bent on continuing alone. María seemed to imply that Ute had asked for it all. I wanted to slap her for it. Or slap someone, do something. Being so helpless was agony. On the way back down with Carlos, I felt myself going mad. Every giant cactus looked like something behind which Ute might be hiding.

And this is where we lose Ute's tracks.

Later, much later, I wrote *Villa Pacifica*. Everything I've written is true, although one thing I learnt in Villa Pacifica is that true and real are not the same thing. As you might guess, I got the idea from Oswaldo's *The Three Lives of Mikel*, which accompanied me home. I flew back to Britain after several weeks of futile search involving the British Embassy and, yes, even a helicopter that flew over the entire park, the mangroves in the south, and all the bays along the shore, looking for Ute, dead or alive. At the time I prayed they wouldn't find her dead. But that's because I didn't yet know the hell of not knowing. A dead body would have been better.

I put the painting in the living room at home, and after many months of staring at it in a stupor, I realized that it wasn't about the lives we have in chronological order. No, it was about the lives we don't have, the turns in the road we don't take. And it was Ute who would have realized this before me. She had humanity and imagination. I had vanity and fancies. She had hunger. I had appetites. She was twice the man I was, and twice the writer I wasn't.

I wrote *Villa Pacifica* so that I could be close to Ute again, and relive everything through her. But I also did it because it was the only way to make sense of what happened in December 2009. You see, the facts by themselves are not reassuring.

Oswaldo Joven did die in 2007. I didn't see his grave up in Agua Sagrada – I didn't think of it at the time – but I looked up his biography.

There is no information on Villa Pacifica on the net or in any guides that came out since then. I travelled back a year later, and couldn't find either Puerto Seco or the Villa. I got on one of those dismal buses, and a bus seller gave me some porn and *El Che* Part I and II to hold while he did his spiel, and I went exactly the same way, but nobody knew of Puerto Seco. I couldn't find that bend in the road.

Here are some more facts. There was an El Niño storm on that coast in December 2006, and not again until last year – 2015. It's true: they only happen every ten or fifteen years. There was no tidal wave or any other climate disaster on that coast in 2009, while we were there.

And here is the strangest thing of all. When I finally left Puerto Seco, without Ute, it was the same day as the day we had arrived: Tuesday, the 15th of December.

All this messed me up in the following few years. I fancied that if time could play tricks on us, we could play tricks on it too. Thus anything was possible. It was possible that Ute was alive, and that she might return to me after a long spell in the mangroves. That she had fallen into a time-trap and was still trying to find her way out back to me. But eventually, such hope destroys the soul.

Everyone was concerned for me and convinced I was deranged with grief. I discussed with an astrophysicist the concept of the wormhole. I told him what had happened, and I told him my theory: that Puerto Seco and Villa Pacifica are in a wormhole, and we got caught up in it. It is always the *year after* the disaster there. Versions of the same events repeat themselves each year. A weather anomaly. A flood. A gringo dies a violent death. Consuelo kills herself. Mikel and Lucía leave. Over and over again. But then, somehow, it all repeats itself – because the place doesn't exist in real time. And it's typical for wormholes that while time passes inside them, on the outside, in the real world of space-time, no time has passed at all. Do you see?

I said. He did, but he also saw a problem. Wormholes *may* exist, he explained, but they are unsustainable. They can't exist in perpetuity. They are momentary lapses of space-time. They do not contain alternative worlds. Do me a favour, he said, see a psychiatrist.

I told the psychiatrist my story. He said I was suffering post-traumatic stress disorder, and I was having a manic-depressive episode, and I was possibly psychotic. He prescribed some drugs.

I wrote *Villa Pacifica*. By doing that, I became the man I should have been for Ute. A man who can reach outside of his own little world. A man who could have saved her and himself. The awful thing is that conditions become ideal a heartbeat too late.

Even now, I feel as if she might be just around the corner. I can't help it. It's not a hope any more, it's a feeling. I haven't thrown out or given away any of her things. Once a month, I dust her shelves of travel guides, all of them out of date. But not Ute.

You see, those we love may leave us, one way or another, and never return. And, gradually, they fall out of date. But those we have loved and betrayed are always near, one way or another.

And that has made all the difference.

Acknowledgements

I AM VERY GRATEFUL TO the Scottish Arts Council, for generously supporting the writing of this novel.

My thanks to Chris Mosse for his moral and literary support in reading an early draft of the novel.

I would not have been able to finish this novel without the love and support of my parents in Auckland, who gave me a home at a time when I felt homeless.